INVITATION
TO ALL COUPLES IN LOVE

We, the citizens of Eternity, take great pleasure in inviting you to hold your wedding at the Powell Chapel.

Remember the legend: Those who exchange their vows in the chapel will remain together for the rest of their lives.

So let us help plan your special day. We've been making dreams come true for more than a hundred years.

Weddings, Inc.

Eternity, Massachusetts.

Dear Reader,

The day after my husband and I were married in London, we flew to New York. We checked into a hotel in Times Square—the only address we knew in Manhattan—and enjoyed a twelve-hour honeymoon. The next morning my husband left to start his new job, and I set out to find both employment and an apartment. Given the state of our bank balance, I had about four days before our money ran out! I had never set foot in the United States until then, but I was young enough—and foolish enough—not to realize what a daunting task we'd set ourselves.

Somehow—probably with the help of an army of guardian angels—we managed to avoid most of the disasters that strike foreign immigrants moving to a big city. By mid-July, we'd both been promoted, our apartment had a table and chairs as well as a bed and we'd saved enough money to celebrate the three-month anniversary of our wedding in grand style. We decided to rent a car and take a trip to New England.

Like so many visitors before us, we fell in love with that part of America. Each day we had the fun of choosing the inn where we would spend the night, and I have vivid memories of the huge, wonderful lobster dinners we feasted on. We'd always found Manhattanites perfectly friendly, but the people we met in New England overwhelmed us with their welcome. It was in these small Colonial towns that we got our first inkling that maybe the United States wasn't just a place we were visiting for a while, but the country we would one day call home.

As you can imagine, with so many pleasurable memories to draw on as background, I was delighted when my Harlequin editor recently phoned me and asked if I would like to contribute to a series of books to be set in a fictional town in New England. I hope you will enjoy the story of Eve Graham and David Powell, two overachieving New Yorkers who find both love and danger amidst the old-world charm of Eternity, Massachusetts. Welcome to their story!

Best,

Jasmine Cresswell

Edge of Eternity

Jasmine Cresswell

Harlequin Books

TORONTO • NEW YORK • LONDON
AMSTERDAM • PARIS • SYDNEY • HAMBURG
STOCKHOLM • ATHENS • TOKYO • MILAN
MADRID • WARSAW • BUDAPEST • AUCKLAND

ISBN 0-373-22297-1

EDGE OF ETERNITY

Printed in U.S.A.

Weddings, Inc.

Join us every month
in Eternity, Massachusetts...where love lasts forever.

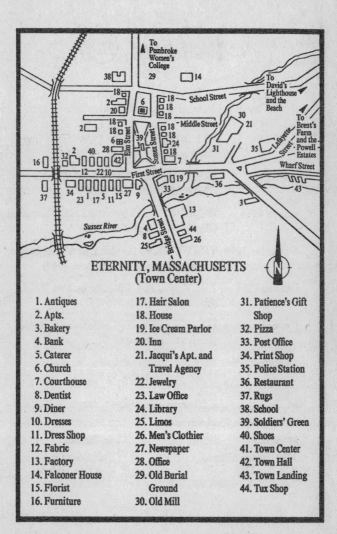

ETERNITY, MASSACHUSETTS
(Town Center)

1. Antiques
2. Apts.
3. Bakery
4. Bank
5. Caterer
6. Church
7. Courthouse
8. Dentist
9. Diner
10. Dresses
11. Dress Shop
12. Fabric
13. Factory
14. Falconer House
15. Florist
16. Furniture
17. Hair Salon
18. House
19. Ice Cream Parlor
20. Inn
21. Jacqui's Apt. and Travel Agency
22. Jewelry
23. Law Office
24. Library
25. Limos
26. Men's Clothier
27. Newspaper
28. Office
29. Old Burial Ground
30. Old Mill
31. Patience's Gift Shop
32. Pizza
33. Post Office
34. Print Shop
35. Police Station
36. Restaurant
37. Rugs
38. School
39. Soldiers' Green
40. Shoes
41. Town Center
42. Town Hall
43. Town Landing
44. Tux Shop

Weddings, Inc.
DIRECTORY

Your guide to the perfect Happily-Ever-After

Prologue

"Give me the gun, Ned." David Powell risked another step forward and held out his hand. He hoped like hell that Ned wouldn't notice the tremble.

"Get away! I'll shoot if you come any closer!" Ned cowered behind the desk, his expression wild, his body weaving, but his grip on the .9 mm pistol obstinately firm. David was seized by a profound sense of irony. Up here, on the thirtieth floor of a Wall Street office building, drama was supposed to be about stock trading and bond issues, not about life and death.

"Killing yourself won't solve anything." David tried to sound calm, despite the fact that he felt about as competent as a novice diver confronting a great white shark. "Ned, you don't really want to do this."

"Yes, I do! I'll be better off dead. What choice have you left me?"

"As long as we're alive, Ned, we always have choices. Suicide is the only decision that leaves us with nothing." David winced at the patronizing tone of his voice. The conversation had taken on a dreadful banality, although his emotions were anything but banal. He burned inside, his stomach churning with an acid brew of guilt and fear. He'd never expected his pursuit of Ned Nichols to end up like this.

Truth was, he'd never thought beyond the need to find out who was stealing the firm's money. *Great planning,* he berated himself. *For this one, you win the big prize.*

Ned laughed bitterly. "You're amazing, David. Totally, amazingly stupid for a man who's supposed to be smart. Don't you realize how wonderful *nothing* sounds to me right now?"

"But only for right now—"

"Killing myself will solve everything," Ned said. "The missing money. The police. My lousy marriage. The whole damn mess."

"Think about your marriage for a moment. Think about your wife." David seized on the opening Ned had given him. "What'll happen to her when you're gone? How do you think she'll feel if you do this?"

"How will she feel?" Ned's mouth twisted into a travesty of a smile. "Hey, don't worry about my sweet lovely wife. I finally figured Amy out. And you know what? She'll do a great job of playing the grieving widow. At least until the funeral's over, and by then you can be sure she'll have some new sucker lined up to *comfort* her."

"I bet she loves you more than you realize." David heard footsteps in the corridor outside the office and wasn't sure whether to curse at the intrusion or pray for an interruption. God only knew what Ned might do if he felt cornered. David spoke quickly, hoping to cover the sounds of approaching people.

"Look, Ned, you know as well as I do that problems aren't solved by running away. Your friends and family just get left to clean up the mess. You're an intelligent person—"

Ned stroked his gun. "Yeah, smart enough to set up the scam, but not quite smart enough to get away with it. My wife won't like that."

"You almost made it," David said, then stopped abruptly. This was ridiculous. Not only had Ned Nichols done his best to steal upward of two million dollars, he'd expended considerable effort to make it look as if David was responsible for the thefts. There was something surreal about hearing himself try to reassure Ned that the scheme he'd devised for ripping off the firm's clients had been an effective one, and that he'd almost succeeded in shunting the blame onto his closest colleague.

David drew a deep breath. "Ned, you're only thirty-five. You have half a lifetime still ahead of you. Don't throw it away."

Ned shrugged, his gaze flat. "Half a lifetime isn't long enough to right this screwup."

The footsteps slowed outside the door, and sweat pooled at the small of David's back. Then the footsteps picked up again, and the person walked on past Ned's office. A reprieve, or a lost opportunity? It was impossible to tell.

David wiped his hands against the sides of his trousers and took another couple of steps toward the desk. Toward Ned and the wavering gun. This was not in the least like a Hollywood movie, he decided. Not only were his hands shaking and his stomach lurching, moisture seemed to be cascading from every pore in his body. Clearly he wasn't cut out to be a hero. In the movies, the hero never seemed to sweat, much less tremble. Bruce Willis saved Washington airport from terrorists without mussing his sweater. Harrison Ford outwitted entire galaxies without needing to change his shirt, so surely David could disarm one slightly overweight stockbroker waving a small handgun. If only he could come at Ned from an angle, he'd have a chance to grab the gun, but the desk was superexecutive size and presented a formidable barrier. Still, he had to try. David sneaked a casual sideways sashay around the desk and toward the window.

Ned noticed at once. "Stay back! I told you to stay back!" He waved the gun frenziedly, pointing it first at David and then at his own head. He cocked the hammer with an ominous click, his breath coming in frightened pants.

"There's no point in carrying on this damn-fool discussion," he gasped. "It's over. I'm not going to let you march me off to jail, and that's all there is to it. You know I'd be better off dead than shut away in prison."

"We can find you a competent lawyer," David said quickly. "Maybe he'll be able to make a deal with the DA, come up with a plea bargain, so you won't have to do time."

"What kind of a deal were you thinking of?" Ned asked sarcastically. "A plea of temporary insanity caused by stress from trying to pay off my wife's credit-card debts?"

At this moment, a plea of temporary insanity seemed quite credible to David, but he didn't want Ned to kill himself to prove the point. He'd managed to get to the corner of the desk. How was he going to distract Ned long enough to get around it?

"You mustn't give up, Ned. Even if your lawyer can't work out a plea bargain, with the criminal-justice system the way it is these days, you're not going to spend more than a couple of years in prison—"

Ned turned white with rage. "You sanctimonious son of a bitch. Only a couple of years in prison! And what the hell am I supposed to do when I get out? How the hell am I going to find a job? And what about my wife? I did this for her, and she'll start filing for divorce the second she sees the first cop walking up the driveway."

David swallowed a comment to the effect that a wife who got her husband hundreds of thousands of dollars in debt, then applied for a divorce, wasn't much of a wife and definitely wasn't worth killing yourself for. What the heck, he thought bleakly. He wasn't in a position to be dishing out advice on how Ned should relate to his wife. His own marriage was such a travesty that he and Eve hadn't made love in six weeks, hadn't managed a friendly conversation in two months. Who was he to judge someone else's marriage, even Ned's?

He was calculating the probability of success if he leaned across the desk and simply lunged for the gun when the phone rang. With the typical ingrained reaction of a long-time stockbroker, Ned glanced toward the phone, almost as if considering picking up the receiver. For a single vital instant, his attention was distracted.

This was the only chance he'd get, and David took it. Propelled by adrenaline and guilt, he threw himself across the corner of the desk, bringing the side of his hand down on Ned's wrist in a karate-style chop hard enough to crack bone. Ned's hand jerked reflexively around the firing mechanism of the gun and a bullet exploded out of the barrel. David slumped against the desk, light-headed with relief.

"Oh my God, I've killed you! My only friend!" Ned burst into tears and collapsed into his leather swivel chair, the gun dangling limply from his injured hand.

"Hey, calm down, you didn't kill me." David removed the gun from Ned's fingers, ignoring—actually not feeling—the pain that ripped from his left elbow to his shoulder when he moved.

The door to the office burst open, revealing the distraught faces of Cyrus Frank, the managing partner, and Jean, his secretary.

"What's going on here?" Cyrus demanded. His gaze fell on Ned, now sobbing uncontrollably, and then rested horror-stricken on David's arm. "My God!" was all he managed to say.

"Don't move," Jean said. "I'll call the paramedics."

"No, don't bother," Cyrus said. "I'll drive him straight to the hospital. That'll be quicker." He visibly pulled himself together and spoke with the crisp authority that came with thirty years of success.

David tried to smile. Beneath his curmudgeonly exterior, Cyrus was a grade-A softie, but Ned needed a lawyer and a good psychiatrist, not the hustle and bustle of a hospital emergency room.

"No need to panic," he said, feeling lassitude consume him now that the major crisis was over. "No damage done. Ned's going to be okay, aren't you, Ned?"

Ned stared ahead, blank eyed, and Cyrus snorted. "He's not the one I'm worried about. It's your arm that needs attention, David, so don't argue. I'm taking you to the hospital right this minute. Come on. Jean can take care of calling the police."

"My arm?" David looked down and was astonished to see blood soaking through the sleeve of his shirt in an ever-widening stain.

Damn, he thought sluggishly. *This was a new shirt.* Several seconds later he came up with another thought.

Ned shot me.

He continued to stare at the red stain, hypnotized by the speed with which it was spreading, while Cyrus walked across the room and took the gun from him, handing it to Jean. "Take care of this, will you? Call security. Ask them to send a man up until the police get here." He slipped his arm around David's shoulder, offering his support. "Let's go, Dave, old buddy. We need to get you stitched up and pumped full of antibiotics."

David shook his head, not in denial, but to clear away the wooziness. "Call Amy," he said to Jean. "And make sure she gets here fast. Jean, whatever happens, don't leave Ned alone, not even to go to the bathroom."

"All right," she said. "I'll take care of things. Don't worry, David. I'll baby-sit Ned until the police get here. Now you go and get that gunshot wound looked at."

"Ned needs a lawyer. And we must call his wife." Had he mentioned that already? "Cyrus, we need to arrange for—"

"Shut up," Cyrus said pleasantly. "*You* don't need to arrange anything. We're leaving for the hospital. Now."

"Go on, David," Jean said, making a shooing movement. "What are you waiting for? You're dripping blood all over the office furniture."

Call Eve for me, David nearly said, but then decided against it. Eve would be getting ready to wind up the evening news broadcast, and she didn't need to have his problems added to the controlled chaos that passed for a normal working environment at New York City's most popular local TV station. He'd explain everything when he got home. Now that the facts about Ned were out in the open, he could finally tell Eve about the two million dollars in missing funds, and how he'd spent the past couple of months working his ass off to uncover the truth about the thefts. Once she knew about Ned's nefarious activities, Eve would understand why he'd spent so many hours at the office on nights and weekends, and why he'd been so vague about what he was doing.

David felt a surge of optimism, of real honest-to-God hope. Maybe this would be a chance for him and Eve to make a new start, to get some of their problems onto the table and begin to heal the hurts they'd inflicted on each other over the past few months.

Despite the throbbing pain he now felt in his arm, the prospect was almost enough to make him smile.

IT WAS A SLOW NIGHT in the emergency room, and David was only the third gunshot victim that evening. To a medical staff where even the newest trainee had already seen and dealt with a hundred bullet wounds, his injury was entirely routine. In less than an hour, his arm had been X-rayed, cleaned, stitched and bandaged.

Cyrus, reassured that his favorite junior partner was not about to expire, took off to confront Ned about his crimes, leaving David to cope with three hours of paperwork and a bored cop who seemed convinced that David was guilty of something, even if only terminal stupidity. The cop passed him to a clerk in the hospital billing department, who recorded David's economic history with extreme suspicion and excruciating thoroughness. When he was finally allowed to go, David wasn't sure whether he'd been more intimidated by the cop or his session with the billing clerk. On balance, he thought the clerk could give the cop several valuable pointers on how to maximize the fear factor during interrogation.

It was well after ten o'clock when he paid off the cabbie outside his fashionable Upper East Side apartment. He felt battered, bone weary, woozy from painkillers and distinctly sorry for himself. His mouth was dry and furry. His arm ached, his head ached, his stomach ached, and his butt ached from sitting on a hard plastic chair with rickety aluminum legs. Absurdly, even his conscience ached, as if somehow he was responsible for Ned's problems and the fact that two million dollars was missing from the firm's accounts.

He rode the elevator up to his apartment, slumped against the wall, nursing his hurt and his uneasy psyche. In a fit of misplaced bravado, he'd refused a sling. Now the muscles in his arm were screaming in protest. Cradling his left wrist, he tried to slip the key into the lock without exerting pressure on his sore muscles. He fumbled for a while and finally managed to turn the key. He closed his eyes for a split second before opening the door, shaken by the intensity of his longing to find Eve waiting inside for him, looking as she had in those magical early days when they'd fallen in love.

Resting against the corridor wall, he remembered with sudden aching clarity how she'd smiled at him on their first date. After they'd eaten lunch, they'd walked through Central Park and she'd stopped to lean against a tree. Her face had been soft and flushed, and her eyes had been warm with invitation. Unable to resist, he'd stepped close and kissed her—a light questioning kiss, filled with the promise of all he wanted them to share when they were finally alone. Now, almost three years later, he could still taste her lips, still feel the hesitant eagerness of her response. Right at this moment, he wanted to recapture the warmth and tenderness of that first kiss more than he'd ever wanted anything in his life. He shifted his weight forward against the door, pushing it open with his good shoulder, praying Eve would be there, praying she would welcome him without a barrage of questions.

She was home, but she wasn't sitting there waiting for him with gentle smiles and eyes misty with love. She was seated at her desk in the corner of the living room, files, papers and flowcharts spread out around her. Every line of her body appeared stiff with tension. She looked up as David came into the apartment, her face pale and her eyes blank. Despite the blankness—or maybe because of it—he could sense the intensity of her anger, like a physical presence in the room. He knew her guarded expression masked emotions so volatile, so fierce, she was afraid to let even a hint of them appear.

He automatically girded himself to protect his own extreme vulnerability. Tonight he simply couldn't take any more hurt. He meant to smile in apology, but he felt his forehead crease into a frown. "I'm sorry I'm late—"

"Don't bother to apologize," Eve snapped, her voice brittle. "Let me guess. You started talking with the guys at the office about Japanese rice futures or some other equally riveting subject and just forgot to call."

Her sarcasm sliced into him, cutting against the pain of his wound like the stab of a knife. For an appalling, terrifying moment, he actually felt tears burn at the back of his throat. Good God, he was a man! He couldn't cry! He turned away so that she wouldn't see the rigid, awkward way he was holding his arm, or the blood spattered on the part of his shirt not hidden by his jacket. To hell with it, he thought resentfully. He wasn't going to beg for sympathy.

"Something like that," he said, voice cooler and less emotional than an ice floe. "I'm sorry."

"That's it?" she demanded, her body ramrod straight, vibrating with the anger she wouldn't allow herself to express any other way. "That's your total explanation for why you left me alone tonight on my—" She stopped abruptly.

"That's it," David said. "There you have it. My total explanation." Misery, anger and fatigue churned inside him so rapidly that he scarcely knew where one feeling began and the other ended. The pain of his bullet wound reached inward, where it met with the pain inflicted by Eve's harshness. The two pains touched, exploding into one giant, throbbing wound.

Eve stood up. Despite the painkilling drugs and his mind-numbing tiredness, he saw that she held on to the edge of her desk, as if to stop herself from shaking. With anger, he supposed. God knows, these days their entire life seemed to be one long silence, punctuated by brief exclamation points of rage.

She was so beautiful he couldn't resist lifting his eyes to her face, searching for some hint, however small, that she still cared. He could have saved himself the trouble. Her gray-blue eyes remained blank, wiped clean of emotion. He wondered what had happened to the beguiling sparkle of laughter that had once seemed an integral part of her expression. Gone, he supposed, to the same mysterious place as their comfortable chitchat and their once-fantastic sex life.

She dropped her gaze to the stack of papers on her desk and made a notation on one of them with her pencil, almost as if he was so insignificant that she just wanted him to go away and leave her free to catch up on her administrative work.

"We clearly don't have anything pleasant left to say to each other," she said, her voice remote to the point of boredom.

"We don't seem to have anything left to say, period." *Tell me I'm wrong,* he pleaded silently.

"You're right," she said. The point of her pencil snapped, and she stared at it, rather than him. "David, this... situation has gone on long enough. I can't bear—" She stopped abruptly. "I want a divorce, and I'll do whatever it takes to get one."

He felt the words like a blow aimed right at his wounded arm. Was that how she saw their marriage? As a *situation?* His pride began to ache right along with his arm and his backside. "There's no need to sound so damned aggressive," he said. "If you want out of this marriage, then go. As you may have noticed, nobody's begging you to stay, least of all me."

Her fingers flattened for a moment against the desk. "I'm well aware of that." She turned her back and spoke over her shoulder. "We should make this as painless as possible. Are you going to move out, or shall I?"

Even though they were already in the middle of it, he couldn't quite believe they were having this conversation. Eve would never leave him. She couldn't. For God's sake, hadn't she loved him only a few short months ago? Love didn't just vanish, did it? His stomach felt hollow. His mind went blank in a fog of fatigue. "Move out?" he said. "Out of the apartment?"

Eve turned around again. She finally smiled, but there wasn't a trace of amusement in the wry twist of her lips. "Okay, David, you needn't sound so horrified. I know this is your apartment, so I'll go. My suitcase is already packed." With unmistakable bitterness, she added, "I had nothing else to do tonight but pack my belongings."

So what kind of shark was biting her flippers? David thought acridly. Why was she sounding as though this mess was his fault? While he'd been disarming a suicidal colleague and getting shot for his efforts, she'd been packing her damned bags to leave him. The injustice of her accusations left David cold with fury. The hollow in his stomach disappeared, replaced by anger, which was a lot more bearable than whatever it was he'd been feeling before.

What does it matter if she leaves? he thought. One-sided love could only take a man so far. His marriage to Eve had been unraveling for months, seriously disintegrating for at least the past eight or nine weeks. Perhaps this was as painless a way to end it as any. For a terrifying moment he understood what Ned had been feeling when he aimed the gun at his head, understood how tempting it was to fantasize about getting rid of all your problems in a single instant of excruciating, redeeming pain.

When he realized the dangerous place his thoughts were taking him, David drew a deep, steadying breath and walked toward the tiny bedroom they'd converted into his study ages ago, when he and Eve had been crazy with love. He clung to his anger, so that there'd be no room for the despair waiting to seize him.

"Fine," he said. "Move out as soon as you're ready. Tonight would be a real good time." He wondered if other men felt this roaring tidal wave of grief when their marriage ended. Wasn't there supposed to be at least a small sense of relief? "Have your lawyer call mine in the morning. Let's make this break clean and fast."

"Sounds like a great idea," Eve said. "The faster the better. Who's your lawyer?"

Good question, but of course he had no answer. Until tonight, finding a divorce attorney hadn't been high on his list of things to do. "Who's yours?" he countered.

"Jeb Goldman."

She'd obviously been planning this divorce for a while, David realized. Not only were her bags packed, but she'd even chosen her legal adviser. A friend of *his*. What the hell.

He didn't care. It was time for them to split. If he was going to feel this hurt, this lost, this lonely, he'd just as soon feel it alone.

"I'll call Jeb tomorrow with a name," he said. "Unlike you, I haven't been making plans."

"Good." Eve didn't rise to the bait, didn't deny that she'd been planning for some time to get a divorce. With acid politeness she added, "Please don't get so busy making your next million dollars that you forget to disentangle yourself from our marriage. Personally, I'm ready to move on with my life without messy complications left over from past mistakes."

"I'm sure you are. Far be it from me to stand in the way of your dazzling future." What did she mean, she was ready to move on with her life? What messy complications? Did she have a lover? Was she planning to marry again as soon as their divorce was final?

He couldn't bear to ask or even to think about it. He strode into the study, slamming the door behind him. He felt a stitch pop in his arm. He pressed his fingers to the blood seeping through his gauze bandage, collapsed onto the sofa and leaned back against the cushions, eyes closed, forehead pounding.

One way and another, this had been a hell of a day.

Chapter One

Even if she hadn't been worried about the possibility of encountering her ex-husband, the town of Eternity would have made Eve Graham nervous. Picturesque tree-lined streets and distant glimpses of salt marsh, framed by winsome Greek-revival buildings, was definitely not her style.

Born and raised in Fargo, North Dakota, a graduate of rural Wooster College in Ohio, it had taken her six months to stop feeling faint every time she descended into the surreal world of the New York subway system. Now, nine years later, she was a dyed-in-the-wool New Yorker who viewed clean streets with suspicion, got headaches breathing air that wasn't polluted and developed instant insomnia unless the decibel level was earsplitting. From her perspective, Eternity flunked out on all major counts.

Jaw clenched—a permanent condition, indicative of nothing in particular—Eve drove along First Street, staring in disbelief as one imitation-antique storefront was succeeded by another. Memories and Mementos. Center Jewelers. Heritage Gowns. Windows filled with bouquets of rosebuds, displays of rings, lacy gowns and satin shoes. The merchants in this town sure had the wedding business covered. Eve felt a twinge of regret that she wasn't going to be producing her usual type of cynical hard-edged exposé, because there seemed plenty of material here just begging to be exploited.

Cynicism, however, was out as far as her report on Eternity, Massachusetts, was concerned. Eve was going to make her story cute and gushing, even if it killed her. After months spent trying to persuade Art Sonderheim that "Roving Report" occasionally needed lighter content, she wasn't about to screw up now that he'd finally agreed to go ahead and test her concept.

It was sheer bad luck that his favorite niece had decided to get married last month in the Eternity chapel and that Art—a man who normally made Attila the Hun look sentimental—had come back to New York misty-eyed over the charming wedding ceremony and the quaintness of the town. Eve and the rest of the "Roving Report" crew had been ordered up to Eternity on two weeks' notice, before glorious New England fall turned into dreary frigid winter. According to Art, if they filmed the story right, it would be utterly captivating.

The fact that Art actually used the word "captivating" had Eve sweating even before she left Manhattan. Her boss's instructions usually tended to be loaded with four-letter expletives, not fancy adjectives. His niece's wedding in the Eternity chapel seemed to have caused a definite crack in the granite organ he called a heart.

In some ways, her boss's spasm of sentiment was the least of Eve's worries. Her number-one major-league problem right now was the fact that David's family had deep roots in the town of Eternity, and she knew—her parents had made sure she knew—that after two years of chasing up and down the coast of Central America, David had recently returned to live in the area.

Given freedom of choice, she would rather film on an anthill in the desert or on an ice floe in the Antarctic, than in the Powell-family chapel. The prospect of encountering her ex-husband face-to-face sent shivers rampaging up and down her spine. And those betraying shivers made her furious. David's current whereabouts were no concern of hers. Despite the fact that her family was forever trying to pass on details about his activities, Eve wasn't willing to listen. She didn't care why he'd thrown away his profitable career as a stockbroker to pursue the risky profession of deep-sea diver. She didn't care why his career on the New York Stock Exchange, which had consumed a hundred percent of his attention during the final months of their marriage, was suddenly of no importance the day after their divorce was final. Presumably he'd become a workaholic because he found their marriage boring. Once the marriage ended, so did his need to obsess about his career.

Eve refused to waste her time worrying about past motives and lost opportunities. After two years of living alone, she liked to believe she'd put her relationship with David into proper perspective. She and her therapist agreed that her ex-husband no longer had the power to wound her, so why was she getting chills and goose bumps at the prospect of seeing him again?

A white-painted sign, decorated with a pair of wedding bells, pointed the way to the Eternity chapel. Eve raised disbelieving eyebrows, then shrugged. What the heck. She had a job to do, which didn't include mockery of the town ambience. Whatever her personal feelings about the institution of marriage, her program on the local wedding industry was going to be sweet enough to send every diabetic in America into immediate insulin overload. Or was it underload? Eve's grasp of the functioning of the human body was somewhere between minimal and nonexistent.

Back in high school, when she discovered she was required to dissect a fetal pig in order to pass biology, she'd switched at once to astronomy. Consequently she was much better at naming stars and planets than she was at identifying the functions of body parts.

Early in their marriage, she'd told David the story of her short-lived biology class, and he'd found it delightful. He'd immediately taken her to bed and given her an erotic lesson in anatomy, earning an A-plus for speed and skill in finding the erogenous zones of an adult human female.

Unfortunately his glow of romantic approval hadn't lasted very long. By the time their marriage ended, he considered the fact that she'd wimped out of biology lab as just one more infuriating example of her refusal to confront life's harsh realities. During the final hideous weeks of their foray into married bliss, he'd insisted that her view of the world was dangerously blinkered and sentimental. With the sarcasm that seemed to drip from her tongue in those days, she'd countered with the acid comment that a desire to have a baby wasn't normally considered proof of terminal naiveté, but she could certainly see how he might consider himself unequal to the task of becoming a father. Blank eyed, stony in his silence, David hadn't cared enough about her taunt to lose his temper.

She often wondered if he'd ever watched her television show since his return to the States. If so, he must realize how much she'd changed from the shy fresh-faced newsreader he'd known. As executive producer of her own syndicated news program, she was no longer a woman who recoiled from the squalor of life's underbelly. "Roving Report" was famous—infamous?—for its hard-nosed investigations. Eve insisted that her crew examine every dirt pile and every maggot in close-up and glowing color. What's more, she was always right there on the front line, directing the mike and the camera lens to make sure she got the best possible view of the writhing mess pulsating beneath life's smooth surface. Nowadays, if asked to dissect a pig, she'd simply have asked where she should stand and which knife would look best on camera. Two years after their divorce, Eve knew she had finally become the ambitious, thick-skinned woman David had always wanted as a wife. She admitted that there was a certain satisfaction in knowing he could no longer have her.

Stopping at the town's only traffic light, she raised an eyebrow when she glanced left and saw the statue in Soldier's Green that honored a veteran of the Revolutionary War. No rushing to keep up with the quirks of modern fashion in this town, she thought in silent amusement. Eternity was apparently well named. Not only did it believe in happily-ever-after, it clearly took a long-term view of history.

She glanced at her watch, fingers drumming on the steering wheel as the light changed and she drove through the intersection. Five o'clock. Her plane had been late landing at Logan, and the traffic out of Boston had been typically horrendous, delaying her still further. She disliked being late for her meeting with Constance Powell. Although she was resigned to the fact that punctuality was almost impossible for people who lived and worked in Manhattan, she suspected that the folks in Eternity adhered to a more old-fashioned standard, and Eve retained just enough of her North Dakota upbringing to know that you didn't keep elderly ladies waiting.

Her temples were thrumming. She reached into her leather briefcase and rummaged around until her fingers closed over the zippered silk purse that contained her pills. Expertly, with one hand still on the steering wheel, she shook out a couple of aspirin and tossed them into her mouth. She swallowed with no difficulty, having learned months ago how to take them without water. The tablets slid down, and her stomach sent up an instant burn of protest.

Her gaze still fixed on the road, she scanned for signs pointing to Lafayette Street while she searched for her antacids. The roll was already half gone, but she stuck a tablet into her mouth and crunched quickly. The smarting sensation in the pit of her stomach eased slightly, but not enough, so she ate another antacid, then zipped up the pill case and shoved it back into her briefcase just as she arrived at the turnoff that led to the Powell estate.

Eve massaged her stomach. Tonight she really would have to remember to eat dinner. Grilled fish, maybe, and a baked potato. Perhaps she should drink a glass of milk before bed or something. Too much was going on in her life to risk a major health problem. With her career poised right on the brink of its next major step forward, she couldn't afford an ulcer.

The Powell mansion was much bigger than she'd expected, a huge gabled mansion built to accommodate the grandiose dreams and oversize family of a successful Victorian merchant. She drove up the long driveway and rounded a corner to the main entrance.

The porticoed front door was framed by two old maples, their scarlet leaves so vivid against the gray October sky that for a split second Eve's breath caught in her throat at the sheer beauty of their blazing branches. She turned away almost at once, reaching into the rental car for her briefcase and walking briskly to the door without looking at the trees. For some reason, their brilliant fall leaves brought a pricking sensation to her eyes. She swallowed hard. Nowadays, unless she was discussing camera angles with one of the crew, she couldn't afford to waste valuable time and emotion admiring a view, however pretty.

The doorbell was answered by an elderly woman wearing wool slacks and a lavender lace-knit sweater set. "Hello," Eve said, smiling and holding out her press card. "I'm Eve Graham from 'Roving Report.' Are you Miss Powell?"

"Yes, I'm Miss Powell, but if you're from the television station, I'm not the person you want. I'm Violet, the *youngest* Powell sister." She patted her neat gray curls in a gesture that was almost flirtatious.

"How do you do, Miss Powell. It's nice to meet you," Eve said.

Violet cocked her head. "You can call me Violet. There are so many Powell sisters, people get confused. First names make it easier to keep us all sorted out."

"Thank you, Violet." Eve stepped into the vestibule, which was paneled in exquisite antique maple. "Is your sister expecting me?"

Violet ignored the question. "You were married to David," she said, not moving out of the vestibule. "It's amazing that we never met you while you were his wife."

"Well, we were living in Manhattan, and David was very busy at the time. I met his mother, of course...."

Violet squinted over the top of her gold-wired glasses, her expression definitely skeptical. But all she said was, "Nice boy, David. Won a scholarship to Yale, you know, before he was eighteen. Brilliant mind, but the poor lad's too handsome for his own good. World's worst communicator."

"Do you think so?" Eve's smile never wavered. There was nothing like on-camera experience for teaching you how to smile no matter what. "However, I'm sure you know that David and I have been divorced for more than two years now, and I'm accustomed to thinking of myself as single."

"Pity. You should have been married in the chapel. Never fails, you know. If you're married there, you stay married. We call it our family miracle."

If she'd stayed married to David, it wouldn't have been a miracle, it would have been a living hell. But Eve didn't want to offend the old lady, so she smiled. Maybe she was good at smiling, but words were momentarily beyond her.

Violet didn't seem to have any problem filling the silence. "I was never married, you know. My fiancé was killed in World War II. At Iwo Jima. After that, well, nobody quite matched up to Dick."

"I'm so sorry," Eve said with genuine sympathy.

Violet turned away. "He was very brave...but it was a long time ago, more than fifty years." She finally gestured for Eve to follow her down the long hallway. "My sister

Constance is waiting for you in the sitting room. We lit the fire in there and it feels very cozy. This time of year, the change in the weather bothers my sister a lot." Violet lowered her voice confidingly. "Her arthritis is acting up, although she won't admit it, of course."

"Oh, dear. I hope I haven't arrived at an inconvenient time."

"We've been waiting for you," Violet said. "Constance has been quite excited."

Eve wasn't sure what that meant. She drew a deep breath, determined to be polite, and not only because the Powell sisters were likely to be important to the success of her project. Life in the concrete canyons of New York City had changed her a lot, but not enough to obliterate the bone-deep lessons of respect for others that she had learned from her parents.

"Perhaps there's no need for me to disturb your sister. If I could just get the key to the lighthouse, I can be on my way."

"Is that where you're going to stay? In the lighthouse? Connie never told me that." Violet stopped and stared at her visitor, her mouth shaping an astonished circle.

"Why, yes, I believe that's where I'm going. Your sister said there's a guest room in the lighthouse and the Powell family archives are stored there, together with a great deal of material about the building of the chapel. It seemed a logical place to start work on the research for my program."

"Yes, I suppose it is."

The old lady sounded so doubtful Eve began to feel worried. "My plans are flexible, you know. I can easily find a room in the local inn if that would be better for you."

Violet straightened. "No, no. No need for that. It's not a problem at all, not if Connie arranged it." Violet gave Eve another swift, sideways glance, then turned and scurried light footedly down the remainder of the hall. "I'm only sixty-five, you see, but Connie's ten years older, and when you get to her age, you have to expect these problems."

Violet might be "only" sixty-five, and the youngest Powell sister, but the threads of her conversation weren't easy to follow. Was Connie's problem her arthritis? Or the fact that she'd invited Eve to spend the next week in the lighthouse? Eve devoutly hoped she wasn't going to arrive at her destination and find nineteenth-century plumbing and a resident ghost haunting the only bedroom. Nowadays Eve's definition of roughing it meant staying in a hotel with room service that stopped at midnight and no valet parking.

Violet paused on the threshold of a pleasant, comfortably shabby sitting room and waved her arm. "Ms. Eve Graham is here," she announced, with a decided emphasis on the *Ms.* "David's wife. From the television program. You know, from 'Roving Report.'"

David's wife. Eve clenched her jaw. It was precisely the sort of linkage she'd been expecting—and dreading. Odd how the simple act of putting a burned-out relationship into words could revive the hurt of old wounds.

Not letting her annoyance show, she stepped into the sitting room. Four interested faces, one male and three female, looked up from their teacups. A frail, white-haired woman, dressed in beige wool challis, rose with painful slowness from her seat by the fire and extended her hand. "Welcome to Eternity, Miss Graham. I'm Constance Powell."

"It's nice to meet you in person." Eve shook the offered hand, careful not to pump too vigorously. Her grandmother suffered from arthritis, and she knew how a friendly squeeze could cause agonizing pain.

"This is my sister June." Constance nodded to a wing chair next to the fire where an apple-cheeked woman sat drinking tea and eating a muffin. "And over there on the sofa you see my other sister Patience, together with a good friend of ours, Louis Bertrand."

Patience, a handsome woman with beautiful white hair piled high and thick on her head, sat next to a dapper gentleman with a neat mustache and a definitely roguish twinkle in his eye. Eve noticed at once that Patience's cheeks were flushed, and she sensed a tension vibrating between her and Louis Bertrand. None of the other sisters seemed even remotely aware of any undercurrents, perhaps because they were all so used to each other's company that they no longer paid each other any real attention.

Louis Bertrand acknowledged the introduction by rising to his feet and bowing with an elegant flourish that reminded Eve of Maurice Chevalier about to burst into song. He took her hand and carried it to his lips, somehow managing to murmur a deft compliment over her fingertips without appearing ridiculous.

Patience Powell, on the other hand, seemed totally discomposed by the simple fact of Eve's arrival. She started to get up, dropped her napkin, rattled her teaspoon in her saucer and sat down again without speaking, her hands fluttering as if she wasn't sure where to put them. Louis Bertrand immediately returned to his seat next to her, and Eve saw him give Patience's elbow a tiny, comforting squeeze.

What in the world was going on? Eve wondered. For some unknown reason, watching the elderly couple, she felt an odd little warming of her heart. If she needed background color for her segment, she'd certainly know where to come for it. Louis Bertrand and the Powell sisters looked like extras sent from Central Casting for the express purpose of adding visual interest to her set.

Constance lifted the teapot with a grace that belied the gnarled knuckles of her arthritic hands. "The tea is fresh, Ms. Graham—"

"Eve, please."

Constance smiled. "Very well, Eve. Please do sit down with us for a moment and enjoy a cup."

With all that she had to do over the next forty-eight hours before her crew arrived on Monday, Eve knew she didn't have time to waste drinking tea. On the other hand, the Powell sisters owned the famous chapel that was at the heart of the Eternity legend, so she might as well sit down and absorb some insider views on the local wedding industry.

"Thank you," she said, sitting on a chair near the serving cart and taking the cup of steaming tea.

"It's nice to have you here," Constance said.

June nodded her agreement. "We're looking forward to your TV program. When will it be shown?"

"We're planning some time around Thanksgiving," Eve said, glancing toward each sister with brisk professional courtesy. It was important to get influential locals on her side, and these matriarchs were the closest Eternity came to a ruling dynasty.

"It's very good of you all to make me so welcome. As the executive producer of 'Roving Report,' I want to assure you that we have no intention of trying to destroy the town legend. As I explained to Miss Constance, our research shows that the Christmas season is second only to early summer as a time for weddings, and we plan to produce a heartwarming holiday piece, dedicated to December brides and their families."

"I saw your program last year on Reggie Perry," Violet said, gazing at a cookie she was holding as if she couldn't quite remember why she'd picked it up. "I went to school with Reggie's father. He dipped my braids in the inkwell and ruined my ribbons. Then he pretended Charles Benham had done it."

Eve's gaze narrowed. The piece she'd done on Senator Reginald Perry had won her an Emmy, and she considered it her best exposé ever—a devastating yet seemingly flattering profile of a womanizing crook at work in the back rooms of the state capitol. The senator had approved every inch of footage, never realizing the destructive, cumulative effect of the material. Eve wondered why Violet had chosen this moment to mention that show. Another symptom of a grasshopper mind? Or a shrewd warning not to try the same trick here in Eternity?

"What did you think of the program?" she asked.

Violet crumbled her cookie onto an embroidered linen napkin. "The trouble with Reggie was that nobody ever disciplined him properly. His father spoiled him, and his mother was frightened of him."

"I'm not sure you've answered my question," Eve said.

Violet looked vague again, and Constance broke in with the assurance of a woman who had spent sixty years interpreting for her sister. "What we mean, Ms. Graham, is that your program amounted to a televised assassination of our state senator. In our opinion, based on years of close acquaintance, he deserved everything that came about as a result of your show. The townspeople of Eternity, however, have done absolutely nothing to deserve the sort of muckraking exposé that is your stock-in-trade. We've taken a great leap of faith by inviting you here and offering you our cooperation. We hope you can be trusted to treat the legend of the chapel and the institution of marriage with the respect they both deserve."

Eve blanched. She was more than willing to concede that her on-camera style was hard-hitting, but muckraking seemed several steps farther down the investigative scale. "Let me assure you again I've no intention of producing a hostile story," she said.

"Even though you don't believe in the legend," Violet said.

"I'm a journalist," Eve snapped. "I don't have to believe every silly fairy tale I hear in order to report on it kindly."

"Does that mean you believe the legend about our chapel is silly?" Constance inquired with deceptive mildness.

"No," Eve lied, regretting her momentary spurt of temper. If the Powell sisters wanted to believe that getting married in their chapel guaranteed a lifetime of married bliss, who was she to tell them they were crazy? Constance Powell had shown her nothing but courtesy over the past few hectic days; the least Eve could do in return was guard her acid tongue.

"I'm sure it's a very meaningful legend to the people who choose to marry there," she said.

Constance looked at her with disconcerting astuteness. "In this day and age marriage needs all the help it can get, even from misplaced faith in old legends, wouldn't you agree, Ms. Graham?"

"Certainly. But, please, you must call me Eve." She had no intention of getting involved in a discussion of the sorry state of modern marriage. Quite apart from the fiasco of her marriage to David, she was so far from being an expert on relationships that she'd just broken off her engagement to Gordon, the assistant producer for "Roving Report," and a man who was almost as kind as he was good-looking. Her friends all thought she was nuts to turn him down and Eve almost agreed with them. Gordon still hoped that their relationship could be rescued, but she was secretly resigned to the fact that some flaw in her character made her incapable of sustaining intimacy.

She flashed the sisters one of her best and brightest smiles, and wondered how long it would be before she could escape to the lighthouse, where she could indulge in the comforts of solitude and her roll of antacids.

Constance returned the smile with one of her own. "Well, then, Eve, could you tell us a bit more about how you're planning to portray our town and the story of our wedding chapel?"

"Of course. The nature of this program is such that it needs to be a cooperative effort. I'm going to be relying on everyone in this room for help as I put the project together, so I would like you to think of yourselves as my temporary partners, with all of us united in the cause of showcasing the very best of Eternity and its legend. This is a small town, not all that far from Boston, and yet the townspeople have managed to retain a unique identity, instead of becoming just another bedroom suburb. There's a lot of material here that could be made interesting to a lot of different audience segments, not just prospective brides."

"Audience segments?" June murmured, stirring her tea. "Does that mean people?"

Eve counted silently to ten, but this time she managed not to snap. "Television producers have to think about the demographics of the audience," she said. "That doesn't mean we forget our viewers are human beings."

Louis Bertrand spoke for the first time. "My dear young lady, we understand completely. As far as I'm concerned, you can count on me as one of your most active supporters." With only slight assistance from his cane, he got up from the sofa and executed another fancy flourish. This one, Eve decided, owed more to Fred Astaire than Maurice Chevalier.

"Thank you, Mr. Bertrand."

"Please, I insist, you must call me Louis." He gave an airy flap of his hand. "You may already know I'm a veteran of several well-received appearances on stage, screen and radio. I would be happy to participate in your project in any capacity you think might benefit from a little extra savoir faire. You can't beat input from a talented local, you know."

Wonderful, Eve thought with a mental groan. This was all she needed. For all his corny ways, Louis Bertrand seemed rather an appealing character with a wealth of stories to impart. In other circumstances, she would have welcomed his interest. But this was Eternity, and she wanted to get in and out of the town as quickly as possible. Before she encountered David—

Eve snapped off that thought before it had time to take hold. She smiled at Louis Bertrand, trying to squash his hopes as kindly as she could. He really did seem a nice old gentleman.

"I appreciate your offer, Mr. Bertrand, but my plan is to focus the program around a couple planning to get married in the chapel."

"But, of course, I understand—"

This time she cut him off ruthlessly. Two years as an executive television producer did tend to leave a person somewhat short in the patience department. "What I really need from all of you are the names of a couple who are planning to get married about two or three weeks from now. I can follow them as they make their last-minute arrangements and interview them about why they're choosing to have the ceremony in the Eternity chapel."

"Perfect," Louis said, not looking a bit put out. "I know the perfect couple."

"You do?" June said, sounding surprised.

"Who?" Violet asked. "Is it someone from town? My goodness, it isn't one of the Van Bassen girls, is it?"

Louis beamed and placed his hand on his heart. "Indeed it is not," he said. "At least as far as I know neither of them is about to commit herself to the perilous path of marriage. The couple I'm talking about is—"

"No, Louis!" Patience interrupted. She tugged at his sleeve, looking horrified. "Good heavens, Louis, whatever are you thinking of? I can't imagine anything more ridiculous."

June turned to her sister with a hint of irritation. "Patience, whatever in the world is the matter with you? You've been squirming around like a cat with fleas all afternoon.

Let Louis finish what he's trying to say. I want to know who's getting married."

Patience subsided into blushing silence and Violet frowned. "Are you feeling all right, Patty? You've been acting strangely this entire week."

"I'm sorry," Patience said in a small voice. "I've been acting strange because I feel so strange." Her blush darkened and she stared at her shoes. "You see, I know who Louis is talking about. It's me. You see, I'm...um...I'm getting married."

"To me!" Louis exclaimed, with a jubilant thump of his cane. "Your sister has agreed to become my bride, and I'm the happiest man in the entire state of Massachusetts!"

His words were greeted with a stunned silence. Constance, June and Violet appeared to have turned to stone. After ten seconds of absolute immobility, they all moved at once, turning to stare at each other in mute, openmouthed shock. Finally, just when Eve was beginning to wonder if she should offer some congratulations to break the embarrassing silence, they all got up and rushed over to hug their sister, exclaiming with delight and chattering like a gaggle of high school students surrounding the homecoming queen.

Louis stood slightly to the side, watching the sisters with much the same air of benevolent possession as a rooster viewing his harem. He did his best to look suitably humble when the sisters finally turned around to shake his hand, but he failed miserably. He looked, in fact, as proud as a young boy who's just picked up his date in a brand-new sports car, and Eve noticed that whenever his gaze rested on Patience, his eyes glowed with an affection so deep and tender she felt her heart lurch. Louis and Patience must both be in their late sixties, or perhaps even broaching their early seventies, so presumably they wouldn't be around to celebrate their golden wedding anniversary. Nevertheless, Eve had a sudden conviction that however many or few years Louis and

Patience might share, their marriage would be rich with happiness and genuine companionship.

"When are you planning to get married?" she heard herself asking during a brief pause in the rattle of questions and exclamations.

"At Thanksgiving, so that all the family will be home," Patience said, her color still high, but her eyes sparkling with a shy pleasure that made Eve realize what a pretty girl she must have been. "So you see, quite apart from the fact that you would never want to film a pair of old fogies like Louis and me, you and your camera crew are going to be gone from Eternity weeks before our wedding takes place."

"But we could come back and film the ceremony at the last minute," Eve said, thinking rapidly. "If the rest of the program was edited and ready to run, it wouldn't be too difficult to integrate footage of your wedding into the final segment."

Louis smiled at his fiancée. "What do you say, my dear? We've waited twenty years to do this, and I would like the whole world to share in our celebration. Shall we take the plunge with millions of television viewers looking on?"

Patience appeared flustered again. "Heavens, Louis, it doesn't bear thinking about. Won't everyone think we're ridiculous, getting married at our age?"

"Are you suggesting they'd prefer us to live in sin?" Louis inquired, the twinkle in his eye a bit more pronounced.

"Louis!" Patience sounded outraged, but Eve saw that her hand crept along the sofa cushions and linked surreptitiously with her fiancé's.

For the first time since Art had pushed the Eternity project onto her, Eve felt a surge of creative excitement. She suddenly saw the possibilities of the program, saw how she could pull together interesting facts about the state of marriage in America today and interweave the bare bones of the statistics with filmed biographies of Patience and Louis. She wouldn't gloss over the appalling national divorce statistics or the misery of failure for the families involved, but she'd point out that there were millions of happy marriages, even in the last decade of the twentieth century, and millions of children who'd grown up feeling nurtured and protected by their parents' love. For visual interest, she could intersperse clips from various weddings held in the Eternity chapel over the next couple of weekends, and the climax of the program could be a two- or three-minute selection of pictorial highlights from the wedding of Patience Powell and Louis Bertrand. It would be a damn good program, she was sure of it, and provide just the sort of leavening "Roving Report" needed to lighten its image.

Eve knew better than to push her point when everyone was still slightly off-balance from hearing news of an engagement that was obviously unexpected, despite the fact that Louis Bertrand seemed to be an old and intimate friend of the family. She would come back on Monday, after she'd done some research, and chat privately with Patience. Louis, camera hog that he appeared to be, was not going to need any persuasion.

"If I could have the key to the lighthouse, I'll be on my way," she said in a low voice to Constance while the remaining three sisters were engaged in a discussion of who was going to call which cousin with news of the amazing betrothal. The discussion between June and Violet was becoming heated, and she grinned, a genuine smile this time, not one of her professional specials. "I have a feeling you may be needed here to referee. Age doesn't seem to be any barrier to disagreement about which relatives to invite to the wedding."

Constance smiled ruefully. "I think you may be right. Cousin Harold has caused more arguments in the Powell family than any two other relatives combined. He married three times, that's the trouble."

"In this day and age, that's not so dreadful," Eve said, hoping to be reassuring.

"Unfortunately Cousin Harold neglected to divorce wife number one before adding wives number two and three," Constance said. She gave a final wry glance toward the sofa and walked, not quite steadily, to the sideboard. "Here you are, Eve," she said, picking up a heavy old-fashioned key. "I think this is what you need." Her gaze seemed to slide sideways for a moment. "I hope everything works out for you while you're here with us in Eternity."

"I'm sure it will." Eve spoke with more sincerity than she'd have believed possible only twenty minutes earlier. "I appreciate your allowing me to stay in the lighthouse. It sounds like a fun place."

June caught the tail end of their conversation, and her head shot up. She stared at her sister. "She's staying in the lighthouse? Do you think that's wi—?"

"Yes," Constance said in a voice that brooked no discussion. "She's leaving now. I'll see you to the door, Eve. No, June, there's no need for you to come with us. I can manage perfectly well on my own."

Constance, despite her arthritis, seemed to be a very determined lady once she made up her mind. Eve was barely allowed to say her goodbyes and repeat her congratulations before she was ushered politely but firmly to the front door.

"I shall expect to see you sometime quite soon. You have my phone number, so just call to set a time. Perhaps Sunday evening, so that we can set a firm time to discuss further the possibility of filming my sister's wedding?" Constance leaned against the doorframe, clearly tired by the speed at which she had escorted Eve down the hall. "It's good to meet you at last," she said as Eve went down the steps to the drive.

"Thank you," Eve said, opening the door of her car. "It's good to be here." To her considerable surprise, she realized she wasn't lying. With the Powell sisters and Louis

Bertrand to anchor her piece, Eternity and its wedding chapel would make a great show.

If the lighthouse had clean sheets and hot water, she thought, the week was going to turn out just fine.

Chapter Two

David zipped up his oldest and most comfortable pair of jeans and thrust his feet into a pair of moccasins he'd bought last year when he was diving off the coast of Central America. Leaving a towel slung around his neck so he could swat the occasional drop of water from his hair, he scuffed into his tiny low-ceilinged living area and hung up his wet suit on the special rack near the kitchen. Then he spread his diving gear over the scarred Formica-topped table he kept especially for that purpose.

It was chilly inside the cottage, but he didn't bother lighting a fire or turning up the central heating. His worry, mixed with a healthy dose of anger, was doing a great job of keeping him warm. This had been an exciting and productive week for him and Matt, but he didn't feel like celebrating.

Grabbing the swing arm of the desk lamp mounted on the old table, he focused a high-intensity beam first on his air tanks, and then on the seals and hoses of the regulator. His scuba equipment was new, good quality and well maintained. He harbored no illusions about the risks involved in excavating a wreck lodged under a deep-sea cliff, and he inspected his gear with meticulous care each time he made a dive. Every single piece of his equipment should have been damn near accident proof, but twice during the past week

David and his partner, Matt Packard, had come close—way too close—to running out of air way beneath the surface of the Atlantic.

The first incident had occurred on Monday. He and Matt had been searching one of the massive beds of eel grass near the wreck of the *Free Enterprise* when he realized that his air supply was about to cut out. Surprised, because he'd already changed tanks twice and it hadn't felt as if he'd been submerged nearly long enough to be short of air a third time, he checked his wrist computer. Sure enough, his sense of time had been right on; he'd only been at the wreck site for eighty-four minutes and his computer informed him that his current tank was good for almost another eight minutes of air.

Unfortunately David's lungs didn't agree with his computer. He sucked air from the reserve supply in his buoyancy jacket and cleared his regulator, but no air flow resumed. He checked the pressure gauge on his air tanks; it still showed they were a quarter full. Computer and pressure gages were in complete agreement that everything was fine. So why the hell couldn't he breathe?

Whatever his instruments might show, something obviously wasn't working right and he needed to replace his tanks immediately. He signaled Matt to let him know he was having problems breathing and swam over to the giant net that was suspended from the dive boat and contained their supplies. Matt joined him, tapping his pressure gage and indicating his surprise that he, too, was out of air.

They strapped on new tanks without making any further attempt to communicate. They'd been diving together almost daily for two years and they didn't need to discuss their options with laborious hand signals. Matt simply glanced at David, who nodded, and they began their ascent. Since the pressure gages on both their tanks had given faulty readings, they wouldn't take the chance that the remaining tanks might not be similarly short of air.

The wreck site was located at a depth of 120 feet, which meant that after eighty-five minutes underwater, they were outside the safety limits for a direct ascent to the surface. But if they surfaced at a steady pace, floating in harmony with the stream of their exhaled bubbles and exerting a minimum amount of energy to propel themselves upward, they could take minimum decompression breaks. As they paused for five minutes at ten meters, David had plenty of time to watch the haddock swim by and contemplate the various unpleasant ways in which it was possible for a deep-sea diver to die. A collapsed lung. Embolism in the brain. Toxic bubbles of nitrogen in the blood. Dinner for a hungry shark. The possibilities were many and varied, but this time he and Matt had gotten lucky.

However many times you'd dived, however many times you'd encountered life-threatening situations on the ocean bottom, lack of air still created a visceral gut-level fear. The urge to kick loose and swim like hell for the surface never entirely faded, but David had lots of experience in controlling his natural instincts. He and Matt had survived far more dangerous situations than this during the two years they'd worked off the coast of Central and South America. The occasion when an overgrown moray eel took a dislike to David's regulator hose and bit a chunk out of it before turning around and hooking its teeth into Matt's leg probably ranked as his number-one unfavorite memory. But that was closely followed by the time rival treasure hunters tried to harpoon him—and would have succeeded if Matt hadn't come charging to the rescue.

This time there were no man-biting eels to contend with, no fresh blood to attract marauding sharks and no rivals with harpoons. The air supply in their tanks held out, and David and Matt took the last ten meters slowly, watched by nothing more dangerous than a few cod. Nevertheless, it felt great to break the surface and draw in gulps of reviving, fresh-tasting air. There was nothing like breathing through a regulator hose to make you appreciate the pleasures of sucking in the real stuff.

Caleb, who owned the specially adapted fishing boat they used as their dive boat, had greeted their premature return with a grunt. "You're back early. What's up? No mermaids down there to keep you entertained today?"

"We had a problem with our air tanks," David said. "Couldn't breathe. We need to check them out before we go down again."

Caleb had responded with another grunt, but his raised eyebrows were eloquent. Like most fishermen, he had a healthy respect for the whims of the ocean and much preferred to remain safely on top of it. Not deigning to comment on their idiocy, he returned to the shelter of the wheelhouse, where he'd provided himself with a comfortable chair and a pile of motorcycle magazines. Caleb might captain a rental boat to earn a living, but his heart belonged to his Harley.

David and Matt took the tanks and pressure gages apart, then checked all the rest of their gear for good measure.

"What's the problem?" Caleb asked, leaning against the railing and viewing the dials, gages, tubes and bits of plastic scattered over the deck.

"I don't know," Matt said. "As far as we can tell, the pressure gages on two of these tanks are defective. The pins jammed. So when we thought we'd totally filled those tanks, we hadn't. Which means we were getting readings showing we still had plenty of air left, when in fact we didn't."

Caleb squinted toward David. "You mean you were down there playin' with the lobsters and you found out all of a sudden you got no air?"

"Something like that," David said.

Caleb shook his head and went back to looking at pictures of motorcycle engines. His silence spoke volumes.

Matt and David exchanged amused glances. "Are you ready to go down again?" Matt asked. "I spotted an interesting-looking chest just seconds before my air cut out."

"Sure." With the imminent threat of winter storms, they didn't have time to sit around and worry about what-might-have-been. The pressure gages could easily be replaced, and no real harm had been done. Within minutes, they had switched to backup gear and returned to the wreck site.

It was on this dive that he and Matt had made their most exciting find since locating the wreck two weeks earlier: a small leather-and-steel chest that held 543 English gold sovereigns, all of them dated before 1860. The documents at Lloyds suggesting the captain of the *Free Enterprise* had been paid off for his cargo strictly in gold looked as if they might be true.

David and Matt hurried back to shore and went out to celebrate their triumph with German beers and fresh crabs trucked in from Chesapeake Bay. In the flush of their success, neither of them had given the failed pressure gages more than a passing thought.

Until today.

Once again, he and Matt had been using sonar to scan the acres of seaweed that surrounded the final resting place of the *Free Enterprise*. Their find this time had been the ship's anchor, encrusted with calcified barnacles and submerged beneath a virtual forest of eel grass. They were cutting away at the seaweed when they discovered a half-dozen sets of handcuffs caught up in the giant links of the anchor chain.

Manacles, David realized, appalled by the size and weight of the cuffs. My God, did they really punish sailors by locking them into these monstrous instruments of torture?

Matt directed the beam of his light directly at the anchor chain and signaled for David to come closer. He saw at once what Matt was indicating. Corrosion made it difficult to be absolutely certain, but it looked as if the manacles weren't just tangled in the anchor chain; they had been deliberately locked to it. What for? David wondered, angling his light at the lock for a better view. The *Free Enterprise* had sunk with the loss of a dozen lives and all trace of its valuable cargo, although the captain and the entire complement of officers had survived. With the ship in danger of going down, why had someone on board taken the time to fasten six heavy sets of manacles to an anchor that was presumably being cut loose from the ship in a desperate effort to stop the vessel from sinking? It made no sense.

To add to the puzzle, David knew that the *Free Enterprise* had gone down within sight of Eternity Harbor and that the survivors had been rescued after displays of great bravery by the townsfolk of Eternity. According to a report in the *Courier,* the local newspaper, the weather on December 9, 1862, had been appalling, with gale-force winds and high seas. Nevertheless, at least in the opinion of the locals, the captain's failure to bring the ship into harbor until too late in the day had been a major contributing factor in the tragic loss of human life. The newspaper's dramatic story, spread over three pages, had been replete with the sort of robust invective that Victorian readers relished and contemporary society considered libelous. David had read the *Courier* report with more than a twitch of wry amusement, despite the grim subject matter. Contemporary society was pretty lily-livered, he decided. As a purveyor of moral outrage, Rush Limbaugh barely registered on the scale when compared to his nineteenth-century forebears.

David stared at the entwined manacle, trying to make sense of what he was seeing. Two questions nagged at him. Why had all the witnesses insisted that the captain could have brought the ship closer into port? And why, when a ship was sinking in a winter gale, would anyone on board waste time and energy locking handcuffs to the anchor line?

They wouldn't, David decided. Unless there had been bodies attached to the manacles. Bodies that someone on board ship wanted to be one hundred percent sure wouldn't be rescued. Bodies that would never even be sighted by the townspeople waiting in the harbor. Bodies of captives? Bodies of prisoners of war? Except this was a merchant ship, and there was no reason for the captain to have taken prisoners.

But what if the bodies thrown overboard had been slaves? Evidence of slavery would certainly be something to hide on a ship that was operating out of a northern port during the Civil War. What if the owners of the *Free Enterprise* hadn't been the loyal supporters of the Union that they seemed? The cargo manifest David had seen in the archives of Lloyds of London certainly suggested there was something very odd in the trading patterns of the ship.

He let the manacle drop and stared at Matt, seeing his own shock reflected in his friend's eyes—the shock typical of late-twentieth-century Americans when confronted with evidence of the brutality of their ancestors. David was anxious to take photographs. He signaled his intent to swim under the ledge to the wreck of the *Free Enterprise*, where he had tethered his camera to the broken stump of a mast. Matt fell in alongside his partner as they swam into the opaque darkness of the wreck.

The beam of the light at David's waist picked out the murky gleam of the fishnet a split second too late to signal a warning to Matt. The torn net, with its almost invisible nylon fibers, floated out at an angle and twined itself around Matt's flippers, clinging with the tenacity of a jungle vine.

David unsheathed his knife and started to cut his partner free, taking care not to pierce the fabric of Matt's wet suit, which would have precipitated its own chain of problems. In the northern Atlantic, at this depth, at this time of year, a damaged wet suit could be life-threatening. Because of the cold, David was wearing gloves and his fingers weren't as supple as he'd have liked. He'd barely snipped through the first couple of lines when a gush of air filled his mouth, almost choking him with its force.

Good grief, he thought, momentarily freezing. *My god-damned regulator valve has stuck!*

Every diving pro had heard horror stories about divers whose regulator valves jammed open, causing the air supply to gush out of the tanks in an uncontrolled flow. In fourteen years of amateur diving and two years as a pro, David had never even met anyone who'd undergone the experience themselves. Now he was facing it. Stuck valves weren't just a rumor. They really happened.

And he was in big trouble.

They were too deep and they'd been down too long to attempt a straight ascent back to the surface. Apart from which, he needed several more minutes to cut Matt free from the fishnet. He signaled Matt that his regulator was malfunctioning and that he was out of air. For a split second, Matt simply stared at him, eyes wide behind his mask.

Fortunately the pair of them had learned to dive together as freshmen in college, and they'd been diving as professional partners ever since David's marriage ended and he quit his job as a stockbroker. Matt didn't need any more information from David to realize the extent of their problem. He unhooked his spare regulator and leaned in close enough for David to share the air in his tank.

Working as fast as his gloved fingers would allow, David continued to cut at the net, separating the nylon strands, thread by painstaking thread. Their difficulties were compounded because Matt's legs were extended behind him and any effort to change his position risked his becoming even more entangled. To further complicate matters, Matt's knife was strapped to his leg-sheath and so was caught up in the knots of the fishing net. What might have been a three- or four-minute job if Matt could have reached his knife, took closer to six minutes with David working alone. He had a few black moments when he wondered if he was ever going to rid his partner of what seemed like an endless tangle of nylon twine.

Finally Matt had been free. They'd linked arms around his air tank and began the ascent, stopping for the necessary decompression breaks and making it to the surface with a joint air supply of less than twenty seconds remaining.

To say the least, the timing had been a damned sight too close for comfort.

David finally finished inspecting his gear. He'd found nothing suspicious, nothing that indicated future problems. He pushed the swing-arm lamp aside and stretched, massaging his forehead, aware of the pounding pressure of his headache now that he was safely home and the emergency was over. He felt tense as a guitar string, thrumming with a foreboding that wasn't entirely rational. What, exactly, was he worried about? Even if somebody wanted to sabotage his and Matt's exploration of the *Free Enterprise,* tampering with pressure gages and regulator valves was a stupid way to do it. Surely any serious saboteur would realize that such methods were much too imprecise to have any real impact beyond temporary irritation? Amateur divers might panic and get themselves into serious trouble, but a saboteur wouldn't expect seasoned divers like Matt and David to panic. So what would be the point of planning equipment failures? The most likely result of this week's accidents was that Matt and David would take more precautions and check their gear even more carefully than usual. Which, in fact, was exactly what they both were doing.

Despite the fact that there was no logical reason to suspect foul play, David couldn't conquer a nagging sense of disquiet. Why the hell did he find today's accident so threatening? He scowled at the failed butterfly valve in his regulator, but he couldn't come up with any better answer than that he didn't like coincidence, and three pieces of equipment failure within the space of five days was stretching the boundaries of happenstance a bit too far.

On the other hand, he couldn't afford to become paranoid. There was no place in the cutthroat world of underwater salvage for divers who'd lost their nerve. And the truth was that equipment malfunctioned all the time. When you were diving every day, the chances of encountering unusual problems necessarily increased. When you got right down to it, all that had happened was that two pressure gages and one butterfly valve had failed. None of the failures caused major problems, and his stuck regulator valve wouldn't have been much more than a passing inconvenience if Matt hadn't been caught in a stray piece of net at precisely the moment David's air supply blew out. And there was no way in the world that anyone could have predicted that Matt's flippers and the fishnet would connect at the same time David's regulator valve stuck.

His assessment of the situation ought to have reassured him. Instead, it increased the nagging feeling that danger lurked somewhere just outside his range of vision, waiting to swim into focus. If he'd been a cat, he was sure the fur on his back would have been standing on end in anticipation of perils hiding around the corner.

He should never have thought the word "cat," David decided resignedly. Right on cue, Cat walked in from the bedroom—a room officially off-limits to felines—and stalked over to the empty fireplace, tail an upright declaration of disgust.

David looked at the poker-stiff tail and scowled. "Cut it out," he said. "I'm not lighting the fire."

Cat stared at him in mute reproach, and David hardened his resolve. "No," he said. "I have a headache, and it's too much effort to walk outside and fetch the wood."

Cat's tail drooped. He huddled close to the empty grate, looking as desperate as Garfield deprived of a year's supply of lasagna. The temperature inside the cottage was at least sixty-five. Cat shivered, his general demeanor suggesting he would expire from cold any minute unless warmed immediately by a six-log blaze.

Muttering curses that definitely would have shocked his mother, David went out to the front porch and carried in an armful of wood, throwing a couple of big logs on top of the kindling already in the grate, and setting the others on the hearth. He couldn't imagine why he'd gone through the farce of pretending to resist Cat's blandishments. He'd lit a fire every night this week for no better reason than that the cat had conned him into it. Why should tonight be any different?

"Satisfied?" he demanded, putting a match to the corner of a twist of newspaper and staring Cat straight in the eye. "Next time you pull that tail-in-the-air trick, I'm gonna take you right back to the pound where you belong."

Cat treated that threat with the contempt it deserved. Gracious in victory, he even condescended to poke the tip of one paw about half an inch toward David. His throat rumbled with the beginnings of a purr.

David refused the offer of reconciliation. He got up, brushing his hands on his jeans, and ambled toward the kitchen. He yawned. God, he was tired! He hadn't felt this exhausted and thick-witted since the night Ned Nichols tried to kill himself. The night Eve left him.

The unexpected memory of his ex-wife brought no pain. He pushed the thought of her aside without difficulty and totally without regret. David had spent months agonizing over his failed marriage, and nowadays he was numb where Eve was concerned. With the advantage of hindsight—that great instructor—he understood what had happened between the two of them. And it sure hadn't been anything earthshaking. They'd been sexually attracted. They'd married too soon. The sexual attraction had worn off, revealing their basic incompatibility. Bingo! End of tedious story.

He opened the fridge door and stared at the shelves, images of Eve smoothly banished. What were his plans for the night? Should he broil a hamburger and enter more of their research data into the computer? Or should he break out the cereal, surf through a few TV channels and do a couch-potato routine?

The couch-potato routine sounded the most appealing. What the heck, he thought, reaching for the box of sugar-frosted flakes and a carton of milk. Since he'd surrendered to Cat's demands and started a fire, zonking out in front of a "Star Trek" rerun seemed like the very best way to spend a solitary Friday evening. Updating his excavation charts could wait.

The sound of a car driving up the road that led to the cottage stopped him in the act of carrying his bowl, spoon, box of cereal and milk carton over to the coffee table in front of the fire. Dumping his armload of goodies onto the kitchen counter, he went to the window and lifted a corner of the heavy, old-fashioned draperies to see who was coming. Other than Matt, who planned to spend the weekend hitting the nightlife in Boston, David didn't get too many visitors, partly because the cottage was situated four miles outside town on a bumpy gravel road, but mostly because he didn't encourage acquaintances to come calling. After two years working on low-budget treasure hunts off the coast of Central America, David had learned that the fewer people who knew the details of a diving project, the better.

It was dark outside, but he caught a glimpse of the car, a Mazda sports coupe, as it shot past the house, heading toward the sea. Almost immediately, he heard the screech of brakes and the sound of a car door slamming, and he realized that his unexpected visitor had ignored the parking spot of sedge and sage grass in front of the cottage and driven around to the lighthouse behind.

Good grief, he thought. Who in blazes would be dumb enough—or maybe drunk enough—to take their car after dark onto a rocky promontory with no guardrails and a six-foot drop-off into the ocean?

He hurried across to the door that connected his reno-
vated keeper's cottage with the old nineteenth-century
lighthouse. Once inside the lighthouse, he fumbled around,
searching for the light switch and muttering a few more
choice curses when he couldn't find it. He was still searching when he heard the scratching at the rusted lock.

David froze, instantly on guard. He stopped his hunt for
the light switch. Instead, he eased his way around the cir-
cular room, taking care to avoid the bumps in the plank
floor and the glass-topped cases that housed Aunt Constance's prized collection of Powell family documents.

The key rattled in the lock. Who the heck could it be?
Surely no experienced wrongdoer would be crazy enough to
throttle their car up a gravel driveway, wrestle with a cor-
roded door lock and still expect to make a surprise attack.
It seemed unlikely, to say the least. On the other hand, this
obviously wasn't a local visitor paying a friendly call. The
ocean-side door into the lighthouse hadn't been opened
since David had taken up residence in the cottage, and
probably not for years before that. Everyone in Eternity
knew that the only access to the lighthouse nowadays was
through the cottage. And everyone in Eternity also knew
that there wasn't any reason to visit the place unless you had
an obsession for musty papers. Papers that recorded such
fascinating details as how much the Powell family paid to
have their roof repaired in 1877, or what arrangements had
been made for serving punch after William Powell's bap-
tism in 1905.

David flattened himself against the rough plaster wall,
wishing like hell he'd picked up the poker from the fireplace. Good Lord, if he'd been this careless during his years
in Central America, he'd have been fish bait before he finished salvaging his first wreck. The familiar rural calm of
Eternity created a false sense of security, but he should have
known better than to let himself relax. Especially in view of
what had happened during his dives this week. In this busi-

ness he brought his own danger with him. Underwater salvage was a competitive affair, and his diving activities could attract the human variety of shark more swiftly than blood attracted the ocean-dwelling variety.

"Thank goodness. Finally! Stupid key."

David heard the muttered words at the same moment the door burst open, shuddering free after years of disuse. The violent bang of the door triggered every self-defense reflex in his body. Even as he launched his attack, a tiny part of his brain registered that the voice he'd heard was a woman's. An even smaller part of his brain registered that the voice had sounded hauntingly familiar. No matter. Adrenaline and instinct overrode everything else. He propelled himself at the intruder from behind, bringing her to the ground with a swift efficient hook around her legs, then straddling her and twisting her arms into a vicious full nelson before she had time to take more than a couple of steps into the darkened room.

The woman screamed once, then went utterly and rigidly still.

David recognized her perfume, the scent of her, before he recognized anything else. *Eve.*

He jumped off her limp body as if he'd been stung by a dozen Portuguese men-of-war. In fact, his body itched with the same warning sensation of poison about to enter his bloodstream.

She didn't move, not even when he released her, but he knew she was conscious with a certainty that went beyond reason. He drew a deep breath, wondering why he felt as though his heart had suddenly expanded to a point where his lungs were crushed. He labored to drag air through them as if he were fathoms deep under the sea.

"Hello, Eve." He finally managed to squeeze out the words. "Would you like to tell me what the hell you're doing in my lighthouse?"

Chapter Three

Her arms felt as if they'd been ripped from their sockets. Her knees had banged on the plank floor with a force that was more or less equivalent to a rookie pilot crash-landing his plane, and she was still shaking from the shock of being attacked. But she'd be damned if she was going to plead for sympathy or understanding from David. She'd played that game for too many months and she'd always lost. Clamping her mouth shut to prevent groans of pain, Eve pushed herself to her feet at precisely the same moment David switched on the lights.

Her stockings had holes in both knees and the jacket of her nifty little designer suit had a rip in the sleeve. The odds were good that she had dirt on the end of her nose. In other words, she looked exactly how every woman prays not to look when encountering her ex-husband for the first time after a bitter divorce.

David, naturally, looked like an advertisement for an upscale line of men's casual clothing. Whatever he'd been doing since their split up obviously agreed with him. In fact, he looked so damn tanned and lean and lithe—so damned *sexy*—she was about ready to kill him. The least she'd hoped for was that he'd have gone bald or grown a beer belly. Instead, he'd matured from thirty-three and handsome into nearly thirty-six and drop-dead gorgeous. She added failure to lose his hair and develop flab to her long list of David's marital sins.

Glaring at him, inwardly flustered because she hadn't expected to feel even the faintest tug of attraction after the painful death of their marriage, she dusted off her skirt, bared her teeth in a feral smile and said the first thing that popped into her head.

"Hello, David. Still having to wrestle your women to the floor before you can get their attention? Sometime you should try saying hi. Boringly conventional, I guess, but you'd be amazed how often it works."

He showed not the slightest reaction to her bitchiness. "What are you doing here?" he asked again, his voice so cool it sounded as if he was only mildly curious about the unexpected arrival of his ex-wife at a lighthouse in the back of nowhere.

Too many of their discussions had ended with David sounding icy and bored while Eve grew more and more tearfully distraught. She was determined not to humiliate herself by following that destructive pattern. Getting a firmer grip on her skittering emotions, she answered with an indifference she hoped matched his.

"I'm supposed to be staying here at the lighthouse for the next week while I tape a segment for 'Roving Report.'" She glanced around the cavernous room, which was empty except for two small display cases, a glass-fronted bookcase filled with leather-bound volumes and a row of metal filing cabinets. Dubiously she eyed the narrow staircase that spiraled around the bare brick and plaster walls. "Are the living quarters upstairs?"

"There's nothing upstairs except an observation tower and a dismantled warning light. The lighthouse was decommissioned right after World War II."

"I don't understand." Eve was puzzled enough that for a moment she forgot to be intimidated by David's presence and spoke naturally. "Your great-aunt Constance insisted I stay in the lighthouse. There aren't two lighthouses in Eternity, are there?"

"No," David said, his voice suddenly taking on a deeper tone. "There's just one."

Eve gave the room another doubtful inspection. "Constance surely couldn't have expected me to sleep here. I mean, there's no bed. No shower..."

"There's an attached keeper's cottage, equipped with all the modern conveniences. Or at least a 1950's version of them." David's voice was dry. "Around here, people say the lighthouse when they really mean the cottage. I'm sure that's where she intended you to stay."

"Fine." Eve felt a wave of relief. She was tired and sore after her fall and she didn't relish the prospect of driving back into town, nursing her bruises. "In that case, I'll bring in my luggage and my bag of groceries."

"You might want to reconsider that," David said.

"Why?"

"It so happens I'm already living in the cottage."

"What?" Eve yelled. She lowered her voice a couple of decibels and tried again. "What do you mean, you already live in the cottage? Do your great-aunts know you're living there?"

"Of course they know."

Eve decided her brains must have been scrambled by the fall, otherwise she wouldn't have felt so bewildered. "Then why would they invite me to stay here for the next week?"

David's smile was entirely devoid of amusement. "Because my aunts are elderly maiden ladies and incurable romantics. I'm sure Aunt Connie imagined that once reunited, we'd instantly fall into each other's arms and say how much we've missed each other since the divorce."

The absurdity of that idea had the contrary effect of lightening Eve's mood. "Well, I guess they were half-right," she said wryly. "We did sort of fall into each other's arms."

David, thank heaven, didn't misinterpret her remark. He actually flashed her a grin that reminded her a little of the old David she'd known years and years ago when they were in love. "Yeah, I guess we did." He hesitated for a second, then added, "I'm sorry about jumping you like that. The locals never use the back door and I expected a marauding beach bum at the very least."

"Heaven help the beach bums." Eve rubbed her arms, which were beginning to throb.

"I'm sorry," David said again. He stretched out his hand and took half a step toward her before retreating. "It's not an adequate excuse, but if you remember, I tend to overreact once my adrenaline starts flowing."

The only occasions Eve could remember David overreacting were in the early months of their marriage, when he'd considered everything about her adorable and sexy. In those long-ago days if she flipped the tab on a can of soda he would say she looked so beautiful he needed to make love to her. If she lifted the weight of her hair off the back of her neck when she was cooking, he'd declare she was ravishing. The pot would be left to burn on the stove while he showed her just what he meant. She felt her cheeks grow hot at the memories, but she wasn't about to share them with David, so she stared at her feet and said nothing.

He waited politely. When she didn't say anything, he spoke again. "Do you think you need medical attention? I can call the doctor, or I could find you some Band-Aids and antiseptic in my first-aid supplies."

"No, thanks. I just need a hot bath, some dinner and a good night's sleep." Eve walked toward the door, feeling sad. It was obviously better that they be polite to each other, but their descent into careful courtesy highlighted the void between them, which once had been filled with love and the beginnings of a rich, warm affection.

"Could you point me in the direction of the local inn?" she asked, anxious to get away from reminders of their failure. *Her* failure. In the end, she'd been the one who'd cracked under the intolerable pressure of weighted silences, career conflicts and David's unexplained absences. *She* was the one who'd demanded a divorce. On her thirtieth birthday. Which David, of course, had forgotten to come home for.

She managed a tiny smile. "Fortunately this town isn't big enough for me to get badly lost. I even have a map in the car."

She sensed David's hesitation, although he wasn't looking in her direction.

"What's the matter?" she asked.

"It might not be quite as easy as you think," he said. "You'd better come into the cottage. Take five minutes to freshen up. Have a glass of something and some aspirin. I'll call the inn to make sure they have a room available before you leave. You don't want to drive for nothing."

Eve's stomach performed a quick nervous flip. "Surely you don't think the inn will be fully booked?"

"Eternity is a wedding town," David said. "That means every weekend literally dozens of people arrive to watch their nearest and dearest tie the knot in the chapel. Midweek isn't so bad, but the Haven Inn runs close to capacity every weekend, even at this time of year, which is sort of off-season for weddings."

"Then I guess you're right. It would be smart to call first, but I'm sure they'll have space for me." Eve didn't want to consider the alternative. "My camera crew had no problems making reservations for next week," she said, trying to reassure herself.

"That's for next week and they called ahead. Today's Friday, the start of the weekend. We'd better check."

Eve wasn't going to let him see that the prospect of walking with him into his home made her panic almost to the point of paralysis. She couldn't understand why this chance meeting was having such a strong physical impact on her.

After all, her parents insisted on keeping in touch with David, and she'd known he was living somewhere near Eternity. Long before she left her office in Manhattan, she'd come to terms with the likelihood of running into him. Why else had she consumed a roll of antacids between taking off from La Guardia and arriving here?

True, she'd spent much of the past week cursing Art Sonderheim for sending her into her ex-husband's territory, but—between curses—she'd indulged in a few daydreams about a reconciliation. A civilized reconciliation that would enable her to get on with her life, and maybe even take the plunge and make a meaningful commitment to Gordon. She'd planned agreeable scenarios where she invited David to a candlelit dinner and they managed a friendly courteous burial of the ugly skeleton of their marriage.

Of course, in her daydreams, they'd always met in a restaurant, surrounded by other people, and Eve had always looked stunning in her most fetching black evening suit. David, by contrast, had looked paunchy and regretful for all he'd lost. Sadly, the reality of their encounter tonight hadn't come close to her fantasy. Still, the basic fact was that she'd anticipated a meeting with her ex-husband—why else had she driven along the town's main street with her eyes darting from side to side like a lizard?—and there was no reason to go into a mental tailspin just because she wasn't wearing an elegant suit and David wasn't potbellied.

"I'd better get my overnight bag if I'm coming in," she said, doing a credible job of sounding bright and cheerful although she couldn't manage to meet David's eyes. "I could probably use a change of outfit before I run into any townsfolk."

"I'll fetch your luggage," David said.

"That's all right. There's no need—"

His mouth tightened with impatience. "For goodness' sake, Eve, let me show you some normal courtesy. The floor's hard, and I used my full weight against you. I'm feeling guilty as hell. For once in your life, can't you just admit that you're feeling bruised and sore without acting as if you've lost a major battle in some undeclared war with me?"

She stared at him as if he were speaking a foreign language of which she understood no more than the occasional word. Her offer to bring in her own luggage had been automatic, a meaningless civility. Why in the world was he glaring as if she'd attacked his manhood, for heaven's sake?

"Feel free to play porter," she said, aware she sounded ungracious, but too dumbfounded to moderate her tone of voice. "I need the small gray overnighter, as well as the garment bag, if it's not too much trouble."

What battle? she wanted to ask him. What undeclared war? She didn't ask, of course. Since they were no longer married, there wasn't any point in probing minor mysteries, minor failures of communication. God knows, she had taken long enough to form scar tissue over the emotional wounds of their marriage. She didn't need to start slicing the scars open now, when she was finally in charge of her life again.

Their divorce hadn't brought the immediate surcease of pain she'd hoped for, and she'd gone into therapy for several months. Under the sympathetic but firm direction of her therapist, she'd eventually managed to put her relationship with David into proper perspective. The sex had been terrific, but they'd had nothing to back up the physical attraction. Eventually David's driving ambition and her own ambivalence about their hectic yuppie life-style had messed up the sex to the point that they'd been left with nothing. Great sex, followed by failed sex, followed by aching emptiness. A sad all-too-common requiem for a modern marriage.

David came back into the lighthouse carrying her luggage. He gestured to indicate she precede him into the cottage. Despite the fact that they were in New England and the cottage was at least a hundred years old, Eve hadn't expected to be greeted by such a homey, snug sort of room. The low-beamed ceiling created a sense of intimacy, enhanced by the forest green draperies, drawn to shut out the darkness. Thick flower-patterned rugs covered most of the maple-wood floor, which was stained an unfashionable but cozy rust color. A beige sofa, piled high with needlepoint cushions, sat solidly in the center of the room, and the fireplace was flanked by two shabby wing chairs, slip-covered in a chintz fabric that might once have matched the bright flowers of the carpet but was now faded into dusky shades of faded rose and moss green. A roaring fire blazed in the old-fashioned brick fireplace, and a black cat with four neat white paws was washing itself on the rag rug in front of it.

"You have a cat!" Eve exclaimed. During their marriage, David's adamant opposition to the idea of acquiring a pet had merely been a forerunner to his even more adamant opposition to the idea of having children.

"No, I don't," David said stiffly.

Eve blinked, but the cat didn't disappear. It yawned, subjecting her to an intense amber-eyed scrutiny. Then, not finding her worthy of further acknowledgment, it stretched itself out full-length on the rug, blissfully exposing its underbelly to the blaze.

"The cat seems to think you have a cat," Eve suggested, bending down and stroking its stomach. It purred with exaggerated joy, lifting a foreleg so that she would have more fur to stroke.

David shrugged. "He's a stray. Turned up on my doorstep and wouldn't go away. I'm planning to take him to the pound as soon as I can find the time."

The cat certainly didn't behave as if he lived in hourly expectation of being evicted to the gas chambers. In fact, he had the snooty air of an animal that knows he's lord of all he surveys. What's more, the rag rug looked out of place in the living room, as if it had been brought in from somewhere else and placed there solely for the cat's convenience. Eve shot a covert glance at David, who was flipping through a phone book, ostentatiously ignoring both her and the cat. Eve smothered a grin and decided not to press the issue.

"Is there a bathroom on this floor?" she said, straightening from her stomach-rubbing duties. "I could certainly use a mirror and some hot water."

"Through the kitchen, first door on your right. It's small but adequate. I'll call the inn while you wash up."

"Thanks. I appreciate your making the call for me." It seemed they were back to scrupulous courtesy. Eve sighed. She was too tired for this brutal politeness, and her stomach was burning again. Astonishingly, despite the burn, she realized she was hungry. It had been weeks since she could remember experiencing genuine hunger as opposed to a resigned feeling she probably ought to eat. She thought of her bag of groceries sitting uselessly in the trunk of her car and stifled another sigh. It must be the sea air giving her an appetite, she decided. The pleasantly bracing tang of salt marsh had been in her nostrils ever since she'd arrived in Eternity.

The bathroom was not only small but also lit by a single dim bulb, badly positioned. However, the inadequate lighting was probably a blessing, all things considered. What Eve could see of herself in the tiny mirror over the pedestal sink didn't encourage a desire for floodlights. Her nifty designer suit appeared seriously ruined. As for her fear of having dirt on the end of her nose, she'd underestimated the problem. She didn't have one spot, she had three: one on each cheek and a long streak of dirt all the way across her forehead. As for her hair, which she'd had the studio hairdresser fix in a sophisticated coil before she'd left New York, the style could now best be described as four protruding hairpins and a straggle of untidy blond fuzz.

She combed her hair and tied it back with a thong she used when she was working out; not glamorous, but tidy. She washed the dirt off her face, then repaired the damage to her makeup as best she could. Finally she changed into wool slacks and a plain cashmere sweater and emerged from the bathroom hoping she looked smart enough to impress David with how well she'd weathered their separation. This was probably the last time they would ever be together, and she wanted to leave him with a more appealing image than torn clothes, disheveled hair and a dirty face.

She realized now that her idea—her fantasy—of a quiet friendly dinner had been ridiculous. If she and David were capable of eating friendly dinners together, they wouldn't have ended up in the divorce court. Her friends kept telling her she needed to open up and express her deepest emotions, or she'd find herself becoming a shriveled stick of a woman, incapable of handling intimacy. Heck, she *already* couldn't handle intimacy, she thought ruefully. Why else would she have screwed up her marriage to David and backed away from Gordon the moment he pressed her for a real commitment?

When she returned to the living room, David was standing in front of the fire waiting for her. One look at his face was enough to warn her that the news from the inn wasn't good. "No luck?" she asked.

He shook his head. "The inn's fully booked all weekend."

Her stomach was not only burning, it was taking a nosedive straight to her feet. "What about a motel?" she said. "Isn't there a motel? Or a guesthouse?"

"The two bed-and-breakfast places are full. So is the motel at the highway exit. There are rooms available at the Colonial Inn in Ipswich, which is a very pleasant place to stay, but it's twenty miles from here."

"Then I guess I'd better start driving." She hadn't meant to sound so darn sorry for herself, but she was bone weary, and at this precise moment a twenty-mile drive to Ipswich sounded like a journey across the Siberian tundra by open dogsled.

She was halfway to the door before David spoke. "You could stay here," he said.

She swung around. "Here?" she said. "With you?"

"There's a spare bedroom," he replied tightly. "I was offering sleeping space, not stud services."

She hadn't meant to sound like a Victorian maiden who feared being ravished. Lord knows, David hadn't made love to her for weeks before the divorce; she had no fear he was going to pounce on her tonight.

"It never occurred to me you were offering anything more than a place to sleep," she said. "I'm just surprised you're willing to have me intrude on your privacy."

"It's no big deal. Besides, it's getting late and it's the least I owe you after Aunt Connie messed up your arrangements like this. I'd call her and tell her exactly what I think of her schemes, except I want to cool off a bit first. My mother taught me I wasn't allowed to yell at little old ladies."

He sounded as if having her stay the night was about as pleasant as opening his home and hearth to a rabid rodent. Eve, who until that moment had had every intention of leaving for Ipswich, perversely decided to stay put. "Frankly, I'm exhausted," she said, "not to mention hungry. If you don't mind, I'm going to take you up on your offer, at least for tonight."

David's face might have been carved out of marble. "I'll be delighted to have you."

"Try to say that without looking as if someone is pushing needles under your fingernails," Eve snapped.

He visibly cut off an angry retort and turned to throw another log onto the fire. "Do you need anything else from your car?" he asked, his voice scratchy with the effort of control.

She cheered up a bit at the discovery he wasn't quite as unruffled as she'd thought. "I have some groceries in the trunk. Basic supplies. Stuff for dinner, that kind of thing."

He straightened, brushing his hands against the seat of his jeans. She looked away. She was about a decade too old to drool over a man's thigh muscles.

"If you'll give me your keys," he said, "I'll fetch the groceries and drive your car around to the front of the cottage. It's not a good idea to leave it with one wheel dangling over a cliff."

She took the keys out of her pocket and handed them over, taking care not to touch his fingers. In the interest of harmony, she ignored his reference to how she'd parked the car. "Could you tell me where the spare bedroom is?" she said. "I'll take my suitcase upstairs and unpack."

"The room on the left," he said. "The door's open, I expect. You'll see an old-fashioned brass bed with a blue spread. The door on the right leads to my bedroom, and the room straight ahead at the top of the stairs is the bathroom, if you want to take a shower. You'll find clean towels under the sink."

The spare bedroom was small, but comfortable, with a full-size bed and plenty of drawer space. The bathroom was white tiled and strictly functional. But by the time she'd taken a long hot shower and hung up her clothes in the cramped closet, Eve's mood had improved dramatically. A CD was playing flute music as she came downstairs, soft and sweetly sad. Handel or Hayden, she couldn't tell which. David had taught her to appreciate classical music, but she was still pretty much of an amateur listener who liked simple pieces of the sort you could hum along to. When they were first married, David had found her humming cute. By the end of their marriage, he wouldn't even put a CD on when she was in the apartment for fear she would desecrate his listening pleasure by breaking into song.

Perhaps the CD playing now was a gesture of reconciliation on his part. Or maybe he'd forgotten how much her musical ignorance irritated him. Whatever his motive, Eve resolved to avoid the temptation to sing along with the flutist. With a little care, she and David would get through the evening without any more embarrassing tension. They owed each other the dignity of behaving like mature adults.

She found him busy in the kitchen, cooking. "I thought you might be hungry," he said. He'd obviously been making resolutions similar to hers. His voice sounded almost normal and he nearly managed to meet her gaze without scowling.

"I'm starving!" she said, wincing at her own false heartiness.

"Good. I cooked the fish I found in your grocery bag and made a salad. Genuine Roquefort dressing, your favorite." He stopped abruptly, clearly not having intended to indulge in reminiscences. Forcing a smile, he waved a foil-wrapped package in her direction. "I even got some garlic bread out of the freezer. I'll heat it if you're ready."

"Great. Terrific. I'm more than ready." Her mouth was fixed into the sort of smile she gave on television when a major disaster was occurring off camera and the audience wasn't supposed to notice.

David broke an awkward little pause. "Well, ten minutes to heat this, and then we can eat." He put the bread into the oven and opened the fridge, pulling out a bottle of beer. "Want one?" he asked.

She hadn't drunk beer since the day her marriage ended, partly because beer was too high in calories, but chiefly because special-reserve California chardonnay and imported white burgundy were the beverages of choice for her crowd. But since David had already dipped the fillets of sole in batter and fried them, this didn't seem to be the moment to worry about a few extra calories.

"Thanks," she said. "A beer would be great."

"Sit by the fire," he suggested, twisting off the cap and handing her the chilled bottle. "We'll have to eat in the kitchen. You may have noticed there isn't a dining room."

"The kitchen's fine by me." If they bent any further backward to be accommodating, Eve thought wryly, they'd both fall flat on their rear ends. As she wandered back to the fire she passed a desk holding a computer and saw his diving gear. "Are you diving again?" she asked. "Isn't it a bit late in the year to dive in this part of the country?"

"We're right on the edge of storm season, but it's been a mild fall. There hasn't been a single frost so far this month, and no winds worth bothering about."

"Hasn't there? I've been traveling so much I haven't really noticed the weather. Although my flights have been surprisingly on time."

"Are you enjoying the travel?" he asked with such careful neutrality that she immediately remembered how often they'd argued about the demands of her hectic travel schedule. In fact, one of his prime reasons for not wanting a pet had been the fact that she traveled so much. Not an unjustifiable reason, now that she came to think of it.

"Work's been interesting lately," she said, then quickly changed the subject. "So where are you diving? You didn't say."

She noticed a tiny pause before he answered. "Matt and I have been fooling around along the coast. Here and there. Neither of us has done all that much cold-water diving and it's an interesting experience. More plant life, more fish, but a lot less colorful."

"Matt is here in Eternity?" Eve asked. "Is he living here at the cottage, too?"

"No, at the motel. But he's in Boston at the moment." David chuckled. "He's showing his latest girlfriend the nightlife."

She smiled back. "Some things never change. Have you met the new woman?"

"Not yet. Although she passed the thirty-day test a couple of weeks ago."

"Wow! And this time Matt's sure it's the real thing, right?"

"Right." They exchanged grins. Matt's women changed so frequently she and David had devised a rule for him: Don't introduce your latest love of a lifetime to us until you've been dating her for at least thirty days.

Eve looked away, tipping the bottle and taking a swallow of icy beer. With an ex-husband, it seemed it was sometimes hard to avoid falling into the trap of reminiscing. "I'd like to see Matt again," she said. "He's a good guy."

As soon as she spoke the words, she wondered if they were true. Did she really want to see Matt again? She'd liked him a lot and enjoyed his happy-go-lucky company, but her memories of him were inextricably tied up with her marriage, which meant they were all laced with regret.

She and David had married on the spur-of-the-moment, with Matt and his woman-of-the-week as their only witnesses. What had his girlfriend been called? Lynn? Linda? Laura? How depressing that she couldn't remember, that she'd been so self-absorbed on her wedding day that Matt and his companion had been little more than a blurred backdrop to her feelings for David.

She remembered sharing a bottle of champagne with Matt and Lynn/Linda/Laura, then she and David had flown off to Bermuda for a heady weekend honeymoon, three days crammed with laughter, sun and sex. Neither of them had bothered to call their families until their marriage was a couple of weeks old. They were so wrapped up in each other that even their parents and brothers and sisters had seemed to fade into unreality.

Looking back, Eve couldn't understand how she and David could have ignored the feelings of so many people who loved them. It was as if they'd floated through the early days of their relationship in a permanent state of intoxication, drunk on lust. She could still remember the nerve-tingling excitement that swept her the first moment she'd seen David. She could still *feel* the anguish of the final weeks of their marriage when nerve-tingling attraction had turned into vicious heart-tearing pain.

"Bread's hot. Dinner's ready," David said.

Eve carried her beer into the kitchen, followed by the cat, who was obviously so well fed that food had to be served on the table before he deigned to show any interest. David slipped him a saucer of tidbits and tried to pretend he hadn't.

"Everything looks great," Eve said sincerely. Fried fish and garlic bread dripping in butter hadn't been exactly what she planned to eat tonight, but her stomach reacted to the prospect of so much hazardous cholesterol with a rumble of pleased anticipation.

"Thanks." David pulled out her chair and sat on the opposite side of the small wooden table. He offered her the bowl of salad. "So what exactly are you doing here in Eternity? You said you were filming a segment for 'Roving Report,' but I can't imagine what about."

"I'm doing a story on the successful wedding cooperative that the town's developed," she said. "And of course I want to include the legend of the Eternity chapel."

He pulled a face at her choice of subject matter, but at least he didn't leap to the conclusion that she was planning to trick the townspeople and produce a scathing exposé. "Sounds like a pretty tame story," he said. "Is it likely to interest your viewing audience? They're used to meatier reports from you. As far as I know, there isn't even much disagreement among the co-op members. They're all working in perfect harmony."

She felt a little spark of pleasure that he'd obviously watched her program. "Meaty" was the word she'd have used herself to describe her work. "I think there's plenty to interest my audience in the story," she said, warming to the project as she outlined it for him. "There are several fascinating stories to develop here. For starters, unlike most small towns close to a big city, Eternity hasn't become just a bedroom community. It's managed to pull all its merchants together into a successful cooperative that both insures the town's prosperity and helps to preserve its unique identity. In the present economic climate, that's a story in itself. An amazing story, in fact."

"True, but how are you going to handle the ridiculous legend my family's built up around their chapel?" David asked. "If you expose it for the myth it is, you'll ruin the town whether you intend to or not."

"Why do you assume the legend's ridiculous?"

He put down his fork, gazing at her in genuine surprise. "Because it is. Because half a brain—a quarter of a brain— tells you that getting married in the Eternity chapel can't possibly guarantee a marriage that lasts a lifetime."

"No, but perhaps couples planning to marry there think things through a little more carefully than people who just rush off to the nearest town hall or marriage mill. That way, they're less likely to make a terrible mistake."

"Are you talking about us?" David asked.

"No, of course not," she said quickly. Too quickly. "I'm just trying to explain the statistics that form the backbone of the Eternity legend. My initial research shows that they're truly amazing, totally off the chart in comparison to national averages. People who marry in the Eternity chapel just don't seem to get divorced."

He shrugged. "So what are you going to do? Film some naive young couple getting set to tie the knot? And end the program with them riding off into the sunset in a cloud of white lace and promises?"

"Not quite." She smiled, remembering Louis Bertrand and Patience Powell. The picture of them surreptitiously holding hands on the sofa brought a warm glow to a corner of her heart. "Give me credit for more originality than that. I'm planning to film a very special wedding."

David broke off a chunk of bread. "Whose?" he asked. "A local couple?"

She nodded and her smile widened. "I'd give you three guesses, but there's no point because I know you'd lose."

"Okay. Tell me."

"Your great-aunt Patience is going to marry Louis Bertrand—"

David dropped his fork. "What!"

"—and they've agreed to let me film the preparations and the actual ceremony, as well."

"You've got to be kidding!" David was silenced by shock and then he chuckled. "So the old rogue talked her into it at last." He leaned back in his chair, obviously delighted. "I wonder if Louis has promised to reform, or if Patience has decided to kick over the traces and live dangerously after seventy years of Yankee decorum?"

"I suspect it's a bit of both. I met them just now when I went to pick up the key from your aunt, and Louis was obviously on his best behavior. On the other hand, I saw a definite sparkle in your aunt's eyes." Eve took another bite of fish and realized she'd eaten the entire piece and her stomach hadn't emitted even a twinge of protest. "Dinner's really good, by the way. You always cooked better than I did."

"Glad you like it." A silence fell. David closed both hands around his beer. A log burned through in a shower of sparks and he cleared his throat. "What happened to us, Eve? We were so happy, and then we were so damned miserable. What the hell happened?"

He spoke quietly, a hint of pain in his voice. Eve found she couldn't look away from his hands, clenched around the neck of the beer bottle. This was it, she thought. The chance she'd been looking for to lay the ghosts of her marriage to rest. "We married for the wrong reasons," she said finally.

"For sex," he said. She didn't disagree, and he scooped bread crumbs into a pile beside his plate. "Is that really all there was between us, Eve?"

"I don't know," she said slowly, wanting to give him the courtesy of an honest answer. "We were both workaholics, and when our careers got in the way, the whole structure of our marriage crumbled because we had nothing solid to build on.'' Strangely enough, the heady sensation of joy she'd felt when she'd first met David had seemed solid, real, capable of withstanding anything. Obviously that had been a dangerous illusion.

Silence fell again, stretching out between them. "Well, at least the sex was fantastic," David said.

He spoke lightly, and Eve understood he was trying to ease the tension that suddenly lay thick around the dinner table. Unfortunately his tactic didn't work. The sex *had* been fantastic. Mind-blowingly fantastic. Her gaze locked with his and she saw heat darken the tan along his cheekbones. She knew what he was remembering, because she was remembering much the same thing. She closed her eyes, but that simply brought the image of their entwined naked bodies into sharper perspective. She quickly opened her eyes again. David hadn't moved, but there was a sheen of sweat on his forehead.

Her stomach felt hollow, her mouth dry. This was crazy! She reached for her beer, but her movements were jerky and she fumbled, sending the bottle flying. She and David both grabbed for the same paper napkin. Their fingers touched. They both dropped the napkin and jumped up from their chairs as if the seats were on fire.

"I'll get a paper towel," Eve said, rounding the table.

David moved at precisely the same moment. They bumped into each other and sprang apart as violently as if they'd poked each other with electric prods. Eve didn't know whether to laugh or to cry, so she stood paralyzed, afraid to move in case she touched David again.

He gave a disgusted grunt and reached for her hands, taking hold of both of them at once. "This is insane," he said, trying to smile, although his breathing wasn't quite steady. "We're behaving like certified morons. We can hold each other's hands without igniting, for God's sake."

Speak for yourself, Eve thought dazedly. If she wasn't igniting, she was coming pretty darn close. With great care, she slid her hands out of his clasp and pushed them into the pockets of her pants, where he couldn't see them shaking. She drew a deep breath and tried for a casual smile. She failed.

"I'll get the paper towels," she repeated. "Why don't you finish the rest of your dinner?"

"Fine." David was on the point of sitting down again when the doorbell rang. Eve realized that the fact neither of them had heard the sound of a car approaching was a measure of how caught up they'd been in their own ludicrous drama. She also realized that the flute music had stopped. Well, at least she'd managed to survive the entire CD without bursting into song. At this point, she should be grateful for small mercies.

David opened the door. "Matt!" he exclaimed. "What's up? I thought you were going to check out the Boston nightlife with your new girlfriend."

Matt didn't come in, but Eve could hear him plainly through the open door. "Amy got called away just as we were leaving. One of her co-workers is involved in some messy family situation. So I went back to the motel. Dave, someone broke into my room. The lock was busted, and the charts are gone."

David swore with creative fluency. "What about the site drawings? Photos?"

"Gone. All of them. We have your copies of course, but someone's on to us, Dave, and now they have everything they need to clean out the site once they find the wreck."

"Hell," David said. As an afterthought he added, "You'd better come in."

Chapter Four

Matt's news was troublesome to say the least, but David's overwhelming sensation was relief. Relief that Matt had arrived before David made any more of a horse's ass out of himself than he already had. Relief that Matt had arrived before Eve realized her ex-husband was suffering from major brain dysfunction, brought on by an acute attack of lust. Why did he feel an overwhelming urge to take his ex-wife to bed when he didn't even like her? When he knew she'd cut him off at the knees the first chance she got? He'd watched Eve in action often enough to be free of illusions; she was lethal when she chose to wield the knife.

"Come in," he said again to Matt, holding the door wide. He tried to find some casual way to mention Eve's presence but couldn't, so he didn't say anything. The old pattern of his marriage reasserting itself with a vengeance, he thought sardonically. Don't know what to say, so say nothing and look like a jerk.

Matt breezed into the cottage in his standard dressed-to-seduce outfit of black jeans, black oversize sweater and Obsession men's cologne. From the skintight fit of his jeans, it looked as if he'd solved the dilemma of whether to wear briefs or boxers by wearing neither.

Matt did an exaggerated double take when he saw Eve. "My God, Evie, is that really you? You're looking wonderful, babe. Simply spectacular. Love that hairstyle, babe. The casual look suits you." He swept her into a hug that David thought went on far too long. Eve, however, gave every indication of enjoying it.

She finally pulled away and laughed up at Matt, her eyes sparkling with some of their old teasing fire. "Hey, Matt, good to see you. You're looking terrific, too, and don't call me 'babe' or I'll report you to the thought police."

"Whatever you say, babe." He grinned at her, then thumped David on the back. "A great buddy you turned out to be. How come you didn't breathe a word about Evie spending the weekend with you?"

David felt stiffer than a steel brace in contrast to Matt's easygoing camaraderie. "Eve's here on business. Her visit was unexpected...."

Matt slanted a hot look in Eve's direction, then smirked at David. "Hope I didn't interrupt anything exciting. If I'd known what was going down between you two, I'd have waited until tomorrow morning to come calling."

"Nothing is going on between me and Eve," David said tightly. "I told you, she's here on business."

"Sure, a real credible story." Matt waggled his eyebrows in the direction of the kitchen, where the remains of their cozy dinner for two were plainly visible.

David was finally smart enough to shut up. He'd forgotten that his friend's attitude toward women lurked somewhere between a hypocritical fifties' condescension and a predatory eighties' conviction that sex was the only reason men and women got together. Eve, despite her feminist views, never seemed offended by Matt's chauvinism and tonight was no exception. She merely rolled her eyes, told Matt his mind would be like a sewer except it was too empty and offered him a beer.

David couldn't understand her indifference. He knew that if he'd given her a leer like Matt's she'd have frozen him with a glance. Hell, she'd have stormed out of the cottage, lashing him with some slogan about his lack of respect for the dignity of womanhood. But Matt acted like a slimeball and she offered him a beer. Go figure, David thought grumpily. He'd never understand her.

"Come and sit by the fire," Eve said to Matt, handing him a frosty bottle of Coors. "Tell us what happened. What do the cops say about the break-in?"

Matt shrugged. "Nothing much. Nobody was hurt and nothing was stolen that's likely to turn up in a pawnshop or a drug deal. Even in a placid backwater like Eternity, the police don't have time to waste on that sort of penny-ante stuff. If the thieves hadn't smashed the door when they were forcing the lock, I wouldn't have bothered to report the break-in, but Joe insisted. He needs an official report, or his insurance won't cover the cost of repairs."

"Where are you going to sleep tonight?" David asked. "I know the motel's full. You're welcome to stay here if you'd like."

"Thanks, but Joe's offered me the spare room in his apartment, and we've already moved some of my things over there."

"Who's Joe?" Eve asked.

"The motel manager. I have an efficiency suite at the motel, two rooms and a bath. That way David and I don't have to spend all night together, as well as all day. It's worked out pretty well so far."

"At least nobody got hurt tonight," Eve said. "Thank goodness you didn't arrive back at the motel while the burglar was still working your place over."

"Yeah, I guess." Matt sounded unconvinced. "Except it would have been great if I could have gotten a glimpse of the guy." Almost to himself he muttered, "Dammit, I thought we'd kept a low enough profile to avoid this." He took a swig of beer and turned back to David. "Whoever broke in didn't pick my place at random, you can count on that. He singled me out, and he was looking for something specific."

David grunted, not disagreeing. "How can you be sure?" he asked, more for confirmation of his own opinion than anything else.

Matt counted off on his fingers. "First off, this guy was no ordinary thief. He didn't touch my stereo equipment or the TV or a bunch of other stuff that would have fetched easy cash from the local fence. Second, the charts were in plain view, right on the table, so they weren't grabbed by mistake, along with something more valuable. Third, any thief who knew enough to take the excavation charts would also know they're useless without another chart to pinpoint surface locations, and this guy obviously went looking for the necessary backup materials. He damn near tore the place apart searching for the rest of what he needed."

"Do you mean that literally?" David asked. "Did he slash the mattress, rip your clothes? What about your diving equipment?"

"Caleb took it to the dive shop for the weekend, thank God. And no, nothing was literally torn. It looked like the thief worked in a big hurry. He emptied drawers, stripped the bed, tossed my clothes out of the closet, but he didn't actually destroy very much. Guess I should count my blessings."

"Damn!" David threw another log onto the fire and watched it catch in a hot red flare. He knew Eve was listening to their exchange with avid interest, but there seemed no point in warning Matt to watch what he said. In the first place, irrational as it might have seemed in view of her profession and their screwed-up relationship, he trusted her not to repeat what she heard. In the second place, it seemed that his and Matt's cover had already been blown.

"Damn!" he repeated. "I worked so hard to spread the story that we're here on extended vacation, doing a little fishing."

Matt snorted. "That may wash with the locals, but we both know it wouldn't deceive a professional salvage operator for five minutes. If word is out in the trade that we've been up here in Eternity since June, the pros are going to assume we've found a hot site."

"It's my hometown," David said without much conviction. "I planted a couple of rumors to the effect that I was having a premature midlife crisis...."

"Yeah, well, I guess somebody wondered if I was having a midlife crisis, too. And once the pros start asking why we're having our nervous breakdowns together, any diver with residual brain function is going to leap straight to the right answer. That we're fit as fiddles and we've found a promising wreck somewhere close to the town of Eternity."

"So why do you think the burglar risked letting us know he's on to us?" David asked. "Seems to me this was a high-risk operation. Whoever broke into your room has put us on guard and gained very little advantage for himself."

"I know," Matt agreed. "There's only one thing I can come up with that makes any sense. Somehow, he heard about the sovereigns we've already found. Maybe he thought we'd already cleaned out the wreck."

David's head jerked up. "He must know we wouldn't be stupid enough to keep thousands of gold coins in a motel room. That's dumber than expecting us to keep a map with a giant X marking the spot where he can find the treasure."

Matt raised his shoulders in a shrug. "He must have anticipated finding *something* in my rooms he could dispose of for big bucks. Otherwise you're right. He wouldn't have risked tipping us off to the fact we're being watched."

David let out a sigh. He picked up Cat and smoothed the fur along his spine, soothed by the hoarse rumble of Cat's purring. "Only three people knew we'd found those sovereigns," he said, voice clipped. "You, me—and Caleb."

Matt winced as he chugged the last of his beer. "Dammit, Dave, it doesn't make any sense for Caleb to sell us out."

"Like hell it makes sense, and you know it."

Matt shook his head. "No, dammit—"

"You like Caleb—we both like Caleb—and you want me to reassure you, tell you you're crazy to suspect him even for a moment. But I can't tell you that." David scowled unseeingly at Cat. "This wreck is in much better shape than we had any right to expect. If it turns out to be carrying everything we anticipate, we're talking huge sums of money. Megabucks. Enough money to tempt almost anyone."

"Almost anyone, but not Caleb." Matt rolled his empty beer bottle between his hands. "It's not just that I've worked with Caleb before and he's always been as honest as the day is long. The fact is he doesn't care about shipwrecks and buried gold and megabucks in profit. Darn it, Dave, you know as well as I do that Caleb wouldn't care if we'd found the lost treasures of Atlantis and El Dorado combined—not unless it turned out that Atlantis had an underwater version of a Harley."

"He sure gives that impression," David said. "But think of the terrific bike he could buy with those golden sovereigns we already brought up from the *Free Enterprise*."

"We've promised him a share of the treasure when it's raised. Why risk a big payoff a few weeks from now—a legitimate payoff—for the sake of a few illegal golden coins today?"

"Because those *few* stolen coins represent several thousand of today's dollars, and I've seen the need for money do terrible things to people." David was seized by a bleak memory of Ned Nichols, waving a gun, sweaty with fear and despair. "Maybe Caleb has an urgent need for cash, right now, without delay. We don't know much about his personal life."

"What's to know? He's in love with his bike. . . ."

"And maybe his ex-wife is tired of the competition."

Eve bit her lip, forcing herself to stay silent. Trust David to assume that if Caleb had gone off the rails, his ex-wife must be responsible.

"I don't think Caleb's ever been married," Matt said.

"But we don't know for sure," David pointed out. "On Monday, I'm going to make a few discreet inquiries into his financial situation. He could have a string of ex-wives and be supporting ten kids through college for all we know."

"Okay." Matt was clearly reluctant to suspect a friend. On the other hand, he knew they couldn't afford to ignore the risk that their operation was being betrayed from within. "Jeez, I hate this aspect of the business, suspecting everyone who doesn't come with an FBI certificate of purity."

David smiled grimly. "Those are the first guys I'd suspect."

"You ex-stockbrokers have real nasty minds." Matt yawned. "Let me know if you need any help with your research into Caleb's background."

"Thanks," David said. "Unfortunately, as you just pointed out, during my stockbrokering days I acquired lots of experience in running character checks and digging up financial dirt. I can probably find out most of what I need by computer."

The references to his old life brought back many memories, most of them painful. He glanced at Eve, who was smart enough to be sitting still as a mouse and more silent than a sleeping snake. Tough luck for her that he could never forget her presence even for a minute. He leaned forward in his chair and stared into her incredibly gorgeous sapphire blue eyes. He willed himself to concentrate on the matter at hand, which was a fortune waiting to be excavated from the wreck of the *Free Enterprise* and Caleb's possible betrayal. The way her eyes used to become a dark smoky blue when they made love was entirely irrelevant to their present situation.

"Eve," he said softly, "your nasty little thoughts are written all over your face."

"I can't imagine what you—"

"Yes, you can. You can imagine perfectly what I mean. I'm talking about the fact that you're an investigative reporter with a reputation for being far too nosy, and Matt and I are a couple of unfriendly guys who like to dive without any interested observers watching the flow of our air bubbles. We especially don't like observers from the media."

Eve was much too clever to continue pretending a lack of interest. "Since I'm an investigative reporter, maybe you should consider letting me help investigate what's going on here. Seems to me, you and Matt are running into some potentially serious trouble."

"Thank you, but Matt and I are accustomed to trouble, and we can manage our investigations without any help from a television journalist."

Her cheeks flushed an enchanting sexy pink. "You needn't sound so damned condescending. I have ten years of experience in ferreting out information people would rather conceal—"

"You're not listening to me, Eve." David knew how viciously competitive deep-sea treasure hunting could be, and he was sweating at the prospect of Eve's getting caught up in the danger. He and Matt were operating legally, as agents for Lloyds of London, but there were plenty of hunters who considered rules and laws about deep-sea treasure as just so many irrelevant printouts in a boring government handbook.

He cupped Eve's face in his hands and forced her to look at him. "If you whisper so much as a single word of what has been discussed here tonight, even to your own mother, I will personally take you down to the wreck site and leave you to find your way back up to the surface. Alone. In the dark."

He was lying, of course, but it was disconcerting to see that Eve seemed to believe him. She blanched. She'd parachuted from planes, gone hang gliding, climbed mountains that would have challenged a goat and even explored underground caverns, but for some reason, despite hours of instruction, she was still terrified by the idea of donning flippers and a face mask, then strapping a tank of air to her back so that she could swim underwater.

"I understand that you need to keep your dive site confidential," she said stiffly.

"Not just the site," David said. "Everything about it. The name of the ship. What we're looking for. What we've found so far."

"As you know quite well, I have no idea what the pair of you are looking for or what you've found. Except that this is obviously a high-stakes deal."

David felt Matt staring at the two of them with amused interest. Obviously the tension between himself and Eve had finally become sharp enough to pierce even Matt's alligator-thick hide.

Matt stretched and gave them a cheerful smile. "I guess this reunion between you two is kind of a recent thing. Some of the kinks still waiting to be worked out, huh?"

"It's not exactly a reunion," David said. "Leave it, Matt." Now that was a ringing clarification of the situation, he told himself. He sneaked a glance at Eve. She was very busy unraveling a thread from the cuff of her three-hundred-dollar sweater. He was a bit surprised she didn't leap in and announce that, except for a chapter of accidents, she wouldn't be staying at the cottage and probably wouldn't be anywhere within a hundred-mile radius of her despised ex-husband. For some reason, she remained silent.

"Sure, sure," Matt said, still grinning with infuriating smugness. "Hey, you know me. The soul of tact in matters of the heart."

Eve perked up at that. "Right," she said. "Matt Packard and Godzilla—the two people I turn to when I feel the need for real sensitivity."

Chuckling, Matt got to his feet. "It's good to have you back, Eve, for however long. Now I'm going to head for home before you decide to hand me a cloth and point me in the direction of the dinner dishes." He waggled his fingers suggestively. "These hands are reserved for more important tasks than washing plates."

"Such as?" Eve asked sweetly. "Holding your overinflated male ego?"

Matt laughed and gave her a swift kiss on the cheek. "Be kind to David," he said softly. "Remember the poor guy is a marshmallow underneath that tough veneer he tries to adopt."

David was speechless. He considered various interesting forms of torture as he watched Matt scratch Cat's head and make for the door, humming a chirpy tune under his breath. He recovered his voice just as Matt was waving a casual goodbye. "If you're free sometime tomorrow afternoon, I'll stop by the motel and we'll decide on what increased security precautions we need to take before our next dive."

He spoke sternly, but Matt grinned, totally unrepentant. "Come on Sunday around seven in the evening," he said. "Amy and I have a busy day planned for tomorrow to make up for all we missed tonight."

"Fine. I'll see you Sunday." David shut the door behind his friend, torn between outrage and resignation. He wasn't envious of Matt's dating plans, not exactly. He never had any difficulty finding female companionship whenever he wanted it, so he was surprised by a sudden feeling of emptiness when he contemplated the long hours of the weekend stretching ahead of him. The thought crept into his mind that it would be great to spend the day with Eve, showing her some of the small-town delights Eternity had to offer. Then in the evening, they could share a quiet dinner. He would open a bottle of their favorite chablis and grill a couple of steaks, and they could picnic in front of the fire.

He quickly corrected the disconcerting trend of his thoughts. He didn't want to spend the day with Eve. Good grief, they'd divorced because they couldn't be together for more than a few minutes without ripping each other's emotions to shreds. Why would he lay himself open to that sort of hurt again? He simply felt restless tonight, in the mood for some female companionship. His mouth twisted in a wry smile. Not to put too fine a point on it, he felt horny as hell. Having an ex-wife sleeping under the same roof seemed to be wreaking havoc with his libido.

Eve was already clearing the remains of their dinner from the table when he walked into the kitchen. "You cooked. I'll clean up," she said when he went to help.

"Sounds like a fair deal." He was determined to keep their conversation polite, friendly and as impersonal as possible. "Would you like coffee?"

"Thanks. That would be nice. We could drink it in front of the fire." She glanced wistfully toward the living room. "I hadn't realized how much I miss having a fireplace in my new apartment."

"Where are you living now?" he asked, scooping fresh coffee into the filter.

She frowned. "Eighty-second and Third. The address is deluxe, the security system is great, and my apartment has all the personality of a packing crate. The only decent room is the bedroom."

"Satin sheets? Mirror on the ceiling?"

She laughed, not seeming to hear the edge to his question. "No, I bought enough bookshelves to line three walls floor to ceiling. The books almost make it look like a room with character." Her hair was coming loose and she refastened the clip that held it in place, pushing a couple of straggling curls off her forehead. Her breasts strained against her sweater, soft and full, unbearably tempting.

David glared at the cat and ordered him out of the kitchen. Cat stared back at him with the contempt he deserved and stalked to the front door, scratching to be let out.

David suddenly laughed. What the hell, even Cat knew he was being ridiculous. He crumpled the paper napkins they'd used during dinner and tossed them into the trash. "What are your plans for tomorrow?" he asked. "Anything I can help with? Do you need directions? Chauffeuring?"

She flushed. "Well, I don't want to inconvenience you..."

"You won't. The most pressing task on my Saturday agenda is a trip to the supermarket to buy milk for the cat."

She smiled faintly. "For the cat you're planning to take to the pound. What's his name, by the way?"

"Cat."

A corner of her mouth quirked upward. "How... original," she said.

He stared at her mouth. "Yeah. I have a richly creative mind."

She looked at him then, not with the teasing warmth she'd shown Matt, but at least without the cold hostility that had marked the end of their marriage. "If you really aren't too busy, I'd appreciate a guided tour of the town. My crew arrives first thing on Monday, and I'd like to have the basic structure for the program worked out by then. That way, they'll know what they need to tape and I'll have an idea how best to frame my interviews."

"You've got a deal," David said, still not quite sure how in the world he'd *volunteered* to spend Saturday with the woman who'd broken his heart.

IF ANYONE HAD TOLD HER before she left Manhattan that she'd spend Friday night sleeping in the same house as David and that she'd spend the next day touring the town with him in his Jeep, Eve would have said that the person was delusional. And yet, here she was. Even more astonishing, she was having a good time.

True, she'd woken up at dawn, oppressed by the unnatural quiet of her surroundings. And admittedly there'd been a certain strain as she and David faced each other over orange juice and the morning paper. Still, the Eternity *Courier* made her smile with its solemn recap of the week's "news," which included such events as a high school football game against the town of Ipswich and a heated vote on the size of the town council's contribution to this year's Christmas decorations. Five thousand dollars could arouse more passion in Eternity than a million dollars in New York City.

David, fortunately, seemed to be taking great care to keep their relationship—if that was the word—on exactly the sort of friendly but slightly impersonal basis Eve wanted. In the bright light of a sunny October morning, she began to hope that after this week she might have a realistic chance of laying to rest the lingering ghosts of her marriage and getting on with the rest of her life. She'd been dreading Gordon's arrival on Monday. Now she almost looked forward to it. Maybe she'd take one look at him and realize she was ready to name a date for their wedding. After all, she thought wryly, wasn't Eternity supposed to be the town of happily-ever-afters?

They visited the famous wedding chapel, then several businesses in town, with David playing tour guide and Eve taking copious notes as to who would make for the most colorful interviews. They stopped in at the travel agency run by Jacqui Bertrand Powell, a pretty woman who was married to David's younger brother, Brent. Even that potentially sticky interview went off quite well, with the conversation focusing on the great news that Jacqui's uncle, Louis Bertrand, was marrying Patience Powell, rather than on the fact that Eve had once been married to David. With considerable tact, Jacqui made no reference to the embarrassing truth that during the entire two years of their marriage, Eve had never actually paid a visit to David's hometown and had only met David's brother when Brent had gone to New York on a brief visit for a fire fighters' training session.

"We've got time for one more quick stop before lunch," David said as they left Jacqui's. "How about a visit to the *Courier* office? You'll probably want to meet Katharine Falconer before you start filming your story. She'll be a good source for you."

Eve was well prepared with background information on the town's major figures. "Katharine Falconer's the owner of the paper, isn't she?"

"Yes, and the editor in chief, too. Her family's had connections to the area for years, but they only bought the paper about forty years ago." He stopped and turned to her. "Why are you smiling?"

"The fact that you used the words 'only' and 'forty years ago' in the same sentence. When you work in television, last week is ancient history."

He looked blank for a moment, then chuckled. "I hadn't realized that I've reverted to thinking like a native. When folks around here talk about the war, they mean the American Revolution. 'Newcomer' means anyone who arrived since the depression."

"So tell me more about this upstart Falconer family," Eve said.

"Upstart? Bite your tongue. Mrs. F. may be a newcomer to the *Courier,* but she likes to remind everyone that her ancestors on both sides of the family came over to the colonies on the *Mayflower.*"

"Once they got here, did they do anything useful?"

"Procreate." David grinned. "She also had an ancestor who was into shipping and competed with my great-great-grandfather in the nineteenth century, so her links to the town stretch back quite a way." He hesitated for a moment and Eve had the impression that he cut off some reminiscence. "Anyway, Katharine's never entirely reconciled herself to being a big fish in the tiny pond of Eternity. The *Courier*'s okay, but she feels a paper like the Boston *Globe* would be more suited to the size and scope of her talents."

"It sounds as if she's a modest woman," Eve said.

"Mmm. Modest rather like Miss Piggy."

Eve laughed. "In that case, I'll bet I can wheedle unlimited access to the *Courier* archives in exchange for the promise of an on-camera appearance for Mrs. Falconer. Thanks for the tip."

"You're welcome. Although you don't have to wheedle access to the archives. They're computerized and accessible to anyone with a computer modem."

"That's great. And surprising."

David smiled. "The twentieth century has reached even this backwater." He parked the car outside yet another building with colonial-style columns and old-world bay windows. "This is it. The *Courier.*"

Eve followed him into a small reception area decorated with striped burgundy wallpaper and set off by dark green carpets. An extremely good-looking redhead was seated at a large desk behind a bank of telephones, sorting through a pile of glossy black-and-white photos. She looked up.

"Yes? Can I help you?" She sounded polite but bored. Then her mouth puckered into an excited circle. "Oh, my! I recognize you! You're Eve Graham, aren't you? From that TV program, 'A Current Affair.' I'm Amy Lewin." In a gesture Eve had seen a hundred times before in similar circumstances, the receptionist moistened her lips and smoothed her hair, adjusting her face into a smile, almost as if she expected a cameraman to spring from behind the draperies and start filming.

Eve held out her hand. "Actually, you're only half-right. I'm Eve Graham, but my program's called 'Roving Report.' It's nice to meet you, Amy. This is a...friend of mine, David Powell. Perhaps you already know each other?"

Eve had spent most of the morning watching the women of Eternity either simper or preen when they talked to David, so she wasn't surprised when Amy glanced quickly at him, then flushed and stared down at her fingernails. David held out his hand and, after a second's hesitation, Amy stood up and shook it. Why the hesitation? Eve wondered.

"Hi, David," Amy said, sounding breathless. "It's a pleasure to meet you. I've heard so much about you."

David gave a groan. "Never come back to live in your hometown," he told Eve in a mock warning. "Who's been talking about me?" he asked Amy with a smile. "My great-aunts? My mother? Whatever they said, it's all lies."

Amy gave a husky little laugh that was surprisingly sexy. "None of the above have been talking to me," she said. "I'm a friend of Matt's."

David feigned horror. "Even worse. Really, I'm a great guy. Honest, trustworthy. Chamber of Commerce seal of approval available on request. Please, Amy, don't believe a word he's told you."

She looked at him consideringly. "He says you're smart and honest and the best friend he could ever have." The phone buzzed, and she sat down to answer the call. "Good morning. *Courier.*"

Eve actually felt sorry for David. She had rarely seen his attempt at charm so ruthlessly trampled on. This must be Matt's latest girlfriend, she reflected, the woman he'd planned to take to Boston last night, before their date got canceled at the last minute. She was very attractive, Eve decided, but much less outgoing and bouncy than the type of woman she'd seen Matt date in the past.

Amy's skin had the magnificent creamy tinge that sometimes accompanied red hair, but a fan of tiny lines at the corner of her eyes indicated she was well into her thirties and several years older than the bimbos Matt usually preferred. Perhaps, after thirty-seven years of playing the field, Matt was seriously thinking of settling down. Even the mightiest warriors fall in the end, Eve thought, hiding a smile.

Amy looked worried when she put down the phone. "I'm sorry to keep you waiting," she said, "but I have to track down Binnie Forsyth. She's our staff reporter," she added for Eve's benefit.

"What's the scoop?" David asked, smiling.

Amy didn't answer his smile. "Someone's dead," she said. She swallowed nervously. "The police think he's been murdered."

"Here? In Eternity?" David sounded more incredulous than horrified.

Amy recovered her poise. She nodded, her fingers busy dialing. "Some kids found the body down on the beach this morning. It was a man. He'd been shot."

A chill rippled over the surface of Eve's skin, leaving goose bumps in its wake. In New York, violent death might be regretted, but it sometimes seemed unavoidable, an integral part of the city landscape. Up here, in the rural peace of Eternity, it was harder to accept the intrusion of deadly violence.

David and Eve exchanged glances. They could hear the phone ringing, and finally the reporter's answering machine clicked in. Amy recorded a message.

"Binnie, you need to get over here right away. A man's been found dead on the beach. Murdered." Amy referred to her notes. "He runs a charter boat but hasn't lived here long, just the past five months. Apparently he moved up from Boston and rented a room from Marge Macdonald. His name's Caleb. Caleb Crewe. Call in as soon as you get this message."

Chapter Five

Caleb's body, shrouded in black vinyl, was being loaded into
a morgue van when David and Eve arrived at the beach.
Officials from various law-enforcement agencies swarmed
around the bloody stretch of sand where he'd been found,
like flies buzzing over rotten food. Detective Pete Pieracini
stood next to his squad car, shoulders hunched, trying, with
little success, to look as if he knew exactly what to do next.
Shoplifting and the occasional break-in were the most violent crimes he was accustomed to investigating, and he was
mad as fire that some big-city jerkoff had committed a
murder on his turf.

The standard yellow tape that marked the crime scene
snapped and billowed in the wind. Their shoes seeping sand,
David and Eve skirted the plastic barricade and made their
way across the beach toward the detective.

"Hi, Dave," the detective said. "I guess I don't need to
ask what brings you out here."

"We heard some bad news about a friend of mine, Caleb
Crewe." David shot a glance toward the cluster of forensic
experts working on the beach. "Unfortunately it looks like
the news was true."

"Yeah, he's dead, more's the pity. Shot a couple of hours
before dawn this morning from what they reckon." Pete was
sweating, despite the fact that a stiff breeze was blowing in

off the ocean. "Didn't realize you and Caleb were acquainted, Dave. He's not from these parts." The detective made nonresidence sound like an indictable offense. "How well did you know him?"

"We weren't close personal friends," David said. "But we'd spent a fair amount of time together. I was out in his boat just yesterday. I guess there's no doubt the victim really was Caleb?"

"No doubt at all," Pete said. "We found his driver's license right next to the body, complete with photo. Age forty, six feet, 180 pounds. And his landlady already confirmed the ID."

"He'd taken a couple of rooms over in Marge Macdonald's place, hadn't he?" David asked.

"Yeah. Jeez, this has been a lousy morning. Caleb's face wasn't messed up too bad, but his guts was all spilling out—" Pete remembered he was talking to an acquaintance of the deceased and stopped abruptly. "Marge got sick to her stomach when she saw him. Couldn't stop crying, and the pathologist ended up giving her a shot. Said it's the first time he's injected somebody who's alive in fifteen years. Jeez!" He mopped his forehead with a grubby handkerchief. "I tell you, it's been like a three-ring circus down here today, and I'm not trained to play ringmaster."

"I guess we're lucky murder's such a rare occurrence in this town."

"We sure are. Wouldn't want to be a cop if I had to do this too often. Don't know how the city guys stand it." Pete stared lugubriously at the police photographer, who was stretched out on his stomach trying to get a final picture of the blood-drenched sand. "I've been with the police department in Eternity for twenty-two years, and this is only our third murder. As far as I'm concerned, that's three too many. I can't believe this happened here."

Eve had been trying to remain quiet and inconspicuous, but she couldn't let that one pass. "Murder can happen anywhere," she said. "People are still people even in a picture-postcard town like Eternity. And some of them are rotten people who do rotten things. Including commit murder."

"I know that." Pete looked at her. "Have we met somewhere, miss? I seem to recognize you."

"This is Eve Graham," David said. "She's a re—"

"A friend of David's from New York City." Eve brought her foot down sharply on David's toes at the same time as she extended her hand to Pete Pieracini. The detective would surely clam up if he realized she was from "Roving Report." "Good to meet you, Detective."

He shook hands warily. "Likewise. Don't get me wrong, Eve. I've got nothing against New York and I realize Eternity isn't paradise. I know we've got our share of all the usual problems. Folks still get drunk, they still have fights with their relatives, and our teens are every bit as pigheaded and pea brained as the kids anyplace else. The difference between us and the big cities is our gossip network. The grapevine out here tends to work real well, and that's great protection for everyone." He cracked a smile. "I guess it's as annoying as all get-out if you want to have an affair with your neighbor, but on the plus side, at least we usually hear about threatening situations before they get totally out of hand."

"I guess Caleb wasn't tied into the network," Eve said. "People didn't know him, so they didn't gossip about him."

"I guess not, although folks in this town usually like to find out the background on strangers. He must've made a real effort to keep himself to himself." Pete stared morosely at the ocean. "This murder will turn out to be drug related, you can count on it. Every damn thing's drug related these days. Jeez, I hope those Boston gangs aren't getting ready to move into our town. They'd destroy everything we've worked for."

Eve felt a surge of impatience. With superhuman effort she bit back a comment to the effect that Pete needed to stop mourning the intrusion of the real world into his idyllic life and get on with the business of finding out who murdered Caleb Crewe. She stuffed her hands into the pockets of her pants and stared determinedly at a boat scudding across the horizon. She reminded herself that she wasn't in Manhattan and that she needed to leave her big-city aggression behind. Despite the reminder, she still felt an almost overwhelming desire to give Pete a swift kick in the pants. She reached for her roll of antacids, popped one into her mouth and crunched down on it. Hard.

"You're sure Caleb was murdered?" David asked. "His death couldn't have been an accident?"

The detective shook his head. "Has to be murder. He was shot in the back with something mighty powerful and fell right where we found him. Probably killed with a .357 Magnum, according to the doc. The murderer fired off two rounds, and the second bullet exploded Caleb's heart."

David winced. "Was he robbed?"

"Don't know. His wallet didn't have any money in it, just his driver's license and a couple of credit cards. But if the killer took Caleb's money, why leave his credit cards?"

"Because the killer was high on drugs?" David suggested.

"Could be," Pete agreed. "But even a thief who's high surely wouldn't be strolling along the beach at two in the morning just hoping he'd bump into someone he could rob."

"Sure sounds unlikely. Two o'clock is when Caleb was killed?"

"The coroner hasn't given a time yet, but that's probably pretty darn close, give or take an hour. The way I see it, Caleb arranged to meet someone and they got into an argument. Then—*bam!*" Pete snapped his fingers.

David frowned. "Who the blazes would Caleb arrange to meet on the beach at two in the morning?"

"You tell me," Pete said. "I never met the guy. Who do *you* think he might want to see without anyone knowing about the meeting?"

"Beats me," David said with perfect truth. "As far as I know, most nights Caleb went to bed early and got up at dawn to tinker with his motorcycle. His heart definitely belonged to his Harley."

"If he was a biker, he must have had biking cronies, right?" The detective looked more cheerful as he pictured some chain-and-leather biker as the murderer. Pete was clearly having trouble dealing with the possibility that a citizen of Eternity had fallen far enough outside the law to kill a man.

"I'm sure he had biking buddies, but I never met any of them." David shook his head. "Sorry, Pete. I wish I could help, but Caleb just wasn't the sort of guy who confided details of his life to his friends. We shared a couple of beers on a Friday night, but basically he was one of your real uptight Yankees."

"Maybe it was a drug deal that went wrong," Eve suggested, tired of waiting for the detective to come up with such an obvious suggestion. "That seems like a logical motive, given where Caleb was found. Somebody could be running drugs by boat and landing them on the Eternity beach at night. Caleb could have been organizing the distribution network in the town. Or maybe some of his biking cronies acted as a courier service to ferry the drugs into Boston. Hell's Angels have been implicated in several major drug busts recently. I did . . . I mean I saw a TV program on it."

David's protest that Caleb wasn't a member of Hell's Angels was drowned out by the detective, who gave a ferocious howl of outrage. "If Caleb Crewe was dealing drugs on my turf, then as far as I'm concerned, the bastard got

what was coming to him. Where the hell was he planning to
sell them? At the high school so's he could screw up the lives
of decent kids? Jeez, I'd like to pull the trigger myself on
some of these guys.''

Belatedly he realized that his comments were hardly in line
with departmental policy on communicating with the public, and he snapped his mouth closed. Even more belatedly
he seemed to realize that he'd given out a lot more information than he'd received.

All formal efficiency, Pete pulled out a notebook and
flipped to a clean page. "Okay, Dave, you said you were out
with the deceased yesterday on his boat." Pete's ballpoint
hovered over the page. "What were you doing? Funny time
of year to go for a pleasure cruise, isn't it? Seas were choppy
yesterday.''

David hesitated a moment. "Caleb took out me and a
friend, Matt Packard. Matt and I were roommates in college and he's visiting Eternity for a while.''

Pete might be inexperienced as a homicide investigator,
but he had the veteran detective's memory for names. "Matt
Packard?'' he said. "Wait, he's the guy who reported a
break-in over at the motel last night.''

"Right. His place was really messed up." David leaned
against the squad car, looking the picture of innocence.
"You don't think there could possibly be a connection between somebody breaking into Matt's hotel room and Caleb
getting murdered, do you?''

"I don't know, but it's a coincidence, and I sure don't like
coincidences,'' Pete said. "Matt Packard was acquainted
with Caleb Crewe and he was robbed the same night Caleb
was murdered. Nobody else in town was robbed and nobody else was murdered. Seems to me that's a situation
worth checking out.''

"Maybe you have a point. As far as I know, Matt's in
Boston right now and won't be back until Sunday night. But

I'm sure he'll be happy to cooperate with you as soon as he returns."

"You don't happen to know where he's staying in Boston?" Pete asked.

"Sorry, I don't. He went with a woman friend." Eve noticed that David made no mention of the fact that Matt had an apartment in Boston or that his "woman friend" was Amy, the receptionist at the *Courier* offices. She decided not to fill in the gaps until she found out why David was so reluctant to discuss his salvage operations.

Pete turned back to his notebook. "Well, then, let's get on with this account of the last time you saw the deceased. You and Matt Packard hired Caleb's boat and went off—where?"

"Out in the bay," David said vaguely. "Around the estuary. Like I told you, Matt's on vacation, so we decided to do a little underwater sportfishing, kind of get the weekend off to a good start, you know?"

"Was it chance that you hired Caleb's boat? Or did you choose him on purpose?"

"We'd already made arrangements with him," David said. "We hired Caleb because we'd gone out on his boat many times before and we'd learned to trust his expertise. He's been working this coast for years. He knows—knew—all the best fishing spots in the area. He knew the navigation charts for this area like you know your way around the streets of Eternity."

"Damn cold to get in the water at this time of year, isn't it?" Pete muttered. "Jeez, you must have damn near frozen your..." He glanced at Eve and fell silent.

"We wore wet suits," David explained. "They're pretty efficient heat insulators." He hurried on, and Eve realized he was trying to avoid further questions by providing an excess of irrelevant information. "Once you get down a few feet you can find some interesting fish. Matt and I use spear guns we designed ourselves. It's a very challenging sport

because the water distorts your vision and you have to learn
how to make allowances for the light refraction when you
aim your gun. Which is a harpoon, of course, not really a
gun at all. And there's plenty of opportunity for the fish to
escape even when you've speared them, which is bad for you
and worse for them, so you have to chase them and try to
complete the kill. Lots of times, you go home empty-
handed.''

"How'd you do on Friday?" Pete asked.

"Okay." David gave a disarming grin. "We're not about
to put the local fishing industry out of business."

"To each his own, I guess. Me, I prefer to stand around
in hip boots and wait for the trout to swim by laughing at
me."

The detective obviously didn't know enough about deep-
sea diving to realize that Massachusetts in October was an
extremely unlikely place for anyone to go underwater
sportfishing, both because of the cold and because of the
almost total absence of game fish after years of heavy commercial fishing. Eve wondered why David was deliberately
withholding information from the detective. He must have
a pretty compelling reason to keep the purpose of his diving secret if even a homicide investigation wasn't enough to
make him admit the truth about his underwater activities.

She listened with only half an ear as Pete ran David
through a list of questions relating to Caleb, trying to uncover a likely motive for his murder. Eve had never met
Caleb, so she had no personal reason to mourn his death,
and her work as a television journalist inevitably brought
her into frequent contact with human suffering. Nevertheless, she was aware of a bleak feeling of regret as she
watched the police photographer finish his task and load his
gear into a white-paneled truck.

The forensic crew had worked fast because the tide was
coming in, and the evidence of Caleb's murder would soon

be washed away by the waves. In a couple of hours, maybe less, Caleb's blood, the churned-up sand and the footprints of the investigators would all disappear, the beach made smooth and new again by the cleansing surge of the ocean. Eve felt strangely sad. A place of death, she thought, deserved a longer memorial than the interval between two tides.

She watched as a woman, one of the forensic crew, trudged up the beach and held out a clear plastic bag containing something small and gold-colored, about the size of a quarter, but oval, instead of round.

"Here, Pete, thought you might want to get a look at this. We found it buried under a thin layer of sand about six inches from the victim's right hand."

"What is it?" Pete asked, squinting through the plastic. "A piece of jewelry?"

"I'm not sure. Looks like a coin."

The detective turned the bag over. "Victoria Regina," he read. "Eighteen sixty-two."

"Victoria," the woman repeated. "She was that nineteenth-century English queen who reigned for years and years, wasn't she? The one who draped all her piano legs in velvet because they were too vulgar to be left naked."

"She's the one," Pete said. "This must be a British coin, then. Course, we've no way of knowing if it has anything to do with the deceased. Could be sheer coincidence we found it near the body." He squinted, holding the bag up to the sun. "Do you think it's real gold?"

"It's shiny and heavy enough," the woman said. "Brass would've gone green years ago. If it really dates from 1862, that is."

"It's probably a sovereign," David said. Eve could see that he was barely restraining his desire to snatch the bag and examine the coin, but nobody else seemed to notice his burgeoning tension. He drew a long, uneven breath, struggling not to sound too eager when he spoke again. "Could I have a closer look, do you think?"

"Don't touch it, even through the plastic," Pete warned. "Hold the bag by the corners so you don't smudge any prints. You know something about old coins, then?"

"Just a bit. It's kind of a hobby of mine." David held up the bag, twisting against the light to give himself the best possible view. "Yes, it's a British sovereign all right. That's the name given to a 22-karat-gold coin minted by the British government right through the nineteenth century and up into the twentieth." He cracked a faint smile. "We ought to get down to the beach, Pete, and start digging. Maybe there's a cache of buried pirate's gold down there."

"Don't waste your time," the forensic investigator said. "We checked the beach out real good. There's nothing else on that stretch of sand but seaweed and crabs."

Pete eyed the tiny oval of gold with new respect. "How much is it worth? Enough to kill someone for?"

David shrugged. "Maybe, given that kids will kill each other over a pair of sneakers or a leather jacket. But it wouldn't be rational to commit murder for the sake of a single sovereign. Its face value was a pound," he explained. "Which in 1862, when this particular coin was minted, equaled about eight dollars, or two weeks' wages for an average working man in England. It's worth a lot more than that now, of course, but not enough to make you rich. Depending on the price of gold and the condition of the coin, a sovereign might fetch eighty bucks, maybe a hundred or so if it's a special date of issue."

The investigator looked disappointed. "You'd need a trunk of the things before you'd be rich."

"I'm afraid so," David agreed.

Pete frowned. "If this sovereign belonged to Caleb Crewe, why the heck did he take it down to the beach?" he asked nobody in particular. "What was the point? Surely he wouldn't be dragging around bags of gold to pay off a drug dealer?''

The forensic investigator shrugged, taking back the sovereign. "Don't ask me. I'm just the dumb hick who wraps the clues up in plastic. You're the detective."

Pete's answering smile was totally without mirth. "Yeah, I can hardly wait to bring my wealth of experience to solving this case." He shook his head. "Maybe it was his lucky piece or something."

"If so, it didn't bring him much luck," David said grimly.

"Ain't that the truth," Pete said with sincere feeling. "Ain't that the truth."

NEWS OF THE MURDER had obviously leaked out all over the town's highly efficient grapevine. Binnie, the reporter from the *Courier,* arrived at the scene of the crime fresh from an interview with the high school homecoming queen. Binnie was young and eager, a graduate of Wellesley who longed to prove herself, preferably by uncovering scandal and corruption in high places. The fact that Eternity was ruthlessly democratic and had no high places to speak of didn't dampen her enthusiasm in the slightest.

She was probably the only person in town delighted to have a murder take place so close to home, and—too excited to remember that a reporter who falls foul of officialdom doesn't collect much insider information—parked her car on a stretch of sage grass at the edge of the beach, slammed the door and ran to confront Detective Pieracini.

"So what's the inside scoop? Any suspects so far? Any motive for the murder?"

If she hadn't made the mistake of whipping out her tape recorder, Pete probably would have answered all her questions without a murmur of protest. Accustomed as he was to cooperation with the local paper, he had none of the big-city cop's instinctive distrust of journalists. But the sudden appearance of Binnie's tape recorder under his nose reminded him that this was no ordinary occasion.

"The department will be making a statement at four-thirty this afternoon," he said. "Now if you don't mind, miss, you'd better move on. We got nothing to say at this time."

Binnie was not so easily defeated in pursuit of her "big chance," and she succeeded in slipping down to the water's edge when Pete was distracted by the arrival of a carload of gawking teenagers. Pete, however, was more than equal to the challenge. He might not have much experience with murders, but he was a dab hand at controlling recalcitrant crowds and pushy citizens.

"Get back up here," he bellowed at Binnie. "And you kids keep off the beach or I'll lock you all up for trespassing. There's no reason for you to be crawling all over the sand. You pay your taxes to have the police do that."

"Come on, Pete," said Binnie, "give me a break."

"You'll get a break," he said. "Four-thirty this afternoon at the police station."

"Let's get out of here," David murmured, under cover of the confusion. He took Eve's hand and headed for the Jeep. Recognizing his need for the warmth of human contact, she didn't attempt to remove her hand from his grasp. She'd filmed dozens of homicide scenes and reported on a hundred deaths equally as violent as Caleb's, but her sense of loss never diminished. If it ever did, she knew that would be the point at which she gave up journalism for good. David must be experiencing her feelings of loss in a far more intense form, since he'd known Caleb and was less accustomed to dealing with the aftermath of murder.

David drove along the coast to a small restaurant in a neighboring town. "We missed lunch," he said. "Are you hungry? They do a great clam chowder in this place."

"Sounds wonderful," she said, surprised to find that she was hungry, despite the large dinner she'd eaten the night before and the unpleasantness of the past couple of hours.

"I'm sorry I dragged you out of Eternity," David said as they settled into a sunny table by the inevitable bay window. The waitress indicated the box of crayons in the center of the table and told them they were welcome to draw on the heavy white paper tablecloth if they wished.

"I know you want to meet some more people in the town so that you can work on the structure of your program for 'Roving Report,'" David said. "But the problem is, if we stopped anywhere in Eternity this afternoon, we'd be mobbed by people wanting to talk about Caleb's murder, and I don't think I'm up to that right now."

"I certainly understand, and we don't have to talk about him if you'd rather not."

"I want to talk about him with *you*," David said. "I just don't want to spend the afternoon inventing clever half-truths, which is what I'd have to do with most of the people in town."

The waitress arrived and David gave her their order for two large bowls of clam chowder and a miniloaf of French bread. Eve selected a blue crayon and began to doodle a series of threatening-looking waves cresting on a barren shore. When she realized what she was doing, she put the crayon down.

David leaned back in his chair, his face pale and weary beneath his tan. "This is one hell of a mess," he said.

"You were doing some pretty fancy footwork to avoid answering the detective's questions," Eve said. "Why didn't you tell him what you really suspect Caleb was doing down at the beach?"

David poked at the ice in his glass of water. "Because I don't know what Caleb was doing down at the beach," he said.

"But you've got a pretty good idea," Eve said.

David's eyes met hers, then slid away to focus on the ocean. "Yeah, I've got a pretty good idea," he said. "I think the son of a bitch was planning to sell us out to a bunch of rival treasure hunters."

Chapter Six

"Treasure hunters?" Eve's breath caught in her throat. "What in the world have you and Matt discovered that's so valuable Caleb risked getting killed for it?"

"Nothing—yet." David looked as if he regretted his momentary burst of frankness. "Besides, Caleb obviously didn't go down to the beach expecting to get murdered. Maybe he didn't realize he was in danger." David picked up the menu and studied it, despite the fact that they'd already placed their orders. "They make the world's best Boston cream pie in this place if you're interested."

Eve had spent the final six months of her marriage dealing with David's unwillingness to confide in her when he had problems. In those days she'd worried herself sick about his failure to communicate, convinced it reflected her inadequacy as a wife. She was no longer willing to waste her energies in such an unproductive exercise. Seized by a twinge of impatience, she leaned across the table, forcing him to meet her eyes.

"Look, David, you can brood in gloomy silence while we eat our soup, or you can decide to talk to me. The choice is yours. Feel free to use me as a sounding board if you think that might help straighten out your thoughts. My job has given me a fair bit of experience as an investigator, and I believe I could make a useful contribution, but I'm not willing to plead for you to confide in me. I'm sick to death of playing the role of brainless bride, begging to be allowed to share in her husband's grown-up worries—'' Eve realized her voice was rising to a shrill complaint and she stopped abruptly.

David looked up from the menu, his eyes blank with shock. "What the blazes are you talking about, Eve? That outburst had nothing to do with Caleb's murder, that's for sure."

"You're right." She drew a calming breath. "I was talking about our failed marriage, I guess." She gave a rueful grimace. "I'm sorry my remarks came out sounding so aggressive. I didn't realize I was still that angry with myself over the way I behaved—over the way I let you behave during our marriage. Anyway, that's in the past and you're right, it's got nothing to do with Caleb's murder—"

"What do you mean, the way you let me behave?" David sounded halfway between annoyed and genuinely puzzled.

"I guess that was another bad choice of words," she said. "I meant that we fell into the habit of role-playing early in our marriage, and I played the role you assigned me without protest. That would have been bad enough, but then I spent the whole time being secretly mad at you for giving me a role I didn't like."

"What role do you think I gave you?" David asked. "Good grief, Eve, I felt way too uncertain of myself to be dishing out role assignments to you or anyone else. I could barely take care of being a husband without trying to prescribe how you should be a wife."

"Maybe that was part of the problem," Eve said. "We were both so overwhelmed that we fell back on stereotypes. Don't beat up on yourself about what happened. I was every bit as guilty as you."

"We were overwhelmed," David agreed. "But why? We weren't kids fresh out of high school, or even young college graduates still wet behind the ears. We'd established demanding careers, we'd had other relationships before we got married. In fact, I'd say we were a pretty sophisticated couple."

"I'm not sure that being sophisticated is a recipe for success in marriage," Eve said wryly.

"What do you advocate?" David sounded brusque. "Naiveté? Ignorance? Teenage marriages?"

"None of the above, of course. Maybe a lot more self-awareness than you and I had, plus a willingness to confront problems head-on, instead of burying them under layers of silent anxiety. The truth is, we were so physically attracted to each other that we never took the time to develop a mechanism for dealing with the rough spots that come in any marriage."

"We didn't seem to have any problems the first year."

"That's because we used sex to solve everything," Eve said with brutal frankness. "When we disagreed about anything, from the color of the sofa cushions to where we should spend the holidays, we'd go to bed and make love. The trouble was, however great the sex, we still needed to decide where we were going to spend the holidays and what color cushions we wanted. And we ended up staying home or not buying furniture or not doing whatever. The reality is that you can't spend an entire lifetime avoiding decisions that may hurt your partner's feelings."

"I guess you're right," David said after a moment's silence. "In retrospect I can see you have a point. By the time we'd been married for a year, we each had this mental list of subjects that were too dangerous to talk about."

"We sure did," Eve said with feeling. "The backlog got to be so huge that to start a real discussion—about anything—was like deciding to take a stroll across a field of unexploded land mines."

"So naturally, every time one of us got brave enough to start an honest discussion, sure enough, one of the mines exploded." David shook his head, his expression disgusted. "When you look back, we were really pretty pathetic, weren't we?"

Eve was astonished to hear herself chuckle. "Yes, but call us typically stressed yuppies. It sounds kinder than pathetic."

"Okay, how did we manage to feel so stressed about something as everyday as being married?" David asked. "Your parents have a great marriage, so did mine. What was our hang-up?"

"With the advantage of hindsight, I've decided our parents were a major part of the problem," Eve said.

"They were hundreds of miles away and never interfered—"

"Not intentionally," she agreed. "But we grew up in homes with very traditional values, and somewhere deep inside we expected our marriage to follow our parents' patterns. You were too much a man of the nineties to consider *asking* me to give up my career, but I'm sure you thought that if I really loved you, I'd simply *volunteer* to stay home and have your babies."

"I was never quite that moronic," he protested.

"Are you sure?" she asked. "I was. Don't misunderstand, David. I'm not trying to point the finger of blame at you, far from it. That was my whole point when I started this conversation. I *accepted* the role you assigned me without a word of protest. In my heart of hearts, I agreed with your definition of how a wife was supposed to behave. So I was more than ready to blame myself for everything that went wrong between us. I felt uneasy about the amount of time I spent at work and downright guilty about having so much professional ambition. So when you started to spend nights and weekends at the office, part of me was mad as hell, but the other part of me accepted your absence as the punishment I deserved. After all, if I couldn't be home for you, waiting with a delicious meal, the bed made and your shirts ironed, didn't I really deserve to have you stay later and later at the office?''

David gave a bleak smile. "Do you want to know why I was staying so late at the office?''

He was going to tell her he'd been having an affair. Eve's hand clenched so tightly around the crayon she'd been holding that it snapped. She didn't want to hear about his ultimate betrayal of their marriage vows, but she'd gained enough self-knowledge since the divorce to realize that it would be better to hear the truth from David than to torment herself with images of adultery that would be all the more vivid for having no roots in acknowledged fact.

"Yes," she said harshly. "I'd like to understand what was going on in your life."

David stared at the black slashing lines he'd drawn on his place mat as if he didn't quite know how they'd gotten there. "Why is it so easy to tell you this now when it seemed so difficult back when we were married? The truth is, the extra hours I spent at the office had nothing whatever to do with the problems in our marriage. Not directly."

"Then what...?"

He smiled grimly. "I was searching for a small fortune in missing company funds. I put in so many hours of overtime because I was working my butt off scanning every damn computer transaction and company record trying to find out who'd stolen more than two million dollars from the stock portfolios I managed for my clients."

"What!" Eve was so startled she nearly knocked over her glass of water. "Good grief! How come nobody ever told me about this?"

"Nobody knew. Being suspected of fraud wasn't a career achievement I wanted to spread around." David's eyes gleamed with rueful self-mockery. "Fortunately my boss had faith in me and covered the missing funds while I conducted my investigation. But I spent the last two months of our marriage with the constant threat of an indictment hanging over my head."

"And you never told me." Eve wasn't sure whether to laugh or cry. "All those days and nights, with this terrible threat looming on the horizon, and you never said a single solitary word to me. Your wife."

"In retrospect it sounds crazy, but your career was taking off to new heights of success, and I was just too damn proud to tell you how much trouble I was in."

"But what happened? Who really stole the money? Obviously you eventually discovered the truth." Eve's eyes widened with apprehension. "Or did you? That wasn't why you quit your job right after the divorce was finalized, was it? I mean you weren't fired for stealing or anything?"

"Thank God, no. Right around the time we split up, I managed to find out what had been going on. After weeks of dreary analyses, I was able to show that one of my partners had not only stolen the money, but had deliberately set out to pin the blame on me."

"David, I'm so sorry. I wish I'd known." Eve was torn between regret that she hadn't been allowed to provide him with comfort and a familiar ache of frustration because he'd shut her so completely out of his life. The questions bubbled up, thick and fast. "Who tried to frame you? I still can't understand why you never told me any of this! What was his motive? And why pick on you to frame?"

"The thefts were carried out by a guy called Ned Nichols. He needed money to pay off his wife's credit-card debts and picked me because the areas in which we traded happened to complement each other."

"His wife had run up two million dollars' worth of credit-card bills?"

"Only a hundred thousand or so plus interest. But I guess Ned figured, while he was at it, some extra spending money would be nice." David cracked a smile that contained no humor at all. "He apologized to me with great sincerity when we met in the courthouse right before his trial. He wanted to assure me that his selection of me as his victim was nothing personal. He really liked me a lot, but I'd been the easiest person to frame, and he'd needed the money so his wife wouldn't leave him."

"Obviously his was a friendship to treasure."

David shrugged. "In his own way I think he really did consider me a friend. But he was crazy in love with his wife and their relationship was so mixed up I think he kind of got torn loose from his moral moorings."

"For heaven's sake, David, stop being so damn noble. The guy behaved like a jerk. A total lowlife. Admit it."

David looked away. "I'd like to, but I can't. Maybe it would be easier for me to put the incident in perspective if Ned were still alive. But he's not. He died in prison."

"Oh, no! Did he die of natural causes?" *Please say yes,* she added silently.

"Unfortunately not." David had drawn a smoking gun on the tablecloth, and he scribbled over it. "He committed suicide about six months into his sentence."

"Oh, jeez. I'm sorry."

"Yeah."

Eve instinctively reached out to put her hand over his. "David, it's a sad way for his life to end, but you know better than to blame yourself for what happened, don't you?"

"Of course," he said. "At least in my rational moments, when I'm wide-awake and busy. Sometimes my conscience isn't quite so cooperative last thing at night when I'm trying to get to sleep."

Eve had thought her emotions were pretty much under control. She found out now they weren't. Suddenly all the old hurt and frustration boiled over. "My God, David, I can't believe you were going through all this garbage and I never knew. How could you have been under such stress and never breathe a word to me about what was going on?"

"We were divorced by the time Ned died."

"But I was your wife when he was trying to frame you! Dammit, didn't I deserve to share in something so important?"

David's mood suddenly lightened and his shoulders lifted in an ironic shrug. "Of course you did. But how come you were offered a job at CBS—a huge career leap—that you turned down without ever mentioning it to me?"

"B-because it...it involved a move to the West Coast and I knew I could never take it," Eve said. "How did you hear about that?" Before he could answer, she found herself laughing, albeit a touch wistfully. "All right, point taken. Heavens, David, for two supposedly smart people, we were a pair of idiots, weren't we?"

"Sure. But probably no more idiotic than half the other married couples in America."

"Maybe in a hundred years or so they'll develop androids so that people can have a trial marriage with a programed dummy before they move on to the real thing."

"Sounds dangerous," David said. "I bet most people would end up preferring the dummy. Hell, any smart person would."

Eve was laughing when the waitress arrived carrying two huge bowls of steaming chowder, a basket of fresh-smelling bread and a dish of butter nestled in ice.

"Enjoy your meals," she said. "Can I get you anything else?"

"No, thanks, this is great." David gave her an absent-minded smile and the waitress simpered. Eve sighed. David's sexual magnetism still worked with a hundred percent efficiency on all females. Including her. She realized that she'd drawn a circle of red hearts around her glass of water and quickly scribbled them out, hoping David hadn't noticed. She didn't want him to read deep significance into a meaningless doodle.

"Are you going to tell me what's going on with you and Matt?" she said when they'd both eaten some soup, which was as delicious as David had promised, thick with chunky vegetables and juicy clams. "What are the pair of you trying to find?"

"Eve, I'll agree to tell you what we're looking for if you'll agree to keep everything I say confidential. Deep-sea salvage is a cutthroat business. You saw what happened to Caleb, so you know that when I say cutthroat, I mean it almost literally."

Eve suppressed a shiver. "You have my word," she said. "Although we shouldn't leap to the conclusion that Caleb was murdered because of his connections to your diving operation. As the detective would be quick to point out, Caleb could have been into drug dealing or a dozen other crimes for all you know."

"He certainly wasn't a drug user," David said.

"Unfortunately that might not stop him dealing drugs to people who, unlike him, aren't smart enough to say no."

"You're right." David frowned. "Well, I guess we'll soon find out if he sold me and Matt up the river."

"How?"

"A team of rival divers'll turn up at the wreck site."

Eve gulped. "What'll that mean?"

David was silent for several seconds. "Danger," he said finally.

Eve's imagination kicked into overdrive as she visualized what that laconic single-word answer might mean. "Did Caleb know enough about what you and Matt are doing to cause you real problems?" she asked, trying to sound cool.

"Enough to cause serious trouble? Sure. Remember the break-in at Matt's motel? We couldn't understand who would want the underwater grid charts when they didn't show where we were diving, only what we'd found when we were down there. Well, if Caleb was behind the break-in, everything makes sense."

Eve understood at once. "Because he knew precisely where you were diving," she said. "He's the guy who took you there every day, so those disembodied grid charts make perfect sense to him, even though they'd be meaningless to almost anyone else."

"Exactly. So if he stole the charts, he had all the information a dive team would need to find the wreck we've been working on and to assess where they should concentrate their search for treasure."

"Locating the wreck is the time-consuming part of the underwater salvage business, isn't it?"

"Usually, although with sonar and underwater robots you can often cut down the search time quite a bit. Of course, using robots also increases the costs exponentially, so Matt and I decided to do our own searching on this project, rather than subcontracting out. We had precise information about where the ship had gone down, and we used a pretty advanced computer program to analyze where the currents might have carried it, but it still took us seven weeks to locate the wreck."

Eve grimaced. "Everything you've said makes it sound almost certain that Caleb stole those charts from Matt's motel room. Nobody else would be able to put them to such good use."

"I guess we'll have a better idea about that if we meet a rival team swimming around the wreck next time we go down."

Eve's soup had lost its flavor. She pushed the bowl aside. "Wh-what will happen when you and the rival team meet up with each other?"

"Nothing as dreadful as you're obviously thinking," David said. "Based on past experience with other treasure hunters, I'm guessing they'll try to negotiate a payoff for leaving me and Matt to work the wreck in peace."

His explanation would have sounded a lot more convincing if she hadn't seen Caleb's body being loaded into the coroner's van a couple of hours earlier. "We're back to my original question," she said. "What in the world have you and Matt discovered in a wreck off the coast of Eternity that's causing all this interest?''

David hesitated for no more than a second. "Gold," he said.

"Hah! I thought so." Eve gave a triumphant smile. "How much gold?"

"As far as our best estimates lead us to expect, about 150,000 gold sovereigns, each of them worth around eighty dollars or slightly more."

"Wow! That's a lot of sovereigns and a lot of dollars." Eve made a rapid mental calculation. "At eighty bucks a piece, that makes twelve million dollars. *Twelve million dollars!*" She shook her head and picked up a crayon to write down the sum. "I must have added a zero. That can't be right."

"Yes, it can," David said quietly. "Twelve million dollars in golden sovereigns is exactly what we're hoping to find locked in treasure chests somewhere in or around the wreck of the *Free Enterprise.*"

"Twelve million dollars!" Eve found the idea of salvaging that many sovereigns more terrifying than exciting. "The money won't be yours, will it? Doesn't underwater treasure belong to the federal government?"

"It depends," David said. "In the normal course of events, the federal government imposes a hefty tax on anything found in its territorial waters. And if the wreck is valuable enough, sometimes the state and the federal governments fight court battles about who has taxing and ownership rights. But in this case, all the governmental authorities are out of luck, whether they're state, federal or city."

"Pete will be annoyed that Eternity isn't going to get a cut."

David grinned. "He'll have to take his lumps, I guess. The *Free Enterprise* was insured by Lloyds of London. It sank in a gale about half a mile outside Eternity Harbor on the night of December 9, 1862, and Lloyds paid off on the claim to the tune of more than a quarter of a million dollars."

"That was a small fortune in those days, wasn't it?"

"It sure was. But the point is, the courts have decided in other similar cases that if Lloyds paid off the claim when a ship sank, then Lloyds owns the wreck if the ship is ever located and successfully salvaged. Which means that the cargo is also theirs, even if the wreck is found in United States territorial waters."

"That seems fair," Eve said.

"Mmm. And that's why Matt and I have been keeping such meticulous records of precisely where we've explored and the exact location of everything we've discovered. The grid charts that were stolen show every inch of the wreck and its environs, because we need to have the backup data to prove in a court of law that the sovereigns we bring up were part of the cargo of the *Free Enterprise*."

"And therefore the property of Lloyds and not of the American government."

"Right. Of course, I have duplicates of all the site charts, so from that point of view, the theft of Matt's copies makes no difference."

Eve was so interested in what David was saying that for a moment she forgot that bringing the sovereigns to the surface looked like a task fraught with life-threatening risks. "Let me get this straight," she said. "Technically speaking, you and Matt are working on behalf of Lloyds of London, right?"

David shook his head. "Not really. Matt and I are what you might call independent contractors, working on a contingency-fee basis. We've told Lloyds what we're doing, and they've given us official permission to act as their agents, so our diving activities are completely legal. But Lloyds isn't paying our expenses, so if Matt and I don't find anything of value, we're out of luck, and out of a lot of money, too. On the other hand, if we locate the sovereigns, Lloyd's has agreed to pay us twenty percent of their total value as a finder's fee."

Eve choked into her soup. "That's more than two million dollars for you and Matt," she said.

David grinned. "Actually almost two and a half. Has a nice ring to it, don't you think?" His amusement faded. "Of course, if Caleb sold us out to a group of treasure hunters who are working outside the law, their profits would be even higher. Provided they don't flood the market with too many sovereigns at one time, they'd be able to keep all twelve million dollars."

"Wouldn't it be difficult to sell that many antique coins without the authorities getting suspicious?"

"It depends how cleverly they passed them into the marketplace. But even if they decided to melt some of the sovereigns down and ignore the antiquity or collectors' value, the coins are made of 22-karat gold, and gold fetches almost four hundred dollars an ounce." David's voice was grim. "That still works out to several million dollars. More than enough money to tempt a lot of people into behaving very badly."

"Possibly including Caleb Crewe," Eve said, feeling sad.

"Yes, unfortunately. Damn, I really liked the guy." David stared moodily into his empty soup bowl.

"Tell me more about the *Free Enterprise*," Eve said, wanting to get David's thoughts away from Caleb's possible treachery. "Since it sank right here in your hometown territory, I guess the story of its fabulous cargo must be the stuff of legend, right?"

"Wrong, actually. In fact, the accounts written at the time the ship went down all indicated that the cargo was mostly what was called in those days 'English finished goods.' Things like Royal Doulton china and Axminster carpets, destined for the Boston luxury market and bought with money made by the sale of American timber in the British markets."

"So where did the gold come from?"

"That's still a mystery," David said. "But I suspect it was a payoff for the illegal cargo that the ship was running."

"You mean the *Free Enterprise* was a pirate ship?" Eve's eyes widened. "I thought piracy on the high seas ended long before the 1860s."

"It did, but during the Civil War, both the North and the South treated each other's merchant ships as fair game for seizing. Or sinking. The *Free Enterprise* was registered as a Union ship, which meant that it couldn't legally trade in Southern goods."

Eve was fascinated. "And you think that's what it was doing? Running the Northern blockade to trade with the South?"

"It seems very likely. By sheer chance, I was helping Aunt Connie sort through some Powell family papers this spring and came across a letter written by my ancestor, Bronwyn Powell. She made a couple of references to the fact that she suspected James Falconer, who owned the *Free Enterprise*, of being a secret Confederate sympathizer. My curiosity was piqued, and I got a friend in London to do some research in the Lloyd archives. He came back with the news that the *Enterprise*'s cargo, as it appeared on the Lloyds manifest, was very different from the cargo that folks in Boston and Eternity thought the ship was carrying. According to the documents my friend discovered, the ship was carrying weapons—and four trunks filled with gold sovereigns."

"It's amazing what musty old records can reveal, isn't it?" Eve said. "Is that why she sank? Because the Union navy discovered what her crew was up to and scuttled her?"

David shook his head. "No, she genuinely foundered during a gale. As far as I know, nobody around here had any idea what Falconer was up to."

"I'm almost glad she sank. Presumably, if she'd succeeded in running the blockade, not only would the Confederate cause have been advanced, but the ship's owner would have made a heap of money out of being a traitor."

"A fortune," David agreed somberly. "The British were desperate for Southern cotton and indigo. The Confederacy was desperate for guns and ammunition. Any ship that managed to make the run in both directions without being intercepted stood to rake in a hefty profit. I'm pretty sure that's why James Falconer took the risk. Money seems to have been a strong motivator where he was concerned."

"James *Falconer?*" Eve was suddenly struck by the name. "That wouldn't by any chance be one of Mrs. Falconer's blue-blooded ancestors?"

"A blue-blooded and probably blackhearted ancestor," David said. "You haven't heard the worst of it. I think James Falconer was not only running the Northern blockade in order to bring guns to the Confederacy, I suspect he was also using slaves to act as crew on his ships."

Eve recoiled. "Oh, no! What makes you think that?"

"Evidence from the wreck. When Matt and I were diving last week, we found the anchor from the *Enterprise*. Locked to the anchor chain were manacles, and nearby, tangled up in the eel grass, we actually found a couple of human shin bones."

"Are the bones significant?" Eve asked. "I mean, several sailors drowned in the wreck, so finding the odd bone or two isn't unexpected, is it?"

"Maybe not, but underwater currents would probably tow any bodies out to sea unless those manacles were used to attach human beings to the anchor chain."

Eve gulped. "My God! It's grotesque! You think he killed the slaves, then attached their bodies to the anchor chain...?"

"I'm not so sure he killed them first," David said grimly. "Here's my theory about what happened. When the ship started to sink, it was in sight of Eternity Harbor. The reports in the *Courier* make it clear that Ebenezer Pinnock, the captain, refused all offers to have local sailors come on board and help him navigate through the entrance to the harbor. Captain Pinnock claimed that his engines were damaged beyond repair and that he couldn't move the *Enterprise* because the sails were also inoperable. I think the truth is he was terrified that rescuers would see he had slaves on board and realize that his ship had been trading with the Confederacy. So rather than risk having the folks in Eternity find out what he'd been doing, he chained the slaves to the anchor and drowned them."

Eve shuddered. "Oh, my God, how horrible! It's ... it's so depraved."

"I guess the captain got the punishment he deserved. When he finally decided that he'd covered his tracks sufficiently to risk coming into harbor, it was too late. His engines really had failed, just as he claimed, and by this time, his mainmast had snapped in the gale. He couldn't save the ship, so he went down with it."

Eve felt not even a smidgen of pity for Ebenezer Pinnock. "I'd have preferred him to be found out in his treachery by the townsfolk. They'd have meted out a better punishment than death by drowning." With a murmur of thanks, she accepted a refill of her coffee cup from the waitress. "What about the rest of the crew?" she asked David. "Did any of them survive?"

"Several of them. Officially six sailors drowned, including Captain Pinnock, but of course nobody knew about the slaves. The rest of the crew was saved by the heroic efforts of the Eternity fishermen who took out their boats to rescue them."

Eve sipped her coffee. "Only one thing surprises me," she said. "People have always loved to gossip and hint at dark secrets, so I'm surprised rumors about the slaves never leaked out."

"James Falconer was a man who knew how to cover his rear end. He was in town the night of the gale, and he saw

the *Enterprise* go down. According to the *Courier,* he hurried the surviving crew members off to Boston by first light
the next day, insisting that they would suffer too much if
they had to face the scene of the tragedy. The wily old fox
was probably rushing them out of Eternity before they could
tell anyone what the ship had been carrying and where it had
been trading.''

''When you've brought up the gold, I'd love to do a program about the ship,'' Eve said. ''It would be wonderful if
we could piece together James Falconer's story and tie it in
to underwater scenes from the wreck. Not to mention the
gold. Sunken treasure always goes over wonderfully with the
viewing audience.''

''You'd have some technical problems getting good pictures,'' David said. ''The water down there is pretty murky.''

''I'll hire you as technical adviser to the shoot,'' she said.
''It's a deal.''

They looked at each other, dismayed at where their discussion had led them. Eve quickly changed the subject.
''Was that sovereign the investigator found on the beach the
first proof you've had that the *Free Enterprise* really was
carrying trunk loads of gold—'' She broke off, looking up
with a slight smile. ''Matt, hi! How'd you manage to track
us down?''

''This is one of David's favorite bolt holes,'' Matt said,
barely managing a quick, distracted smile. His face was pale
and drawn taut with grief. Tension kept his body twitching,
as if little jolts of electricity were being shot randomly
through his muscles. ''This sucks big time,'' he said to David. ''Amy told me what happened. Caleb...'' Matt's voice
cracked, and he stared out of the window. Eve had the impression he was afraid to blink in case he started to cry.

''We tried to call you,'' David said. ''Joe at the motel
thought you'd already left for Boston, but we knew that
couldn't be true, because Amy was still at the *Courier* office.''

"Yeah, our great time in Boston was postponed again."
Matt's voice was flat. "Amy had to work this morning. The
other girl called in sick." He rubbed his forehead, pinching
the bridge of his nose in an effort to relieve the pressure.
"Jeez, Dave, for ten years I thought I'd really known Caleb,
but now I'm wondering if I ever knew him at all. It's a rotten feeling."

"The pits," David agreed harshly.

"What was he up to?" Matt shook his head in bewilder-
ment. "What the hell was he doing down on the beach at
some ungodly hour this morning?"

"There seem to be three possible options," David replied, his voice bleak. "I guess you'd call them the not-so-
good, the bad and the absolute worst."

Matt hooked a chair with his toe and pulled it up to the
table. "Let's start with the worst scenario first," he said.

"All right," David agreed. "Here it is. Caleb had made
contact with a team of rogue treasure hunters, and before he
died he'd already passed on to them the location of our dive
site. He also made them a present of the grid charts he stole
from your motel room last night."

Matt's cheeks turned sickly gray. "If he's done that, we're
in deep sh—deep trouble."

"We sure are."

All smiles, the waitress approached their table. "Dessert, anyone? Sir, could I bring you a menu?"

Matt waved her away without even turning around to
look. "Dammit, Dave, Caleb would never sell us out. He
couldn't sell us out. He was a friend, not just some guy
renting out his boat."

David didn't reply. His silence stretched out, painful in its
implications. After several tense seconds, Matt sighed. "All
right, I'm not going to argue with you. Let's approach this
from another angle. If Caleb sold us out, why the hell did
he get murdered? What was the point?"

This time David didn't hesitate. "To silence him," he said. "The only rational explanation for Caleb's murder is that there was a falling-out among thieves. Something must have gone terribly wrong with last night's deal or Caleb wouldn't have been killed."

"Why not?" Eve asked. "He presumably wasn't selling you out to a bunch of Sunday school teachers with high moral standards. Maybe this rogue team of treasure hunters planned all along to murder him as soon as they had the charts and knew the location of the wreck. That makes him one less person to pay off."

"It's unlikely," Matt said, shaking his head. "The last thing a rival team would want is to alert us to the fact that they're interested in our dive site. Ideally they'd just want to get in, loot the treasure and get out again before anyone knows they've located the wreck. Their interest would be in keeping Caleb alive and us innocently unaware we've been screwed."

David pushed his coffee cup aimlessly around the border of his place mat. "The police forensic team found a gold sovereign on the beach right by Caleb's hand. Did you hear that?"

"No!" Matt frowned. "Where the hell did he get it?" Reluctant understanding dawned in his eyes. "You think he stole it? From us?"

"I don't know where he got it," David said. "The date on the sovereign was 1862."

Eve couldn't see why the date was so significant, but Matt's breath drew in on a sharp hiss. "Good Lord! That's two years later than any coin we've found so far!"

"Yes. I guess he's found another source."

Neither David nor Matt said anything more, and Eve couldn't bear the silence. "So where did Caleb get the sovereign?" she asked. "If the date means he couldn't have stolen it from you, what's the big deal?"

"Maybe nothing," Matt said.

"Maybe everything," David said, sounding weary. "It could mean that Caleb and his gang have already plundered the wreck. If they found the gold, it would explain how Caleb came to be in possession of a sovereign dated 1862."

"But I thought you said Caleb didn't dive?" Eve said.

"Yes, that's what we thought," David replied grimly. "Maybe he couldn't. Or maybe we've been fooled coming and going."

"He can't have located the gold!" Matt exclaimed. "Why would anyone break into my motel room and steal the excavation charts if they've already found the treasure?"

David shook his head. "Not to mention leaving Caleb's body in the middle of a beach where it was bound to be discovered. Why the hell did they do that?"

Eve's head shot up as she realized David had touched on an important point. "You're right," she said. "Why *did* they leave Caleb's body on the beach? There's a good chance whoever killed him arrived by boat. So why didn't they take the evidence of their crime out to sea when they left? They could have zoomed a few miles out into the ocean, tied the body in a weighted sack and tossed it overboard. Chances are Caleb wouldn't have been found for weeks."

Matt leaned back in his chair, looking slightly less stricken now that his mind was focusing on the puzzle presented by Caleb's murder, rather than the savage reality of his friend's death. "The murderer might have been scared off by someone before he could dispose of Caleb's body, I suppose."

"At that hour?" David said. "In that spot? And if some upstanding citizen scared off the killers, why hasn't he or she come forward?"

"Maybe they're embarrassed?" Matt suggested. "If the witness was somebody conducting an illicit love affair or a teenager who'd sneaked out of the house, he might not want to speak up."

"It's possible," David said. "God knows, people have kept quiet about murder for the most appallingly trivial reasons."

Matt took a crust of bread from the basket and munched on it absently. "Leaving aside the fact that I still can't believe Caleb agreed to sell us out, how could a straightforward deal go so badly wrong that murder was the only way out for the treasure hunters? Heck, we're talking a real simple trade here. Caleb provides grid maps and navigation charts. The rival team pays him. End of deal, end of story."

"Maybe they couldn't agree on the price?" David shook his head, rejecting his own explanation. "But Caleb wasn't a fool, far from it. He'd never go to meet someone alone on a beach in the dead of night without having negotiated a price for what he was selling. Not to mention some solid guarantees to protect his own ass."

"How do you know?" Eve said quietly. "Both of you are basing your judgment about how Caleb would behave on your relationship with him as a friend and partner. But that's the whole point, isn't it? If Caleb got killed when he went down to the beach to sell you out, then it seems to me you have to face up to the other side of the same reality."

"What's that?" David asked.

"That you didn't know very much about the real Caleb Crewe. And that you'd better get to know more about him pretty damn quick if you want to save your multimillion-dollar hoard of gold coins."

Chapter Seven

After a lot of debate back and forth, David and Matt reluctantly agreed that they had an obligation to let the authorities know about the possible links between Caleb's death and their attempts to salvage the cargo of the *Free Enterprise*. Using Matt's car, they drove straight from the restaurant to the police station to make a report. Eve took David's Jeep and drove back into town to continue setting up interviews for the arrival of the "Roving Report" crew on Monday morning.

She worked hard, taking copious notes, soaking up the feel of the town and its citizens. At twilight, she stopped to watch a young bride and groom emerge from the chapel and pose for photographs to a chorus of enthusiastic cheers from family and friends. Usually her reaction to such a scene was a sardonic groan at the disillusionment lying ahead for the newlyweds. Today, for the first time since her divorce, she found herself offering a heartfelt wish that the couple might enjoy many years of shared happiness. Perhaps that was the secret of the chapel's success, she mused. Its legend allowed people to hope in an age clouded with cynicism.

By the time she let herself into the cottage it was dark and a light rain had begun to fall. She was aware of an odd sense of homecoming as she flicked the switch and the cozy crowded living room flooded with light. The cat jumped off

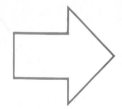

NO COST! NO OBLIGATION TO BUY!
NO PURCHASE NECESSARY!

PLAY "LUCKY 7" AND GET FIVE FREE GIFTS

HOW TO PLAY:

1. With a coin, carefully scratch off the silver box at the right. Then check the claim chart to see what we have for you—FREE BOOKS and a gift—ALL YOURS! ALL FREE!

2. Send back this card and you'll receive brand-new Harlequin Intrigue® novels. These books have a cover price of $2.99 each, but they are yours to keep absolutely free.

3. There's no catch. You're under no obligation to buy anything. We charge nothing—ZERO—for your first shipment. And you don't have to make any minimum number of purchases—not even one!

4. The fact is thousands of readers enjoy receiving books by mail from the Harlequin Reader Service®. They like getting the best in romance fiction conveniently delivered to their home and they love our discount prices!

5. We hope that after receiving your free books you'll want to remain a subscriber. But the choice is yours—to continue or cancel, anytime at all! So why not take us up on our invitation, with no risk of any kind. You'll be glad you did!

You'll look like a million dollars when you wear this lovely necklace! Its cobra-link chain is a generous 18" long, and the multi-faceted Austrian crystal sparkles like a diamond!

DETACH AND MAIL CARD TODAY

PLAY "LUCKY 7"

**Just scratch off the silver box with a coin.
Then check below to see the gifts you get.**

YES! I have scratched off the silver box. Please send me all the gifts for which I qualify. I understand I am under no obligation to purchase any books, as explained on the back and on the opposite page.

181 CIH AQWQ
(U-H-I-11/94)

NAME

ADDRESS   APT.

CITY   STATE   ZIP

7 7 7	**WORTH FOUR FREE BOOKS PLUS A FREE CRYSTAL PENDANT NECKLACE**	

 WORTH THREE FREE BOOKS

 WORTH TWO FREE BOOKS

 WORTH ONE FREE BOOK

the back of the sofa and stretched lazily, his mouth expanding into a cavernous pink yawn.

"Hello, Cat," she said, making her way into the kitchen and dumping her purse on the corner of the counter as she walked by. "I guess your master isn't home yet."

Cat didn't deign to reply to the obvious. Eve scratched his ear. "I'm going to cook dinner for your owner. Something special to take his mind off what happened to Caleb."

Cat's eyes fixed on her with an expression of profound feline scorn. She smiled ruefully, then shrugged. "Okay, you're right. I'm a lousy cook, and David isn't going to forget about Caleb anytime soon, but it's worth a try, isn't it? Besides, this cottage makes me feel...domesticated, I guess. In a place like this, cooking a hearty dinner actually seems like fun."

Apparently "dinner" was a magic word to the cat. He stalked into the kitchen, whiskers twitching. Rubbing against her legs, he whisked back and forth several times until her wool slacks were coated with hair. A purr started to rumble in his throat. Eve stroked his back, muttering complaints about the cat hair decorating her slacks, but secretly enjoying the sensation of being greeted by a friendly living creature.

"David's overfeeding you," she said, giving him a final pat and swooshing him away. "Go take a run around the house—you're way too fat." She closed the blinds on the kitchen window, shutting out the darkness and the drizzle, which was beginning to turn into a steady downpour of cold rain.

Cat reacted to the uncalled-for comment on his girth by walking straight to his bowl and looking pitiful when he discovered it was empty.

Eve laughed. "Okay, I get the message. You're starving and I'm a monster. Sorry, but you'll have to wait for your dinner until David gets home. I don't know what he feeds you. In the meantime, let's decide what we're going to cook tonight.''

She pulled open the freezer door and stared at an unpromising collection of prepackaged meals and plastic containers that seemed to be filled with ancient foodstuffs liberally coated with ice crystals. In the end, she selected a package of ground beef that looked as if it might, with luck, have been bought within the past week or two and set it in the microwave to defrost. The pantry yielded rice, a can of tomatoes and a container of chili powder. The fridge was stocked with surprisingly fresh cheese, a couple of shiny green peppers and a wizened onion. Eve decided that gourmet meals had been made of less.

"Chili," she announced to the cat. "My best recipe, and about the only meal David has the ingredients for. Obviously it's fate that I got home first tonight. What we have here is a perfect meeting of talent and opportunity."

Cat stared at her. Or rather, if truth were told, at the package of ground beef she'd just taken out of the microwave. His whiskers vibrated with longing. Eve hardened her heart and found a skillet, setting the meat to brown over a low heat.

"I had an interesting meeting with Bronwyn Powell this afternoon. She's David's sister, you know, and a justice of the peace. She performs a lot of the weddings in the Eternity chapel, including the one today. She tried hard to be nice although I'm sure she doesn't approve of me. She was polite, but she thinks I must be mentally deficient to have divorced her marvelous brother."

Cat gave his empty bowl a yearning lick.

Eve sighed. "Face it, Cat, as a conversationalist you lack a certain something, but as a moocher you're first-rate." She couldn't find any tins or bags of cat food, so she put a spoonful of half-cooked ground beef into his bowl and mixed it with chunks of stale bread. Cat devoured the offering as if he hadn't seen sustenance in days.

"Beats the yucky stuff that comes in tins, huh?" Humming as she arranged the ingredients for her chili on the counter, Eve reached for the chopping board. Her mood was surprisingly upbeat in view of Caleb's murder and the possible threat to David's safety. Bronwyn's quiet courtesy had helped to remind her that the world had plenty of good people along with the few bad ones. She had also learned from Bronwyn that David's mother was out of town for ten days, which meant that Eve didn't need to wrestle with the idea of whether or not to visit her former mother-in-law—a major relief. Divorce certainly threw up some interesting social dilemmas, she reflected wryly.

Cat had given up waiting for more food. Ears pricked, he marched out of the kitchen and jumped onto the battered table where David kept his scuba equipment. Eve watched his progress from the corner of her eye, ready to scold him if he tried to get back onto the counter to steal food.

Some incongruity—maybe a rippling movement of David's wet suit caused by the thump of Cat's tail—suddenly attracted her attention. Her humming stopped in midbreath and she swung around, really looking at the dark corner for the first time since she'd entered the cottage.

"Oh my God!" Eve dropped the paring knife with a clatter. Her training as a diver was minimal, but she didn't need much familiarity with scuba equipment to recognize that David's gear had been viciously damaged. His wet suit had been slashed in half a dozen places, leaving insulating rubber and plastic hanging in forlorn shreds. His regulator hoses had been cut into strips, and his face mask looked as if it had been smashed with a hammer. The fingers on his gloves had been snipped and his flippers hacked into small pieces. In fact, every single item had been spoiled in one way or another.

Rinsing her hands and grabbing a towel, Eve walked over to the table. The ruination looked even worse on closer inspection, a savage display of angry destruction. Nothing could be salvaged, she was certain. David would have to outfit himself from scratch before he could dive again.

She felt anger on David's behalf before she felt fear. She was poking gingerly through the shards of splintered metal and glass when she was struck by the realization that if all this equipment had been destroyed, someone must have invaded the cottage to do the destroying.

And that someone might still be here.

The warm glow of light in the kitchen no longer seemed cozy. Instead, it seemed a threatening spotlight, illuminating her in its glare. Instinctively she stepped backward, huddling against the table as she peered into the nooks and crannies of the kitchen and living room.

The ground floor of the cottage was small enough to check out in a couple of sweeping glances, but it was irregularly shaped, with lots of jutting walls and niches. The fact that the place appeared empty of intruders wasn't as reassuring as it might have been in her boxlike New York apartment.

Eve swallowed hard, fighting back an attack of panic as she crept along the narrow hallway to the main-floor bathroom. She knew it was stupid to tiptoe when she'd been banging pots and pans around for fifteen minutes, announcing her arrival to anyone who wasn't deaf. Still, the need to crouch, to be quiet, was intuitive. Heart pounding, she flung open the bathroom door and sighed with relief when she was greeted by silent emptiness.

Of course there was no one here, she told herself. There was no logical reason to suppose the person who destroyed the scuba gear was still in the cottage. Why would he hang around once his dirty deed was done? If he'd been anywhere nearby when she arrived home, he'd have gone after her the moment she came through the door.

A soft thud from overhead instantly banished her attempt at calm. She grabbed the poker and raced up the stairs, trying to achieve a compromise between speed and quiet. Outside David's bedroom door she paused, straining to hear the slightest sound.

There were no more thumps, but she heard the faint rustle of moving cloth and her palms grew slippery around the poker. Was somebody hiding behind the curtains? Crawling under the bed?

Belatedly it occurred to her that even if the intruder still lurked in David's bedroom, she would be crazy to burst in and challenge him. Much as she wanted to confront the person who'd vandalized David's diving gear, a poker was no match for a gun, and the intruder would almost certainly carry a gun.

She ran downstairs again and dialed the police with shaking fingers, her back turned to the wall and her gaze fixed on the stairs. She wondered why she was feeling so shocked, so violated. Caleb's death should have warned her not to trust appearances, however beguiling. She'd allowed Eternity to wrap her in its small-town embrace and lull her into a false sense of security. She wouldn't make that mistake again.

She heard the sound of a car approaching on the gravel road just as she finished dialing. She lifted the blinds and saw Matt's car, the hood ornament gleaming in the spill of light from the porch. Ignoring the response of the police operator, she let the receiver drop back into its cradle as David got out of the car, waving a quick goodbye to his friend. Eve pulled open the front door in time to see Matt swing the BMW around and race off, scattering gravel.

"David, I'm so glad you're home!" She hadn't realized how badly she wanted to see him until he was actually there on the doorstep. "I guess Matt decided not to come in?" She tried to smile, tried to sound in control, and failed miserably.

"He and Amy are finally getting together for their heavy date. Matt was just about panting. The police kept us far longer than we expected." David stepped into the cottage, shaking off a shower of raindrops. He pushed the front door closed with his foot, reaching for her all in the same motion. "What is it?" he asked. "Eve, honey, what's the matter?"

Honey. Strange how natural, how right, that sounded. "Your diving gear," she said, fighting a crazy impulse to burst into tears. "Oh, David, it's totally destroyed! Someone got into the cottage and vandalized it. And I'm afraid the intruder might still be here. I heard someone—something—moving around upstairs in your bedroom!"

He muttered a curse, and then another, more forceful. "Stay here," he ordered, brushing her cheek in a quick, reassuring caress. He took the stairs two at a time, using his foot to push open the door to his bedroom and immediately springing back to flatten himself against the corridor wall.

Eve held her breath. For two or three seconds there was complete silence, then Cat strolled out of the bedroom and rubbed David's legs briefly before continuing on downstairs and sitting on 'his' rug in front of the fire.

"I guess Cat was the intruder you heard," David said. Cautiously he entered his bedroom, disappearing from Eve's view. A minute or two later, he reappeared. "Everything seems okay," he said as he came downstairs. "Although I'm pretty sure I closed the door to my room when I left this morning, specifically to keep Cat out."

"You did, I remember. So whoever vandalized your diving equipment must have gone into your room, too, and then left the door open when he came out."

"Nothing seems to have been stolen or even disturbed. I checked the closet and my chest of drawers." David put his arm around her shoulders and walked her to the table where his ruined equipment lay scattered. He viewed it in silence for several long moments, then turned her in his arms and held her close. "They did a pretty thorough job of destruction, didn't they? Thank God whoever did this wasn't still here when you got back."

She shivered. "It looks...vicious," she said. "Almost demented. The way he ground up the glass from your face mask..."

"As long as you're all right, that's all that really matters." His arms tightened around her. "Thank God you weren't hurt."

"But you've lost all your equipment, hundreds of dollars' worth! Thousands!"

He cupped her face in his hands, smoothing out her frown with his forefingers. "Honey, don't look so stricken. It's only plastic and aluminum, with a few fancy bells and whistles tacked on. Fortunately we can buy plenty more of that. All we need is money."

"A lot of money," she pointed out.

"Last I heard, the dive shop takes credit cards." He pressed his finger against her nose, willing her to smile. "I have one of those fancy gold cards with a hologram in the corner. It's about time I gave it a workout."

His good humor calmed her fears, but for some reason, she found her throat clogging up and the tears she'd locked inside welling up in her eyes and spilling down her cheeks. She felt herself go hot and then cold with embarrassment, but still the tears wouldn't stop. She wiped her eyes on the sleeve of her sweater. More tears appeared.

"Eve, sweetheart, don't cry." David used his thumbs to staunch her tears. He looked uneasy. Tears had always reduced him to a state of flurried incoherence, and Eve had tried never to cry when he was anywhere near. They'd freely shared laughter and passion. The darker emotions they'd kept to themselves.

But this time the more she tried to stop, the harder she cried. "Eve," he said, sounding desperate. "Eve, honey, tell me what's the matter."

"It was my birthday," she sobbed. "It was my birthday, dammit!" The tears gushed out, a positive Niagara of grief.

David appeared puzzled, as well he might. "Today?" he asked. "But your birthday is in May."

She swallowed over a hiccuping sob. "Not today. The night you didn't come home for dinner. The night I asked you for a divorce...."

"I know, honey." He looked stricken. "Eve, I'm sorry. I realized later that it was a special occa—"

She interrupted, choking out the accusation that had haunted her for two years. "It was my thirtieth birthday, and you didn't even bother to call!"

Eve realized there were a lot of excuses he could make for not having called, chief among them the fact that he'd been trying to save himself from the threat of a criminal indictment. But he made no excuses. He just stared down at her, not saying a word, his blue eyes shadowed with regret. She sensed the hesitation in him, the reserve, and knew there was something he was holding back.

Dammit, he was doing it again! Eve's tears stopped as suddenly as they'd started and her cheeks began to burn, but not entirely with anger. To her dismay, the potent combination of fear and frustration she felt began to change. The simple fact of David's nearness left her hot and shivery with physical desire. Torn between excitement and despair, she acknowledged that it had always been like this between them. Any intense emotion, happy or sad, eventually seemed to transform itself into a white-hot flame of sexual need.

David felt the change in her the moment it occurred and recognized the cause. Why not? He'd had years of practice in responding to her sexuality, years of practice in fanning the flame of her desire. His fingers trailed down her cheeks and brushed across her mouth, which—inevitably—had started to tremble.

"I guess it would complicate things if I kissed you," he said huskily.

"It would complicate things," she said. "A lot."

His head bent a little lower and his voice thickened. "Sex is never the answer to anything."

"Never," she agreed. "Absolutely never."

"We sure found that out during our marriage."

"We proved it conclusively," she said, but she didn't move away. Her hands crept up and linked behind his head. David closed his eyes. Her hips started to rock toward him, but she caught herself in midsway, freezing into stillness, terrified of where they were headed.

David sighed restlessly, pulling her against him. "I've missed you, Eve." His mouth was no more than a millimeter from hers. "God, I've missed you."

She had just enough sense left not to respond to that remark, but he closed the infinitesimal gap between them, anyway. He touched his mouth to hers and her lips parted in instant hungry response.

He tasted of the cold and the rain and a hundred nights when they'd shared the wonders of a sexual passion that seemed to have no limits, no beginning and no end. Eve felt a wave of longing start in her toes and surge through her entire body. Shuddering in his arms, she pulled up his damp sweater and pressed her mouth to his skin, drinking deep of the taste and texture of him. The thud of his heart slowed and melded with hers. In the space of a kiss, their bodies had readapted to a single unified rhythm.

When she realized they were lying on the sofa, she couldn't remember how they'd gotten there. Worse, she didn't really care. David was muttering frenzied love words, covering her neck and shoulders with feverish kisses. She preferred not to reflect on the fact that declarations of love didn't mean much when spoken in the throes of unslaked passion.

"Yes," she whispered. "Yes, David, please make love to me."

"I want you."

"I want you, too. So much." She melted deeper into his embrace, molten with longing, soft and sleek with need.

His hands shook as they pushed her slacks over her hips and fumbled when they reached for the clasp of her bra. His mouth closed over one of her nipples just as she found the buckle of his belt and unzipped his jeans. He was rock hard. She was already shivering on the brink of climax.

They pushed aside the last remnants of their clothes, scattering underwear over the floor and sofa as she pulled him on top of her. He slid into her, and she wrapped her legs around him, waiting for the deep strokes that would carry her to the culmination hovering so tantalizingly on the horizon.

He brushed her hair out of her eyes, his gaze fierce as he looked down at her. "My God, Eve, it's been torment without you. Without this."

"I know. I've missed you, too."

David's voice was hoarse. "It feels like a million years since we made love."

Eve didn't—couldn't—answer. She was suddenly seized by an edgy, restless sense of danger, as if some sixth sense warned her of emotional hazards lurking frighteningly close. Only a few moments ago they'd both agreed that sex was never the answer to problems in a relationship. So why was she setting herself up to reopen all the old unresolved issues? The painful unhealed wounds?

Perversely, the half-realized threat of danger did nothing to cool her physical needs. On the contrary, it seemed to add the final spark that set the conflagration burning out of control. Instead of escaping while she still could, she countered the sense of danger by grasping David's head between her hands, pulling his lips to hers and thrusting her tongue into his mouth. He shuddered, convulsing in response.

Yes, she thought on a sigh of silent exultation. Now, at last, she felt whole. In David's arms she would finally ease the gnawing hunger that had been building inexorably ever since she'd landed on the floor of the lighthouse and found herself trapped beneath him. Trapped beneath the powerful, muscled body that for some reason seemed to have a unique capacity to drive her wild.

She arched her hips, inviting him more deeply into her. His face contorted into a spasm of pleasure as he accepted her invitation and thrust hard, claiming possession.

In the arid years since their divorce she'd forgotten that sexual desire could be fierce enough to leave her barely breathing, suspended between agony and bliss. She'd forgotten that the need to mate could be as compelling and as elemental as the longing for water after days wandering lost in the desert. Forgotten that when David held her the universe stopped in its tracks. Forgotten that when he cupped her breasts and kissed her throat she felt stars explode and her soul shatter. Dear God, she'd been so careful never to let herself remember! But now the past was uniting with the present in a dazzling star burst of pleasure. David was tormenting her with exquisite reminders, forcing her to remember the forbidden past, enticing her to walk with him into an unknown future.

The tremble of ultimate release started deep inside her as David plunged, prolonging the exquisite moments. She soared with him into the secret universe only he could find. A place of magic and dark velvet softness. A place of light and rainbows and shimmering joy.

For a few endless, blissful moments, Eve knew that in David's arms she had found perfect happiness. For an instant carved in time she realized she would never find this much happiness with any other man.

Then reality returned. She sat up and opened her eyes.

A FEW SECONDS before she said anything David knew Eve was going to deny the reality of what had happened between them. The little pants of her breath hadn't quite stopped, and her body still quivered with the aftershocks of her pleasure, but her hands suddenly pushed against his shoulders, forcing him away. Her eyes flew open and she stared at him with something close to despair. Then she turned her head away, hiding her face in the sofa cushions.

Although he knew she didn't want him to touch her, he couldn't resist letting his hand trail down her spine, relishing the way she quivered at even this light caress. Her skin was perfect: smooth, still golden with the remnants of a summer tan. Incredibly, despite the intensity of their sexual encounter, he already felt aroused again.

She shivered, her breath quickening, even though she refused to look at him. David knew precisely the odd combination of physical response and mental rejection she experienced as his fingers stroked her back. Knew, because his own feelings were just as ambivalent and just as strong.

"David, please let me get up." Her voice was muffled since she chose to speak to the sofa rather than to him.

He dropped his hand and moved away, but only to the end of the sofa, sitting by her feet. He wondered what the hell they were supposed to do now. The sex they'd just shared had been spectacular, perhaps the most wonderful of his entire life, but where did that leave them? Whatever naive delusions he'd harbored when they first met, he'd wised up enough by now to realize that great sex didn't make a great marriage. He and Eve had enjoyed mind-blowing sex for more than a year after they got married, but that hadn't stopped them heading for the divorce court with the emotional wounds they'd inflicted on each other still fresh and painful. Since David wasn't a masochist, presumably the incredible sex he'd just enjoyed with Eve wasn't cause to rush out and apply for an immediate renewal of their marriage license. But wasn't it cause for *something?*

What kind of man was so out of touch with his needs that he didn't know how he felt or what he wanted? How could he possibly *not* know what he felt about this person—the woman he'd married and divorced? The idea of being confused about his feelings at this stage in the game was patently ridiculous. But his heart was hammering and his stomach churning. And the honest-to-God truth was that he didn't know why.

He watched as Eve scrabbled among the sofa cushions, obviously searching for something. He fished her bra from between two pillows and held it out, gaze carefully blank. Much as he loathed not being in control of his feelings, he loathed revealing his uncertainty even more. "Is this what you're looking for?" he asked.

"Thanks." She snatched the bra and put it on, hunching away from him as she cupped her breasts and fastened the front hook. He found the simple everyday action unbearably erotic. Hell, he thought, a smidgen of humor returning, that wasn't surprising. He found everything Eve did unbearably erotic.

He waited until they'd both scrambled into their clothes before he said anything else, hoping Eve would feel less vulnerable and less defensive when she was dressed. Then he took her hands, holding fast when she tried to tug them away. Growing up in a big affectionate family, he'd always assumed that important relationships took care of themselves. In his child's view of the world, mothers and fathers and brothers and sisters all loved each other simply because they were family. And this view was never challenged, because in his family, it had been true.

Only when his marriage was already well down the road to failure had he realized he might sometimes need to put complex feelings into words, however hard that might be. And only after his divorce had he understood another, subtler truth: the harder it was to find the right words, the more likely the words were needed.

"Eve," he said softly, "thank you for what we just shared. Making love to you, well, there's been nothing else like it in my life, ever. It was . . . wonderful."

"You're welcome." Her pulse fluttered beneath his fingertips. She ran her hand over her face, hiding a blush more of frustration than embarrassment. David found it comforting to realize that, despite her poise and fluency on camera, she couldn't always find the words she needed, either.

"I didn't mean that the way it sounded." She drew a shaky breath. "David, the sex . . . the lovemaking . . . was wonderful, but I still think it was a mistake. I mean, there's no . . . context for what we did."

"I know." During their marriage he'd always felt compelled to sound decisive, knowledgeable, in control. Masculine. Now he saw his bluster for what it had been: the arrogant posturing of a man afraid to reveal his uncertainties. He turned her hand palm up and carried it to his face, pressing it against his cheek. "I know one thing, though. When two people can give each other so much pleasure every time they make love, there must *be* a context."

She drew her hand away, not roughly, but almost sadly. "Maybe not, David. Maybe the only context is that we make great sexual partners." She stood up, looking down at him with troubled eyes. "We're forgetting how badly we hurt each other when we were together. The lovemaking was great. But the pain and the horrible silences in our marriage were real, too. After . . . after what just happened between us, it's too easy to forget the silence and the hurts."

"Neither of us seems to be finding them easy to forget. In fact I'd say we've both done a great job of remembering. We're scared to death to get close to each other again in case we inflict more wounds."

Eve gave a tiny smile. "Let's face it, David, we have reason to be scared." She gave a tiny gasp. "I don't think I could survive another two months like the last two of our marriage."

"Maybe we've both learned something about the importance of communicating," he suggested.

"Have we?" Eve seemed on the brink of walking away, then she shrugged and turned to face him. "All right, David, let's communicate. I still want to work in television and you'd like me to stay home. I still want to have a baby, and I think I can manage that without sacrificing my career."

"And what's going to happen to the baby when you go back to work?" David snapped. "Who's going to take care of this child of ours when you're away on assignment, filming drug lords and crack addicts and deposed dictators whose armed thugs are likely to rough you up if they don't like your questions?"

"I think you just proved my point," Eve said, her smile fading, leaving only the sadness behind. "The gaps between us, our disagreements about what we want out of marriage, are too wide to be bridged. You want a homemaker, David, and I want something . . . much more complicated."

He was very much afraid she was right, although part of him—his libido?—wanted to insist she was wrong. He ran his hands through his hair, hot and scratchy with frustration. "Dammit, Eve—"

She touched a finger to his lips. "Let's not talk about it right now."

"But that's what we always did. Decided not to talk."

"No." She shook her head. "When we were married, we didn't *decide* not to talk. We fell into resentful silences."

"And this is different?" he asked, raising an eyebrow.

"Sure it is." She risked a faint smile. "At least now we've openly acknowledged the sort of problem we're facing, and we've agreed that taking the problem to bed and burying it in sex won't work."

"It may not have worked," he muttered. "But the burial process sure was a lot of fun."

"Only for a while. Look, David, we need to spend some time thinking about solutions that might work for us. Maybe we can come up with something. Maybe we can't. But yelling at each other isn't going to help, and making love again is only going to confuse the issues." She drew a deep breath. "We simply mustn't make love—have sex—again, David. We can't. It's too confusing."

The way he felt right now, confusing the issues with sex sounded like a terrific idea, probably the best idea he'd had in months. He managed to smile. "If we can't find a way to be married to each other, maybe we could agree to spend one month a year on a desert island making love." He wasn't sure if he was being facetious.

She laughed. "Now that's a really tempting proposition. You're a truly magnificent lover, David."

Her whole face lit up when she smiled. Looking at her, David knew that a month of lovemaking would never satisfy him. After a month in bed with Eve, he would simply be left craving more of the same. Which brought him right back to where this wretched conversation had started. He scowled, stumbling through his thoughts, trying to decide how he could persuade her to accept his point of view when he wasn't sure what his point of view was.

Eve gave him a quick, light kiss on the cheek. He resisted the nearly overwhelming impulse to grab her. "We'll talk again," she said softly. "But not now, David." Her breath caught in a little hiccup that was almost a sob. "Not now, David, please."

"Okay." He accepted her desire to change the subject, albeit reluctantly. He might be mixed up, but he was smart enough to know he wasn't capable of handling a renewed attack of her tears. "Did I see signs of dinner in the kitchen?" he asked. "What were you planning to make?"

"Chili," she said with evident relief. "Chili and rice. It'll take about an hour, though. I'd barely gotten started."

"I'll help. I can chop and grate with the best of 'em."

"Great. That should speed things up. I'm hungry again, even though we ate lunch late." Eve sounded unnaturally bright and her smile was obviously forced. David wasn't sure whether he wanted to rail at her for refusing to face the reality of what they both felt, or whether he wanted to kiss her for being so adorably stubborn. Or was that simply two different facets of the same want? He ordered himself to stop asking dumb questions and applied himself to chopping green peppers with grim determination.

"Tell me what happened at the police station," Eve said as they settled into the rhythm of slicing and dicing.

"The police were interested in what Matt and I had to say, to put it mildly."

"Did they tell you what's happening with their investigation?"

"Not much. They've contacted Caleb's sister and she's going to make the funeral arrangements. Joyce—that's the sister—maintains her brother despised drugs and would never deal in them."

"That doesn't surprise you."

"No, I agree with her. Other than that, we didn't learn much. Pete Pieracini was obviously feeling guilty about his loose tongue down on the beach today. To compensate, he very nearly turned himself into a walking, talking edition of the police guide on how not to blab to citizens. He insisted that the investigation was on track and the Boston police were digging up useful background information on Caleb Crewe."

"I'd love to know the detective's definition of useful."

David grinned. "That's easy. Anything that links the motive for Caleb's murder to big-city Boston criminals."

She added onion and chopped peppers to the garlic browning in a pan. "You'll have to tell him about the destruction of your diving gear."

"Yes, I'll make another report tomorrow morning." He grimaced. "The police station's beginning to feel like my second home."

Eve stirred a can of tomatoes into the ground beef and lowered the flame beneath the pan. "Why would anyone want to destroy your equipment, David? And how did they get into the cottage? They must have had a key because the lock wasn't smashed."

"Half the town of Eternity probably has a key to this place," David said. "My aunts dish 'em out to any friend, relative or passing acquaintance who needs a place to stay."

"Maybe we should change the lock," she suggested.

"I'll call a locksmith in the morning. That won't keep out anyone who's determined to get in, but there's no point making things easy for intruders."

"Maybe he could check the bolts on the windows at the same time," Eve said. "Although we're probably closing the barn door after the horse has bolted."

"Not if it keeps you safe," David said, surprised and embarrassed when he heard his voice turn husky with emotion. He was overwhelmed by the sudden need to hold her, a need that was only partly sexual. Unable to resist, he put his arms around her waist, nestling his face against the smooth skin of her neck. She felt warm and womanly and unexpectedly fragile. He pulled her closer, the urge to protect instantly transforming into an urge more explicitly sexual. "God, Eve, you're so beautiful."

She trembled and the wooden spoon she was holding slipped from her fingers. "Don't," she whispered. "We agreed...no more...not tonight...."

"Then walk away from me," he said, dropping his arms to his sides.

He felt the shudder of her indrawn breath. She took a single step, then stopped. He didn't dare move in case she took another one. The silence in the kitchen stretched out, a hollow dome, vibrating with conflicting emotions. When he couldn't stand the tension any longer, he reached around her and turned off the stove. Then he held out his hand and led her without speaking toward the stairs. This time he wanted to make love to her in his bed, with soft pillows and warm covers and all the time in the world to show her what he was feeling.

She gave a little sigh, half acceptance, half regret, and let her head fall against him as they climbed the stairs. Outside his room she hesitated again, and he stepped across the threshold, silently inviting her in. She followed him into the room, but he could see his own turmoil reflected in her troubled expression. Eve was too honest not to acknowledge the desire she felt, but he knew she hadn't come to terms with the disparity between her sexuality and what her common sense told her.

He risked breaking the spell by speaking. "Eve, this isn't just about sex."

She met his gaze. "Maybe that's why I'm so scared."

He smiled wryly. "Me, too." He didn't want to look away from her, so he reached behind him to turn back the covers on the bed. Still with his gaze locked on hers, he tossed back the comforter and the top sheet. But as he stepped forward to take her into his arms, her face froze in an expression of total horror.

"Eve?" He tried to hold her, but she pushed him violently away. "Eve, honey, what is it?"

She gagged, literally unable to speak. Then she pointed to the bed, closing her eyes.

He swung around to look, not sure what he expected. A rat stared back at him, dead eyes hideously vacant, its gullet spilling out of its slit throat, intestines exposed by the surgically sliced belly. The fat black body was already frozen into stiffness, and its pink tail formed a curved question mark of naked flesh against the beige sheets.

Hastily he threw the top sheet back over the grisly sight. Arm around Eve's waist, he hurried her from the room. "Wait for me downstairs," he said. "I'll take care of cleaning it up."

"I'm all right." She spoke through stiff lips. "It was the shock, that's all." She cleared her throat. "Would you... would you check the bed in my room?"

"Sure." He went into the guest room and pulled back the covers. A rat, a mirror image of the one in his bed, stared at him with sightless eyes. David stared back, momentarily transfixed. Then he realized he was wiping his hands against the seat of his jeans, as if trying to rid himself of contamination. Tight-lipped, he returned to Eve's side.

One look at his face told her what he'd found. "There was another rat." Her words were a flat statement, not a question.

"Yes. I'll take care of it. We'll need clean sheets. Clean everything, in fact."

She hardly seemed to hear him. Her blue eyes appeared enormous against the pallor of her face. "David, what's this all about? Who could have done this to you?"

He felt a twitch of gallows humor. "Well, not Caleb Crewe."

"My God, David, this isn't a joking matter. This is a serious hate crime. You must tell the police right away. A person would have to be mentally unbalanced to slit the throats and bellies of two huge rats and put them in your beds. And crazy people are dangerous." She wrapped her arms around her waist, shivering. "My God, they were enormous! I've never seen a rat that big before."

Knowing Eve, he doubted if she'd seen many rats, period. For himself, finding the dead rats in his beds had filled him with feelings of rage and a determination to find out who was responsible. Watching Eve, the rage dissipated and David was overcome by a renewed wave of tenderness.

"Come on, let's go downstairs," he said, taking her hand and holding it for a moment against his cheek. "You're ice cold, honey. Why don't you build us a fire, which will please Cat no end, and I'll call the police."

She drew a deep, hard breath. "Lord knows, I'm always happy to be of service to the cat," she muttered.

He admired her courage all the more because he knew how squeamish she was. If the rats had bothered him, he knew they must have devastated her. He gave her hand a comforting squeeze.

"I'm glad you're here, Eve," he said, surprising himself by the simple truth of his words. "I'm really glad you're here."

Chapter Eight

Detective Pieracini, commenting darkly that Eternity seemed to be in the midst of a crime wave ever since Eve had arrived in town, conducted a thorough inspection of the cottage and asked numerous questions, none of them leading anywhere as far as Eve could see. He arranged to have the table where David stowed his gear dusted for fingerprints, and concluded his visit by warning them both to take the incident seriously.

"As of now, it's my opinion the murder of Caleb Crewe will turn out to be connected to your attempt to salvage valuable cargo from the *Free Enterprise,*" he informed them earnestly. "Mr. Crewe seems to have been associated with some very nasty folks, and you'd better be prepared for the worst. I'm going to call the Coast Guard and request that they patrol the area around your dive site, David. We want to know if anyone turns up there over the weekend."

David started to protest that he wasn't anxious to draw attention to the site, but the policeman cut him off. "Look, you may want to keep the exact location of the wreck a secret, but that's crazy in view of what's happened. From what you and your friend Matt Packard told me, if Caleb Crewe handed over those charts to some crowd of underwater criminals, sooner or later they're going to turn up and cause trouble. Probably sooner rather than later. So if you

take my advice, you and Matt will be very cautious before
you do your next dive. I don't know much about scuba
equipment and such, but I bet there's a lot of opportunities
for the pair of you to get into a whole heap of trouble when
you're swimming around a wreck hundreds of feet underwater."

On this ominous note he departed. Eve was exhausted,
but the prospect of going to bed was unappealing, to say the
least. Pete had taken charge of the rats, whether to dispose
of them or send them for postmortem examination, she
preferred not to inquire. To her chagrin, she was discovering that it was one thing to film the seamy side of life and
quite another to live through it. Her recently acquired veneer of cool sophistication was, it seemed, just that. Deep
down inside, she was still the same wimpy Eve Graham
who'd ducked biology class and never went to a movie unless she was sure it had a happy ending.

She helped David remake the beds with clean linen, swal-
lowing a twinge of nausea at the smears of blood on the
sheets. Unfortunately the clean linen did nothing to obliterate her mental pictures of the dead rat, hairless tail curled
obscenely among the covers. If she'd been alone, she
wouldn't have bothered with dinner, but David said he was
hungry, so they set up a card table in front of the fire and
she served up the rice and chilli, willing to push food around
her plate and pretend to eat rather than admit to a churning
stomach and shaky nerves.

Surprisingly, instead of giving her indigestion, the spicy,
piping-hot food seemed to help her relax. The normal everyday pleasure of eating a good meal in front of a warm
fire somehow muted the repulsiveness of what they'd discovered upstairs in the bedrooms. At first she responded
only mechanically to David's attempts at conversation. By
the time they were sipping cups of after-dinner coffee, she
realized she was truly engrossed in explaining how she and
a two-man crew from "Roving Report" had managed to

film a Central American dictator at the very moment an insurgent army stormed his summer palace in the mountains.

During their marriage, Eve would never have admitted to the dangers she'd encountered in capturing such an incident on film. Ironically, despite her prevarications, David would have read behind her silence and been coldly furious at the risks she'd taken. Tonight, perhaps because she was no longer his wife, he seemed more able to accept the hazards of her profession. He simply asked interested questions about how she'd persuaded the dictator to grant her an exclusive interview and expressed his admiration for the brilliance of the program that resulted. "You deserved your Emmy," he said.

"Thank you." She smiled, flushed with pleasure. Tucking her legs under her, she settled further in the big shabby armchair. "Now it's your turn. Tell me what you've been doing these past two years. Why did you leave your job with Cyrus Frank? You always seemed to enjoy being a stockbroker."

"I did enjoy it up to a point, but our divorce, and the showdown with Ned Nichols, gave me a real need to step back and reevaluate my priorities. Matt had just spent six months working in the Galapagos Islands on a marine-research project, and he was determined never to go back to being a lawyer. He convinced me I should spend some time with him diving in the Gulf of Mexico. I asked Cyrus for a three-month leave of absence, and he agreed. Three months was all it took. By the time my leave of absence was up, I was hooked."

"On the diving?" Eve asked. "Or on the lure of finding underwater treasure?"

"Both," he said.

"It's an odd combination, stockbroker and deep-sea diver."

He smiled. "Do you think so? I've decided that the two professions have a lot in common. They're both jobs where you need to have a cool head and steady nerves. You have to be willing to do lots of meticulous research and careful comparative analyses, but in the end, you also have to be willing to play your hunches. That's how you get the big payoff in the end. Like here in Eternity with the *Enterprise.*"

"Sure," Eve said. "A two-and-a-half-million-dollar payoff in this case. Always provided the Calebs of the world don't murder you first."

"We don't know yet what Caleb was up to or why he was murdered," David pointed out. "And if you've read a newspaper recently, you may have noticed that hunting for underwater treasure isn't the only way to get yourself killed these days." He hurried on before she could dispute his point. "Anyway, after three great months in the Gulf of Mexico, Matt and I decided to formally quit our 'real' jobs and team up as full-time divers. We did some intensive research into wreck sites, moved south and started working off the coast of Guiana."

"With anyone else, I'd try to look intelligent," Eve said. "With you, I'll come clean. I haven't the faintest idea where Guiana is."

"It's a strip of coastal land between Venezuela and Brazil. The British, French and Dutch all had colonies there at one time or another. Matt and I uncovered a promising lead and went to Holland to follow up with research. We found rock-solid evidence that a group of insurgent peasants had sabotaged a Dutch colonial tax ship and that it sank only about twenty miles from the harbor, which made the salvage prospects much easier."

"Sounds exciting. Did it work out? Did you find a treasure trove of tax money and turn into instant millionaires?"

"I wish." He smiled ruefully. "We didn't find a thing. Not even a trace of the hull, much less a ship laden with treasure. Which doesn't mean it isn't down there somewhere, just that we didn't manage to look in the right place. Matt and I spent six months and far more money than we could afford, and came out with a big fat nothing. But, hey, it was great fun and we learned a lot.''

David's face was alight with enthusiasm, and Eve felt a surge of affection as she looked at him. He'd been a workaholic overachiever all his life, going from high school to college to graduate school and then plunging straight into the competitive world of the New York financial markets, virtually without pausing for a break. Along the way, he'd acquired a scholastic record replete with *A*s, a scholarship to Yale and the 1978 number-one ranking in Massachusetts for long-distance swimming. Eve had a suspicion that his search for lost treasure ships made up to him in some ways for the fun he'd missed during a lifetime spent pushing himself to the limits. Living up to his own and his family's expectations had left no room for enjoying life.

Even she had been guilty of piling on the pressure, she realized. During their marriage, there had been constant competition between the two of them for professional success. Funny how a mere two-year separation could change perspectives and priorities. Looking back, she couldn't imagine why climbing the career ladder had seemed so consumingly important.

If she'd made these self-discoveries while they were still married, they might have been worth discussing. Now there seemed no point in raking over problems divorce had made irrelevant. ''Where did you go after Guiana?'' she asked, genuinely interested in hearing how David had filled the months since their divorce.

''Matt and I headed into the Caribbean. We worked for a couple of commercial exploration companies for a while, because we were too poor to work for ourselves. Then one of those scruffy characters that hover around the fringes of the diving world approached us in a bar and sold us an 'ancient letter' that described a fierce battle fought in 1832 between a Brazilian tax ship and three pirate ships near Belem." His eyes gleamed with repressed laughter. "There was a chart attached showing exactly where two of the ships supposedly sank. Loaded with treasure, of course."

"And you bought that load of nonsense?" she exclaimed. "Good grief, I can't believe you and Matt fell for such a corny scam!"

"We only paid fifty bucks, and I don't think either of us was entirely sober at the time." He grinned, showing a total lack of shame. "Besides, it just goes to show that virtue and sobriety don't always bring their own rewards."

"Don't tell me," she groaned. "The letter turned out to be genuine, right?"

"It sure did, and the chart showing where the ships sank was amazingly accurate. We'd only been diving a couple of weeks when we located the Brazilian frigate and one of the pirate ships within a half mile of each other. The pirate ship even had a ball still in the cannon ready to be fired."

"What about the treasure?" Eve could feel her eyes growing wide. There was something about tales of Caribbean pirates and sunken galleons that made a child out of even the most hardened reporter.

"Unfortunately the gold was long gone," David said. "We found remnants of a dozen rotted wooden chests and about three gold doubloons, but that's all. The ocean currents are strong there, and the coins were scattered so widely that we hadn't a hope in hell of finding them."

Eve sighed. "I'm disillusioned. I have this Disney World picture of swimming down to a sunken galleon, sails still fully rigged, and discovering a treasure chest, lid open and piled high with gold. And a rope of pearls hanging over the side, of course, gleaming with a soft pink luster."

David laughed. "It's a great fantasy. Usually what the salt doesn't corrode the sea worms eat or barnacles calcify."

"So the end of this exciting tale is that you struck out again, despite the great 'ancient letter' and your old sea chart. There's a moral to this story, David."

"Not exactly. We were incredibly lucky. We didn't find any gold, but the hull of the frigate was partially buried in silt, which helped to preserve it, and eventually we located a small metal object jammed between two collapsed ribs. The object turned out to be a golden casket, considerably worse for wear. But inside the casket, wrapped in layers of oiled cloth, was a jeweled tiara we believe can only have been intended as a gift for a princess in the Portuguese royal family."

"Because it was so fancy?"

"It was *very* fancy. At the center of the tiara were three four-karat diamonds, each surrounded by ruby flowers and clusters of emerald leaves. The circlet was fashioned from a hundred more diamonds and a few sapphires just to break the monotony."

"Ivana Trump, eat your heart out," Eve said. "What did you do with it?"

"We sold it at fabulous profit to a Korean art collector who has a passion for Portuguese history. We made enough on the deal to cover the costs of the entire Brazilian expedition and to finance our operation here in Eternity."

"You seem to have had a great time these past couple of years," Eve said, realizing she sounded rather wistful.

"It's been interesting, that's for sure," David said. "Although there've been moments when I've wondered about that Chinese curse. You know, the one that says, *May you live in interesting times.*"

A subtle, frightening curse. His words brought Eve back abruptly to the problems of the present. It was approaching midnight, and she would soon have to go upstairs to bed. To curl up in a bed last occupied by a dead rat. Interesting times, indeed. She swallowed hard, trying to ignore the unpleasant mental image. "I've really enjoyed hearing about your exploits," she said, "but it's getting late. What time do you have to be up tomorrow?"

"Not too early, since it's Sunday. I'd like to get started on checking into Caleb's background, but I'm not sure what I can do over the weekend, beyond talking to Marge Macdonald."

"She's his landlady, isn't she? Won't the police already have questioned her?"

"I'm sure they have. But my questions might be a bit different from Pete Pieracini's." David shrugged. "It can't hurt to ask the questions, even if she doesn't tell me anything new."

"No, I guess not." Eve cleared her throat. "I'd like to go with you, if I could. This rat thing makes whatever's going on somewhat personal as far as I'm concerned."

"I'd like your company," he said. "Your expertise as an interviewer should help a lot in putting Marge at ease."

"Great, that's settled then." Eve jumped up from her chair. "Well, if it's all right with you, I'm off to bed. Okay if I use the bathroom first?"

David wasn't deceived by her bright smile. He got up, pulling her into his arms. "Sleep in my bed," he said softly. "That's the best way I know to banish the pictures of those rats we're both trying so damned hard not to see."

For a moment she allowed herself to luxuriate in the thought of spending the night wrapped in David's arms and waking in the morning to the enticing caress of his lovemaking. Then she sighed and pushed away from him. "Thanks for the offer," she said huskily. "But a few things in this world are even more frightening than dead rats."

David looked at her, his eyes dark, his expression guarded. "What scares us so damn badly, Eve? What are we running from?"

She knew the answer to that one. "Pain," she said. "Pain that nearly destroyed both of us."

David didn't respond with words, but his hands dropped
to his sides and he stepped away from her. It was all the answer she needed. It meant that, in his heart of hearts, he
agreed with her. The fierce tug of attraction between the two
of them was a problem to be overcome, not the basis for a
renewed relationship. Slowly, sadly, Eve turned and walked
upstairs.

MARGE MACDONALD appeared to be in her late thirties. She
had beautiful thick brown hair, the yellowed complexion of
a committed smoker and thighs that were half a size too
large for her pants. Despite the fact that her face looked as
if it was accustomed to laughter, she greeted David and Eve
with a reserve that bordered on hostility.

"We really appreciate your taking the time to talk to us
this morning," David said.

For once his charm had no visible effect. Marge's gaze slid
over him, dull and indifferent. "Come on in," she said,
"but I don't know what you want from me. Like I told the
detective, Caleb kept himself to himself and never caused no
trouble, not to me nor to nobody else."

"He was very good at his job, too," David said, standing
back to let Eve and Marge precede him into the chilly parlor that was clearly never used except on formal occasions.
They sat down in high-backed chairs with prickly tweed
cushions. Marge lit a cigarette and dragged on it nervously.

"What do you want to know?" she asked. Her tone of
voice suggested she might or might not be willing to provide them with answers.

"Caleb and I had been diving together for several
months," David said. "We got on well together, but I
wouldn't say I really knew him as a person. He worked hard
and he seemed to spend most of his free time fixing up his
Harley." He gave a small smile. "I guess a man can't get into
much trouble doing that."

Marge's expression softened. "Yeah, he loved his bike. Every Saturday morning, seemed like he had some new gadget to fool around with."

The glow in the landlady's eyes alerted Eve to the idea that Caleb had possibly played a larger role in Marge's life than temporary lodger. "You're going to miss him," she said quietly.

"Yeah." Marge had all the vaunted New England capacity for understatement. She crossed her hands and stared silently down at her lap.

With years of experience as an interviewer, Eve realized that they would never get any information from Marge unless they could somehow forge a bond of sympathy. And she guessed the best way to arouse the landlady's sympathy was to make her aware of the danger David and Matt faced in the wake of Caleb's death. The catch was to find a way to do that without accusing Caleb of having committed a crime.

"Marge," she said, leaning forward in her chair, "David and I wouldn't have bothered you this morning, but the truth is we're frightened. Or at least, I'm frightened, and I believe David darn well ought to be. We think Caleb's murder is part of something bigger."

"Yeah," Marge's voice was bitter. "The sergeant keeps yammering on about that. Drugs, he said. Caleb would never deal drugs, and that's a hundred percent sure. His ex-wife was hooked on speed, diet pills, caffeine, codeine, the works. Couldn't go through the day without chugging down handfuls of pills. Took so many amphetamines she walked through a window thinking it was the door. Broke her arm, but luckily for her it mended pretty good. Then she went right back to popping the pills. That's why Caleb divorced her—years ago now. He despised drug dealers. He says—said—it was some scuzzy bartender, anxious to make a bit on the side, who'd gotten his wife hooked on the speed. Caleb called drug dealers hollow people, with no souls."

Eve and David exchanged a quick glance. So Caleb had been married, after all, albeit a long time ago. "I agree with you," Eve said to Marge. "I don't think Caleb's murder had anything to do with drugs. I'm sure his death was connected to the shipwreck David and his partner are trying to salvage. The three of them were working to recover some valuable cargo from a ship that went down off the coast here more than a hundred years ago. Did you know that?"

A faint spark of curiosity lightened the misery in Marge's expression. "Caleb never said nothin' about salvaging a wreck."

"He understood it was important not to talk about what we were doing," David said. "This is a competitive business, and we prefer to avoid any gossip. Let me tell you what's been happening over the past couple of days." He went on to explain about the stolen charts, his ruined diving gear and the rats in his beds. Marge listened without any reaction until he got to the part about the dead rats.

"My God!" she said, coughing on a lungful of smoke. "My God, that's sick!"

"Not as sick as murder," Eve said. "Marge, help us out. Those rats make me wonder if whoever killed Caleb has a personal grudge against Matt and David, as well."

"Why do you think that?" Marge asked.

"I can't believe an ordinary intruder would waste time putting dead rats in David's beds. He might tear the place apart looking for something to steal, but he wouldn't have any reason to waste time turning back beds and then carefully remaking them so that the puffs of the comforter concealed the shape of the rats' bodies."

Marge reached for another cigarette. "I can see what you're saying, I guess, but I don't see as how I can help any. How does me talking about Caleb help to find the person who's harassing you?"

"You can help a lot," she said. "You may be able to show us the link between what happened to Caleb and what happened to Matt and David."

"Suppose there isn't no link?"

"Then no harm has been done to anyone, certainly not to Caleb. If the police have the wrong idea about Caleb, you need to set the record straight, or everyone is going to go chasing off in the wrong direction. I bet Caleb let down his guard with you, told you more about himself than he did other people."

"We were . . . good friends."

"Then help us find out who killed him," Eve pleaded. "Did he seem worried about anything recently? Was he having financial problems? Menacing phone calls?"

Marge hesitated for a moment. Then she got up and walked over to the window, lifting a lace curtain and staring out toward the sea. "He didn't have no money problems," she said. "And it wasn't his ex-wife, neither. She and Caleb hadn't spoken in years, that I'm sure of."

"How can you be sure?" David asked.

She let the curtain drop back into place. "Well, there wasn't no reason for them to be in touch, was there? Caleb went into the navy right out of high school. Came out three years later and married his high school sweetheart. No kids, and they divorced a couple of years later. That was because of the pills she popped, like I told you. She cleaned up her act, married some guy from Missouri and they got kids of their own now. Neither one of them was carrying around any grudges and the divorce was finalized more than ten years ago."

"It certainly doesn't sound as if she plays any part in Caleb's life these days," Eve agreed. "Do you happen to know her name?"

"Shelly. But I don't know Shelly what. Like I keep telling you, Caleb and I never talked about her. Wasn't nothin' to talk about."

"How about friends?" David asked. "Did he make many friends since he arrived in Eternity? Apart from you, of course."

"He used to hang out over at the Kowalsky's garage now and again, talking bikes with the guys. But he liked to go into Boston if he had the night off. We'd go dancing. Had a real good time. Caleb was a great dancer, although you'd never have expected it, him being so quiet and all." Marge covered her eyes and turned away from them to stare blindly at the peaceful view through the windows. "We'd talked about getting married, you know. We got on real well together."

"I'm so sorry," Eve said. "I really am."

"Yeah, well, guess there's no use in crying over spilled milk. He's dead." Marge found a tissue and blew her nose. Her gaze slid sideways. "You really think someone out there might hold a grudge against you folks? A big enough grudge to kill you?"

"Yes," Eve said with complete honesty. "After last night, I really think that's possible. After all, Caleb was murdered, wasn't he?"

"Wait here," Marge said. She disappeared from the parlor and came back carrying a metal cash box with sharp edges and a flimsy lock, the kind that could be picked up in any discount store. "This was Caleb's," she said. "It's got some of his personal papers in it."

David looked surprised. "Didn't Detective Pieracini want to take it away with him?"

Marge flushed. "I never told him about it. Well, the way he was carrying on, seemed like he'd decided Caleb *deserved* to be murdered. I thought, nuts to you, Pieracini. Why the hell should I help make your life any easier? You know what I mean?"

"Would you allow us to look through the box?" Eve asked quickly, before David could suggest something appallingly ethical like turning the box over to the police.

"Just in case there's something in there that David might be able to recognize as being important."

"Sure, that's why I brought it down. You go ahead."

Eve opened the box. It contained the sort of things she would have expected: A record of monthly fees paid on Caleb's condo in Boston; a bank statement that showed a balance of two thousand dollars in his current checking account—healthy, but not excessive; a wad of receipted bills; tax records; the maintenance logbook for his Harley; and a loose-leaf notebook.

"You take the notebook," David said. "I'll check his bank statements and see if I can spot any significant transactions."

Marge was looking more uncomfortable by the minute, so Eve leafed as quickly as she could through the notebook, in case Marge changed her mind and snatched it back.

Caleb had apparently used the notebook as a combination memo pad and address book. She flipped through reminders to visit the dentist, buy his sister a birthday present and a notation that someone called Jed was getting married at Thanksgiving. In the alphabetized address section, she found an entry for a Shelly Hunsicker, in St. Louis, Missouri. His ex-wife? She wrote down the address and phone number without comment, trying to be as inconspicuous as possible so as not to alarm Marge Macdonald.

The only other names she recognized were David's and Matt's. In the very back of the book, just as she was closing it, she saw the almost illegible indentations of a few words and numbers, scrawled at an angle. Caleb had probably written down a note to himself on another page, then torn out the page, leaving behind the impression of his writing.

She took the notebook over to the window, lifted the curtain and squinted at the words with the help of the extra light. The first word looked like a name, and definitely began with an *A*, but the rest of the entry was too faint to read. She rummaged in her purse and found a lead pencil.

"What are you up to?" David asked, coming to stand beside her.

She ran her pencil very gently over the impression. "Trying to read this note Caleb wrote," she said. After a few seconds she handed him the page. The scrawled message now appeared in clear white against the pale gray of the pencil:

Amy. 8:30/Sat. (617) 555-6484

David looked at Eve and said, "The Boston area code is 617."

"Amy," Eve said. "Amy Lewin? And why would Caleb have been meeting her?"

Marge's voice spoke from behind them. "Caleb never had no calls from a woman named Amy, not while he was staying here. Only woman who called him regular was his sister. Joyce."

Eve wished Marge wasn't quite so quick to jump on every imagined insult to Caleb's memory. "Then this number's probably not important," she said. "Amy will likely turn out to be his dental hygienist or something." She committed the message to memory and held the notebook out to Marge. "Thanks very much for letting us see Caleb's personal papers. You might want to let the police take a look, as well. After all, they're the experts, and you want to do all you can to help them find Caleb's murderer, don't you?"

"I guess." Marge's mouth wobbled and she dashed her knuckles across her eyes. "Problem is, the police keep acting like Caleb's committed a crime. They seem to forget he's the person who got himself killed. He's the *victim* in all of this, not the guilty party."

"You're right, but you have to understand the police perspective." Eve risked a light comforting touch on

Marge's arm. "They're trying to come up with a motive and they're bound to ask themselves what Caleb was doing on the beach at such a late hour. You told them you've no idea—"

An almost imperceptible jerk on Marge's part caused her to stop in midsentence. "Marge?" she questioned softly. "Do you know why Caleb went down to the beach so late at night?"

"Not exactly." Marge drew a shaky breath. "Something was bothering him that night. Been bothering him all week, in fact. He didn't get home until almost nine, and I was annoyed, because we'd planned to go out to dinner. Anyways, it was too late for a big meal, so we decided to go get a hamburger over at the bar. That's when we heard there'd been a break-in at the motel. Caleb wasn't all that interested until I asked Hugh—that's the bartender—if it was a wedding guest who'd been robbed. The economy of this town being what it is, we don't need no motel break-ins, right?"

"Right," Eve said, steering her gently back on track. "But did the bartender know who'd been robbed?"

Marge actually smiled. "In this town? In the bar? You gotta be kidding. Hugh, he knows all the gossip. The government should give him a pair of binoculars and get rid of their spy satellites. Hugh would keep 'em up-to-date on the news and save billions of dollars into the bargain."

David spoke with careful patience. "How did Caleb react when he heard that it was Matt's motel room that had been broken into?"

"He was upset," Marge said. "Didn't show it much, but I could tell. He made an excuse to leave the bar and we went home. He couldn't settle down to nothin'. When I went upstairs to bed, right around midnight, he said he'd come later. He had to go out because he had a job to take care of."

"Did he tell you what kind of job?" Eve asked.

"Not exactly. I kinda got the impression he was going to take out the boat." Marge seemed surprised by her own words, as if she hadn't realized what she'd been thinking until she said it. She frowned. "I was miffed, let me tell you. Didn't really speak none after that. Just said goodbye and started walking up the stairs. Caleb, he muttered something about how he wished he never got himself involved with her."

She fell silent again. "With her?" Eve prompted.

"Yeah. I wouldn't mention none of this, because it's of no account, except you seem so interested in that Amy woman."

"We're very grateful for any information you can give us, Marge, we really are."

She took her pack of cigarettes out, then shoved it back in her pocket. "Yeah, well, anyways, when I asked him what he meant, he said I had no cause to be jealous. He'd sooner live with a barracuda than this woman who was causing him problems. Then he said something about how she'd found herself bigger and better fish to fry than him."

"But he never mentioned her name," David said.

"No." Marge seemed to look inward for a moment. "That turned out to be the last time we ever spoke. When I thought about it afterward, seemed to me like he'd taken a lot of trouble not to say her name."

Marge seemed to regret admitting so much about a man whose reputation she was determined to defend. She took the papers and stuffed them back into the box. "Well, I've got nothing else to tell you, so if you don't mind, I need to get over to my sister's house in Ipswich. I'm going to spend a few days with her."

She was clearly not prepared to reveal anything more, however innocuous, and pressure would only make her hostile. "We appreciate the time you've given us," David said. "Thanks for talking to us."

Eve spoke softly as they walked to the door. "Marge, will you think about what we've told you, about how David and his partner may be in danger, and if you remember anything more that might help to explain what Caleb was doing down on the beach, would you call us?"

Marge didn't reply, but at least she didn't refuse outright. "Here's my card," Eve said, scribbling the phone number for the cottage next to her name. "And this is where I'll be staying for the next few days." She smiled encouragingly. "Keep us in mind, okay?"

David added more thanks and tried not to show his impatience as they got into the car. He hadn't said a word to Eve about seeing the name Amy in Caleb's notebook, but she knew he was worrying about the same thing she was.

As soon as they were out of sight of Marge's place, David stepped on the accelerator and sped to the nearest public phone, which happened to be in the local gas station. They got out together. "The number was 555-6484, right?" he said, reaching into his pockets for change. "Darn, can you give me some more quarters?"

Eve held out a fistful of change. "Help yourself."

David dialed. "It's ringing," he said. "So at least it's an active number."

Eve heard a young female voice answer the phone. "Good afternoon, this is the Fish Dish, Boston's finest seafood restaurant. How may I help you?"

David's face fell. "Damn!" he muttered, hand over the mouthpiece. "Hi," he said, lifting his hand. "I'm looking for a friend of mine whose name is Amy. I, er, believe she works there. Is this her shift by any chance?"

"I don't think we have anyone called Amy working for us, but I'm new around here. Hold on a minute, please."

Several tense seconds ticked by. An older woman's voice came onto the line. "May I help you?"

"I'm looking for Amy—she's a friend of mine," David said. "I believe she works in your restaurant."

"What's her last name?"

"I don't know." David's mouth tightened. "I mean I think her name might be Lewin. Amy Lewin."

"I'm sorry, I can't help you." The woman hadn't sounded friendly from the start, and now her voice became noticeably cooler.

"Tell them she just got married," Eve whispered. "Suggest she might have a different last name."

Matt rolled his eyes, but he complied. "What I meant to say is, Amy just got married. I'm an old school friend of hers, you see, but she got married recently and I can't remember her new husband's name."

"We have no one by the name of Amy Lewin working at this restaurant." The woman sounded hostile.

"I'm sure she isn't using the name Lewin anymore," David persisted. "I just need to know if you have any employee at all called Amy."

"We have no one called Amy working for us." The woman hung up with a definite bang.

David held out the phone so that Eve could hear the buzz of empty static. He grimaced ruefully. "Well, I sure managed to extract lots of useful information with that call," he said as they walked back to the car.

"Maybe there was nothing to extract. Ms. Fish Dish could have been telling the simple truth. They have nobody called Amy working at their restaurant."

"Or she might have been cautious. Unfortunately in an age of lunatics, weirdos and stalkers, you can't blame her for not handing out personnel information to every Tom, Dick and Harry who happens to call."

"All right," Eve said. "Let's assume Amy doesn't work there. Why did Caleb have the number written down? There was a date and time, too. Do you think they planned to meet there?"

"Could be." David shrugged. "Or maybe Amy called Caleb when she was eating a meal at the Fish Dish and asked him to call her back because she ran out of quarters. In fact, that's the most likely explanation. He scrawls the number in the back of his notebook and then tears out the page when he's finished the call because he knows he won't need the number anymore."

"You're probably right." Eve sighed. "Anyway, I guess we shouldn't get hung up on finding her. We have no reason to suspect she's connected to Caleb's murder. Half the world's population is female. Even if he was planning to meet a woman the night he died, it probably wasn't Amy. And we have no reason to suspect that this Amy is the woman Matt's dating."

"I guess this is what detective work is all about," David said wryly as they got into the car. "Hours spent tracking down leads that fizzle away or turn out to be totally irrelevant."

"On the bright side," Eve said, "I found an entry in Caleb's address book for a woman called Shelly Hunsicker, who just might be the former Mrs. Caleb Crewe."

"Great. Maybe she'll turn out to be bursting with juicy information. Maybe she's gone back on drugs and shot him in a fit of heroin-induced paranoia."

"I have her phone number and plenty of quarters. Do you want to call?"

"Let's go home first," David said, driving out of the parking area. "We can phone in comfort from the cottage."

"Sure." Eve buckled her seat belt. "Is it worth swinging by the motel to see if Matt got back from his date? You need to fill him in on what's happened since last night."

"He won't be back yet," David said, overtaking a Cadillac filled with a cluster of fuchsia-clad bridesmaids. "We spent so long with the police yesterday afternoon that he and Amy decided . . ." His voice died away.

In the sudden silence Eve could hear the rush of blood thrumming in her ears. She looked at David. He looked back. He slammed on the brakes and pulled the Jeep over to the side of the road.

"Dammit, it's no use pretending we aren't worried," Eve said tersely. "We both think it could be Matt's Amy whose name was in Caleb's book, don't we?"

"Possibly." David's voice sounded tight.

"What do you know about her?" Eve asked. "Other than the fact that Matt's crazy about her?"

"Nothing much, except that he's been dating her for almost three months. She's divorced, midthirties, good-looking. I met her for the first time yesterday morning." He pulled a face. "But you know that. You were with me."

"Isn't a bit odd that Matt hasn't introduced you to her yet?"

David frowned. "Yes, although we've been working such long hours there hasn't been much time for socializing, except on weekends. And they like to spend the weekends in Boston at his apartment."

"Is that where she's from? Boston?"

"I'm not sure. She isn't a local, that's for sure, or I'd have known her in high school. From something Matt said, I have an idea she arrived in town about the same time he did."

Eve thought back to the previous day when the news of Caleb's death had been called into the *Courier* office. "If Amy knew Caleb, she's a terrific actress. She gave the distinct impression she'd never met him. Remember how she looked down at her notes to remind herself of his name?"

"No," David said. "No, I don't remember, but I trust your memory because you're trained to observe that sort of thing." He drew a deep breath. "We need to be careful. We don't want to weave some sort of wild conspiracy theory just because Caleb and Matt both know a woman called Amy. Even if they both know the same woman called Amy, it doesn't necessarily add up to anything suspicious."

"But it might," Eve murmured. "If she and Caleb were working in cahoots, think how useful it would be if Amy seduced Matt. She'd be able to feed Caleb all sorts of insider information."

"Matt's much too smart to shoot off his mouth to every woman he happens to sleep with," David snapped.

"What about a woman he's fallen in love with?" Eve shot back. "You know how vulnerable people are right after they've made love. Each time she might get just a snippet or two of information out of Matt. But if she puts all those little snippets together, she and Caleb could accumulate everything they need to know in order to locate the treasure."

David drew to a halt at the town's only traffic light. "Are you suggesting Amy is the person who stole the charts from Matt's room?"

"It's a possibility worth considering, don't you think? Who would know better when it was safe to break in?"

"Why would she need to break in?" David demanded. "She probably has her own key."

"Maybe. But three months isn't that long for a guy, especially Matt, to give a woman a key to his place."

David clenched his jaw. "I think we're building an Everest-size mountain on the basis of a few words scrawled in Caleb's notebook," he said finally. "We have no reason to assume Matt's girlfriend and Caleb's Amy are one and the same. We have even less reason to assume she's some conniving Mata Hari, sucking secrets from Matt and spewing them out to Caleb."

"True, but isn't it worth at least asking her a few questions?" Eve said.

"We have no authority to interrogate her."

"Who said anything about interrogation? We can leave a message at the motel inviting her and Matt to dinner."

David turned onto the gravel road that led to the lighthouse. "And then what?" he said.

Eve shrugged. "Then we'll ask her how well she knew Caleb Crewe."

"And if even half of what you've suggested is true, do you expect her to answer truthfully?" David didn't bother to hide his skepticism.

Eve smiled somewhat sadly. "Of course not," she said. "But I've had years of experience in detecting when people are lying. Invite Matt and Amy to dinner, and I guarantee before the evening's over, I'll be able to tell you precisely how well she knew Caleb Crewe."

Chapter Nine

In response to Eve's invitation, Matt and Amy arrived at the
cottage shortly after seven. Matt breezed in, his normal ex-
uberance somewhat muted, carrying a giant pizza box and
a six-pack of Diet Coke. Amy followed behind, her quiet
personality overshadowed.

"Hello, gorgeous." Matt gave Eve a halfhearted peck on
the cheek. "Here's the pizza you ordered. Double cheese,
extra onion and no salami, as per instructions. It might need
a couple of minutes in the microwave, but the Cokes are ice-
cold. Am I a great guest or what?"

"You're a great guest," Eve said, taking the pizza and the
six-pack so he could remove his jacket. She smiled at Amy,
who was hanging back, seeming a little shy. "Hi, Amy," she
said. "Come on in and get warm. I'm glad you and Matt got
back from Boston in time to stop by tonight."

"We were glad to come." Amy hung her down vest neatly
on one of the pegs by the door. She went into the living
room and held out her hands to the fire. "This is lovely,"
she said. "It's chilly out tonight and there's nothing more
comforting than a real fire, is there?"

"Nothing," Eve agreed, thinking how stunning Amy
looked. At work on Saturday, her hair had been twisted into
a businesslike coil at the nape of her neck, concealing its
extraordinary color and thickness. Tonight she'd left it

loose, and it tumbled around her shoulders in a riot of shining chestnut curls. The forest green sweater she wore with her jeans was a clever choice; it not only highlighted the creamy glow of her complexion, but also flattered her figure by emphasizing the generous curves of her breasts and the slender column of her throat. Despite the lush sensuality of her appearance, however, Eve got no sense that the woman was deliberately flaunting her physical attractions.

Amy might be unaware of the effect she created, but Matt was staring at her with an expression of naked longing, and Eve felt her stomach knot with apprehension. If by some horrible chance it turned out that Amy had been conspiring with Caleb Crewe to strip the *Free Enterprise* of its treasure, then Matt was going to be devastated. How dreadful it would be if the first woman he'd ever seriously loved turned out to have betrayed him.

Pressing her warmed hands to her cheeks and smiling contentedly, Amy sat down in one of the armchairs by the fire. Matt watched every movement, every tiny gesture, as if hungry for the sight of her. Amy seemed unaware of his scrutiny, which Eve found astonishing. How could she not feel the waves of Matt's sexual need beating against her?

The desire was so strong, at least on Matt's side, that Eve felt like a voyeur. "Would either of you like a beer?" she asked, anxious to break the tension. "Or maybe a glass of wine?"

"No, thank you." Amy smiled politely. "I don't drink very much alcohol. I'll wait and have a Coke with my slice of pizza."

Matt blinked, and with a visible effort brought his attention back to Eve. "I'll wait, too," he said. "Where's Dave? What's going on with you two, anyway? He sounded real uptight on the phone."

"He's upstairs," Eve said, "talking to Caleb's sister. She's just arrived in town and she's very upset."

"Caleb's sister is here?" Matt sounded appalled.

"Not actually in the house. She's staying at the inn. Apparently the innkeeper gave her David's number and she called a couple of minutes before you arrived."

"Boy, am I glad David's the one handling that phone call!" Matt's expression tightened with anxiety. "I can't imagine what I'd say to her."

"You'd tell her that you're very sorry Caleb is dead," Amy said quietly. "It's always best to keep condolences simple, and it's important to tell the truth, even when someone's died. Maybe especially when someone's died."

"You're right, honey." Matt sat down on the sofa, leaning across to take Amy's hand and looking at her as if she'd imparted some great nugget of wisdom.

Boy, did he have it bad, Eve thought, torn between amusement and alarm.

"Matt is really upset about Caleb's murder," Amy explained to Eve.

He smiled sheepishly. "Translation—I've been a royal pain in the ass for the entire weekend. We came back early from Boston because I was feeling so down."

"It's tough," Eve agreed. "How are you coping, Amy? Did you know Caleb well?"

She looked mildly surprised at the question. "I didn't know him at all."

"I'm sorry," Eve said. "I must have misunderstood. I thought Detective Pieracini said something about finding your name in Caleb's diary." Well, she thought, that was only a slight stretching of the truth.

"How odd." Amy sounded genuinely puzzled. "I can't imagine why Caleb would have my name written anywhere, unless it was connected with my work. I take all the orders for the classified-ads section at the *Courier*. Maybe he placed an ad, although I don't remember ever speaking to him." She frowned. "I'll check my records as soon as I get back to work. It's kind of creepy knowing your name is in a murdered man's diary."

If she was faking, Eve thought for the second time, then she had to be the world's best actress. "I'm sure it's not important," she said. "Don't worry about it, Amy."

"That's easier said than done until we find out who killed Caleb," Matt said. "I can't get him out of my mind. You know what it's like when you get a picture stuck in your head and nothing will budge it?"

"I sure do," Eve said. "And Amy must be tired of hearing about the murder already. I'm sure the staff at the *Courier* are working nonstop on the story."

"They've never had so much news in one weekend—" Amy broke off. "Oh, here's David."

"How did it go with Caleb's sister?" Eve asked softly.

He grimaced wearily. "About like you'd expect, maybe a bit worse. She's arranging the funeral for next Thursday in Boston." With visible effort, he shook off his dejection and walked into the living room, followed by Cat. He clapped Matt on the back. "Hey, buddy, you look about as chewed up as I feel." He held out his hand to Amy. "Hello, Amy, nice to see you again."

"Hello, David, how are you doing?"

If Eve hadn't been watching Amy so closely, she would never have noticed the slight tightening of Amy's lips or the split-second hesitation before she returned David's handshake. Why? Eve wondered. She'd noticed the same infinitesimal reluctance to take his hand when they'd first met at the *Courier* offices. Had Matt said something that caused Amy to view David with a distaste too strong to conceal? What in the world could that have been? Or was Eve giving too much significance to what might be no more than Amy's natural shyness?

"So what's up, Dave?" Matt said, getting to his feet to put another log on the fire. Cat eyed the action with approval and took up his favorite position on the hearth rug. "Why the urgent phone call? We're delighted to share a pizza with you guys, of course, but you sounded like you wanted more than casual dinner companions when you called."

"I need to fill you in on what's happened over the past twenty-four hours," David said.

"Nothing bad, I hope," Amy said politely.

"Not good," David said. "Sometime on Saturday, a vandal broke into the cottage and destroyed my diving gear."

"Your gear? All of it?" Matt's voice was blank with shock.

"All of it. Every single piece, from wet suit to mask and every other damn thing you can think of. It's going to be a couple of days before I can replace most of it."

"Oh, no!" Amy exclaimed. "That's dreadful!"

Matt and Amy exchanged horrified glances, then he muttered something obscene under his breath. Eve was still watching Amy closely, but she couldn't detect even the faintest sign that her surprise was faked. She'd interviewed too many beautiful women guilty of hideous crimes to allow herself to equate Amy's good looks and sweet smile with a guarantee of innocence. But Amy was betraying none of the telltale signs of guilt or uneasiness that Eve had trained herself to look for.

Obviously shaken, Matt got up again and paced around the sofa. "Was anything stolen?" he asked. Then he pulled up short, struck by a prospect of fresh disaster. "The charts! My God, they didn't take your copies of the charts, too, did they? How about the computer? Was that vandalized?"

"No, the hardware wasn't smashed and I keep the software locked in the safe."

Matt grimaced. "That's not much of a safety precaution, is it? Your safe's a rinky-dink kind of an affair to a professional thief."

"I'm not sure this job was done by a pro. In fact, whoever did this didn't steal anything at all as far as I can tell."

Matt thrust his hands through his hair and then into his pockets. "This whole situation is weird. Really weird. If nothing was stolen, what did they—he—expect to achieve?"

David shrugged. "Heaven knows. Maybe a delay in our diving schedule? A chance to plunder our wreck before we can get down there again?"

Matt shook his head. "If they're professional divers, they couldn't be that stupid. It may take you a while to replace your gear with exactly what you *want*. But they must know you can get everything you *need* at virtually any dive shop in Boston."

"You're absolutely correct, and I'm fresh out of ideas as to what this might be about," David said.

"Okay with you guys if I change my mind and have a beer?" Matt went to the fridge and pulled out two bottles. "Want one, Dave? Eve?"

"Sure," David said.

Eve shook her head. "No, thanks." She was already having trouble zipping up her slacks. Another couple of days of beer, fried fish and pizza, and she'd split a seam.

Matt came back, carrying the beers in one hand and two cans of Diet Coke in the other. "So the vandals didn't steal anything," he said to David. "They just destroyed your gear, right? Was their method the same as at my place? Did they smash the locks to get in? Muss up all your clothes?"

"No," David said. "He—or she—didn't touch my clothes and seems to have gotten in with a key—"

"What?" Matt spluttered into his beer. "With a key? But who could have...? Surely a *woman* wouldn't have done this?"

"Why not?" Eve said, looking at Amy. "Hacking up a wet suit requires a very sharp knife, not brute strength. A woman could have done this as easily as a man."

Amy laughed. "Take care, Eve. You're trampling on some of Matt's favorite prejudices. He's such a total chauvinist he can barely visualize women as doctors or lawyers, let alone criminals.''

''That's not true,'' Matt protested. Amy simply raised an eyebrow, and he grinned somewhat sheepishly. ''Well, okay, maybe there's a grain of truth in what you're saying. But anyhow, male, female or whatever, how in the world did they get a key to the cottage?''

''With no difficulty at all,'' David said wryly. ''My great-aunts hand out keys to this place like Halloween treats. Any thief who wanted to gain entry could steal a key from a dozen different places.''

''Always providing he's from Eternity and knows where to look,'' Matt said.

''Yeah,'' David concurred. ''I guess we can conclude that the person who vandalized this place was a local.''

Matt gave a brief bark of laughter. ''I'll bet Pete Pieracini wasn't a happy camper when he came to that conclusion.''

''He sure wasn't,'' David said. ''These are tough times for poor old Pete and his vision of Eternity, the fairy-tale town with no crime.''

''Don't forget to tell them about the rats,'' Eve said, getting to her feet. ''I'll heat up the pizza while you fill them in on that horrible story. I'd like to get the gross stuff over with before we eat.''

''Rats!'' Amy sat up, showing more animation than she had all evening. She glanced around nervously. ''Do you have a problem with rats out here? I'd have thought the cat would scare them away.''

''These weren't live rats.'' Succinctly David explained about the rats in the bed.

Amy made little murmurs of distress as he told the story, and Matt was struck speechless. ''My God,'' he said when he regained his voice. ''David, what's going on here? What the hell is going on?''

"I don't know," David replied. "Last night, Eve and I both jumped to the conclusion that the same person—or people—who killed Caleb must have destroyed my diving gear and put the rats into my beds for good measure. But the more I think about it, the more ridiculous it sounds."

"Why?" Amy asked, still looking perturbed. "Surely there must be a connection. I mean, all these incidents are happening one right after the other—bang, bang, bang."

"Even so, I'm not sure there has to be a link," David said. "We keep saying Eternity isn't the sort of town where two sets of criminals could be at work at the same time. But why not? Eternity is just a regular town with a quaint legend about its wedding chapel. It isn't a sanctuary from all the problems of the real world."

"That's true," Matt said slowly. "Besides, if you think about it, Dave, we're dealing with two very different sorts of crime. Murder is big-time stuff. But what's happened to you and me isn't all that bad, not really."

"I disagree," Eve said. "The rats were pretty bad."

"Yeah, but I guess if it wasn't for Caleb's murder, we wouldn't be feeling so damned uptight about everything. The rats bothered you so much because you instinctively considered them a personal threat. Caleb is dead. These rats are dead. Next time, *you* might be dead."

Eve looked at him with respect. "You know, I never expressed it to myself that clearly, but you're quite right. That's precisely the connection I was making, although I didn't realize it before." She brought the reheated pizza in from the kitchen and set it on the coffee table, along with a stack of paper plates and napkins. "Help yourselves, folks."

Matt flipped the top on a can of Coke and handed it to Amy. "We need to remember that, despite all the Jacques Cousteau mystique and Mel Fisher panache, underwater salvage operations are a business. Some people conduct their diving business more ethically than others, same as in any other line of work. But if you're going to make money at this job, you can't afford to take unnecessary risks. That holds true whether you're planning to make your money on a legal salvage job or an illegal salvage job."

"What's your point?" Amy asked, returning a string of melted mozzarella to the top of her pizza.

"My point is I can see why a rival treasure hunter might end up killing Caleb Crewe, but I can't see why he'd put those rats in David's beds. He would be running a totally unnecessary risk. And why? What could he possibly hope to gain?"

"Don't ask me," Amy said, shivering. "I'm hopeless at understanding the criminal mind."

"I don't believe there's an entity we can call the criminal mind," Eve said. "One of the things I've learned as a reporter is that the right combination of circumstances can push regular everyday people into committing the most incredible and unlikely acts. Sometimes they're acts of enormous courage, like when a mother fights to save her children from an impending disaster. Other times they're hideous acts that grow out of the darkness of failed and twisted relationships. More often than you'd expect, the heroes and the villains I've interviewed were regular everyday people until something threw their lives out of kilter."

"I guess you're right," Amy said. "Still, speaking personally, I can't imagine committing a serious crime. Not because I'm so virtuous," she added quickly, "but I'm scared witless by authority figures. Give me a parking ticket and I'm convinced I'll be clapped into federal prison if I don't pay up on the spot."

Matt grinned. "Never do that, honey, or they'll arrest you for trying to bribe a cop."

Amy looked stricken. "Can they do that?" She laughed at herself before anyone could answer. "Okay, I'm being totally ridiculous. You don't have to tell me."

Cat, probably attracted by the sliver of uneaten pizza resting on the paper plate balancing on the arm of the chair, jumped onto Amy's lap and began kneading her stomach, eyes fixed on the prize. Amy wrapped the pizza in her napkin and placed it firmly out of reach. "It's not good for you," she said, scratching him behind the ears.

Cat, recognizing the undeniable voice of authority, gave up yearning after the unattainable and curled up on Amy's lap, squirming ecstatically as Amy ran her long supple fingers over his fur. "You're a beautiful animal," she said. "What are you called?"

"His name is Cat," David said. He shot Eve a defiant look. "He's a stray. I'm going to take him back to the pound as soon as I get a few spare moments."

Amy gave a little gurgle of laughter. "You're certainly not going to take him back to the pound," she said.

"Of course he won't," Eve agreed. "David's all fierce bluster wrapped around a marshmallow heart. Cat just about owns this cottage, and he knows it."

Amy chuckled again. "Sorry, Eve, *he* doesn't know anything. David's cat is a female, and my best guess is that she'll be delivering her kittens about three weeks from now."

"What!" David's howl of outrage might have been appropriate if someone had just told him that his Jeep was totaled and his house had burned to the ground. Eve wasn't sure whether to laugh at his panic or be embarrassed that she'd spent hours stroking a pregnant cat without noticing it was female.

"And to think I've been accusing the poor lady of being fat," she said. "Oh, Lord, we'd better take her to the vet for a checkup, and then we'll have to find homes for a bunch of kittens."

"We?" Matt asked, chugging the last of his beer. "Does that mean you and David are getting back together? Congratulations."

"Oh, no, heavens no," Eve said, flustered by her slip of the tongue.

"Not a chance," David said, a split second later.

He needn't sound so damn certain, Eve thought, irrationally hurt. The truth was that events had forced her and David into such an intimate routine over the past couple of days that the nightmare ending to their marriage sometimes fell out of focus, bringing images of happier times into view. But obviously David wasn't allowing his common sense to be blurred by romantic daydreams of recapturing past happiness.

Amy broke the embarrassed silence that had fallen over the group. "This cottage is built right onto the back of the lighthouse, isn't it?"

Everyone accepted the change of subject with relief. "Yes," David said. "There's a connecting door in the hallway near the kitchen. If you haven't visited the lighthouse, you should come back during the day and do the tour. As you'd expect, there's a magnificent view from the observation turret."

"I'd like that. I know your great-aunts sometimes take tourists around in summer." Amy gave Cat a final stroke and returned her gently to the hearth rug. "Actually I mentioned the lighthouse because I was wondering if either of you had thought to check it out since the break-in."

David and Eve exchanged glances. "We didn't give it a thought," David said. "Chiefly because there's nothing in there except Powell family records and dismantled equipment."

"I didn't realize that," Amy said, sounding almost apologetic for having brought the matter up.

"I'm glad you said something," David said. "Now that you've mentioned it, I guess I should take a quick look around to make sure whoever vandalized my diving gear didn't decide to take a whack at the family records. Aunt Constance will be devastated if somebody's spoiled all those grocery lists and medical bills from the nineteenth century."

"Are you going to check now?" Eve asked.

"Why not?" David took a flashlight from the kitchen drawer and led the way to the connecting door into the lighthouse. He found the light switch, and the chilly cavernous room sprung into view.

Until the light came on, Eve didn't realize she'd been holding her breath. She exhaled, her gaze traveling slowly over the glass display cases, the trunks and the walls of metal shelves stacked with cardboard boxes, specially designed to hold archival materials. Not a rat, alive or dead, in sight. Thank God.

"Everything seems normal," Matt said, glancing quickly along the shelves.

David opened a filing cabinet. "Nothing but dust here," he said, sounding as relieved as Eve felt.

Amy had wandered over to the display cases in the center of the room. Eve realized she was staring at one of them in almost hypnotized silence. Her stomach immediately churned in sick anticipation.

"What is it?" she asked, coming close to Amy but deliberately not looking inside the case. She'd seen more than enough rodent entrails for one weekend.

Amy gave a little jump, quickly turning around and positioning herself so that Eve couldn't see the cabinet. "Nothing," she said. "Honestly, nothing at all."

The lie was patent. "Amy, I'd like to see what's in the cabinet."

Amy pulled a face. "I don't think you do, Eve," she said wryly, but she gave up protesting and moved aside.

Eve looked into the cabinet. For a split second, she didn't recognize what had bothered Amy so much. Then she saw the photographs. There were two of them, set neatly in the top two corners. One was of her, the other of David. Or at least the heads belonged to her and David. Their smiling faces had been carefully superimposed on pictures of two naked, hideously battered bodies.

Eve blinked, then swallowed hard. "Matt, David, get over here." Her mouth had gone so dry she was amazed she could speak.

"What's up?" The men came quickly, their voices dying almost instantly into silence.

"Oh my God!" Matt said. His voice broke on the words. "How did they get in here?"

"I think they're laser prints made on a copying machine," David said. "Which means almost anyone could have produced these at one of those self-serve print shops."

"Anyone with a sick mind," Matt said.

"The lock on the display case has been smashed." David lifted the glass lid and was about to take out the pictures when Amy stopped him. "Don't," she said. "There may be fingerprints."

"I'm going to call the police," Matt said. "Those photos are obscene. There's no other word for them." He and Amy walked hand in hand back into the cottage.

Eve realized she'd started to shake and couldn't stop. "Let's get out of here," David said, putting an arm around her shoulders. "You okay?" he asked quietly as they walked back into the cottage.

"Terrific. Peachy keen." Her pretense of composure collapsed, too brittle to be sustained. She turned her face and buried it in his sweater. "No," she said. "I'm not okay. Those photos make me feel sick to my stomach."

"That's two of us, then," he said. His arms tightened around her and he held her close, rocking gently. After a minute or two, she felt his fingers stroking her hair, but he didn't speak, just held her, giving her comfort by the silent strength of his presence. Her nausea slowly faded.

She should have known such tranquil harmony wouldn't last. Not between the two of them. David framed her face with his hands and looked down at her, his gaze intent. "Eve, I want you to go back to New York," he said. "Until we find out who's behind all this garbage, you're not going to be safe staying here in Eternity."

Eve stiffened. She pulled away from him, thinking sadly that if he understood anything about her character, surely he wouldn't dare to make such a suggestion.

In the bad old days of their marriage, her hurt would have turned into instant hostility. Tonight she was determined to do better, to explain her motives for wanting to stay in Eternity, rather than attacking his motives for wanting her to leave.

"I couldn't cut and run even if I wanted to," she said. "David, you must see that. My crew's arriving first thing tomorrow morning, expecting to find me here. I have a program to produce that's already been scheduled for airing the first week in December. That means deadlines to meet and footage to tape right now."

David's mouth tightened and he half turned away. "I know your career always comes first," he said, his voice acid with sarcasm. "However, if you could bring yourself to give just a smidgen of consideration to the fact that a psychotic murderer seems to be stalking you, I'd sure appreciate it."

"How about you?" she demanded, her good resolutions flying out the window. "Are *you* moving out of town? Or is this yet another example of your desire to send the little woman to safety while brave macho David toughs it out with the bad guys?"

"Don't be so damned ridicu—" He stopped himself in midword, banging his fist into his palm. Then he shoved both hands into his pockets and scowled at her, eyes dark with the struggle to speak calmly. He sucked in a lungful of air. "I'm sorry," he said. "You're right. I was applying a double standard. If I can stay because I need to get on with my diving operation, you can stay because of your TV program."

She was so stunned by the admission that she couldn't think of a word to say. David's gaze became quizzical.

"Speechless, Eve? Gosh, I never thought I'd see the day. I guess I should try being humble more often."

"It suits you," she said. She smiled, then reached up and touched him lightly on the cheek. "Don't get too reasonable, or I might start to like you."

"An interesting twist on our relationship," he said. "Are you sure it would be so bad if we liked each other?"

She thought of the two painful years she'd spent getting over him. "It would be . . . frightening," she said. As soon as the admission was made she regretted it. She turned abruptly and walked to the kitchen, where Matt and Amy seemed to be in the midst of a low-voiced argument of their own. They swung apart, and Matt greeted her with barely concealed relief.

"Did you reach Detective Pieracini?" she asked.

Matt nodded. "He's on his way."

Amy shot a glance at Matt that seemed almost defiant. "And a lot of use he'll be," she said. "Unless whoever did this signed his name on the back of the pictures, the police won't have the faintest clue about what's going on."

Eve wished she could disagree. Unfortunately she thought Amy had the situation summed up just right.

Chapter Ten

The detective, Matt and Amy finally left. David helped Eve gather up the congealed remnants of their meal. "I think Pete's planning to request a transfer to someplace less crime filled," he said, stashing paper plates and napkins into the garbage. "Like L.A. Or maybe the South Bronx."

Eve managed a small smile. "We should stop making fun of him. The poor guy has probably had almost no sleep for the past forty-eight hours, and he's doing everything he can. All anyone could do. Sherlock Holmes wouldn't have much luck in making sense out of this situation, either."

"Maybe there is no sensible explanation," David said. "Maybe we're trying to see cause and effect when there's no logical sequence to discover."

"What's happened doesn't feel random or senseless," she said. "It feels deliberate and...vicious."

He scowled. "Yes, I agree. Unfortunately."

She could see David struggling not to lapse into bad habits, such as ordering her back to the safety of New York City, and she resisted an unexpected impulse to walk over and hug him. She decided to change the subject. "What did you make of Amy tonight?"

"I'm not sure, and that worries me. I couldn't quite get a handle on her."

Eve nodded in agreement. "She worries me, David. I've conducted interviews with CIA agents who are more forthcoming than she was. I don't even know if she's attracted to Matt."

"Neither do I," David admitted. "Although it's plain enough he's crazy about her."

"About the only thing I could say about her with any degree of certainty is that she doesn't like you."

"And that doesn't make a lick of sense," David said. "As you know, I met her for the first time a couple of days ago. We've never exchanged a single word of private conversation."

Eve shrugged. "Well, I guess we're not going to solve the mystery tonight, so we may as well go to bed."

The word "bed" resonated in the sudden quiet. She'd been so busy resisting her feelings of affection that she'd walked right into another, much more dangerous trap.

David pounced on the opening her subconscious had given him. He straightened and turned to confront her, unleashing the sexual power she now realized he'd been straining to control. He was a tall man, and he'd always been strong, but the years of diving had honed his body to a muscular strength that was, quite literally, breathtaking. He didn't touch her, didn't even move close, but she couldn't look away. "Eve, sleep with me tonight."

She heard the note of harshness in his voice and realized that it was caused not by the arrogance of demand, but by the fear of rejection. David's sexual charisma had always been overwhelming, but never predatory. Even in the darkest moments of their marriage, he'd never used the power of his sexuality to subdue her, only to respond to her own desires.

She touched her hand to his cheek, not sure what she was going to say, but the feel of his stubbled cheek was so achingly familiar that she instinctively leaned toward him, brushing his mouth in a soft kiss.

Slowly, his eyes on hers, he combed his fingers through her hair. "I've never felt this way about another woman, Eve. You know that, don't you?"

She knew it and was scared as hell. Nervousness caused her to babble. "Maybe that's why we shouldn't do this. God knows, I'm not ready to handle... We've had a rough few days.... My shrink says never to make important decisions at a time of crisis...."

"She sounds like a smart woman," he said. "Last time we reacted to a crisis, we got divorced."

"Was that a mistake?" She stumbled over the question. "And anyway, how do you know my shrink's a she?"

He smiled. "I took a wild guess. And yes, I think we gave up too quickly on our marriage." He lowered his head and pressed his mouth against the sensitive skin of her throat. She closed her eyes on a low moan. Their bodies flowed together, melding from shoulder to knee. "Eve, let's go to bed."

"David...don't..." Her nails dug into his back.

He found the clip of her bra and rubbed his thumbs gently across her nipples. "Don't what?" he asked.

She gave a shuddering sigh. "Don't stop," she said.

BY MONDAY MORNING, Eve was so exhausted by the emotional roller coaster she'd been on that the prospect of starting work seemed almost like a minivacation. She had arranged to meet Gordon and the rest of the crew fifteen minutes after they checked into the motel. She arrived promptly at ten and discovered that the town grapevine had worked its usual infallible magic. Everyone in the motel, including her crew, knew not only about the murder, but also that she was staying with her ex-husband in the lighthouse cottage, where two dead rats and two obscene photographs had just been found.

After listening with what she considered superhuman patience to the film crew's chorus of tactless questions, Eve's temper finally frayed. "The next person who asks me how those damned photos got into Constance Powell's display case is fired, got it?"

The crew snickered, monumentally unimpressed by her threats. "Testy this morning, aren't we?" the cameraman said, grinning. "Anyway, you can't fire us. We've got a union."

"Watch me," she said grimly. "The way I feel this morning, the pleasure of firing one of you guys would make a strike seem worthwhile. Now get this gear over to the Powells' house. We have a tight schedule. Let's stick to it." The crew, no more worried than before, departed for their van.

"You sound like you've had a rough weekend," Gordon said, tucking her hand into the crook of his arm. "I told you before you left New York that you needed me to come up here with you. You know you don't do well in the boonies."

"I'm not sure how your being here would have prevented Caleb Crewe from getting murdered," she retorted as they got into her rental car. "Or even how you'd have stopped some lunatic dumping a pair of dead rats in David's cottage."

He made soothing noises. "Mike's right, you *are* testy this morning. But I can understand why. Poor you. You must be feeling devastated by all that's happened. And having to spend so much time with your ex, too. That must be like salt rubbed in the wound."

With a little shock of surprise, Eve realized she wasn't feeling in the least devastated. Actually she felt great, despite her fatigue and her inability to understand the way David had behaved last night. In fact, she was secretly delighted that Gordon had been safely stashed in New York over the weekend. Which probably said something wretched about her character since he was the kindest man imaginable and she ought to be grateful for every minute spent in his company.

"I'm fine," she said, giving him a smile. "But let's concentrate on work now, please. If I never hear the words 'murder' or 'rat' again it'll be too soon."

She should have known better than to expect the Powell sisters to have put the excitement of the weekend murder behind them. They all clustered around, demanding the latest information. Finally Eve managed to persuade them to sit down, so that the crew could start adjusting microphones and setting up lighting.

Eve never liked Gordon better than when she worked with him, and this morning his enthusiasm was particularly infectious. As the associate producer on "Roving Report," he was responsible for the technical aspects of filming a story, and he had a magic touch for setting up cameras and microphones in just the right places to capture unexpected facial expressions and details of the setting that would have escaped less-talented eyes. Eve prided herself on her acute powers of observation, but she had no doubt that when she viewed Gordon's film of the Powell sisters and their cozy sitting room, she would see both the room and the people in an entirely new light.

He also had a skill that amounted almost to genius for persuading people to forget they were being filmed. Today he had the added advantage of the sisters' being already agog with the double excitements of the murder and Patience's wedding. He guessed that the more meticulously he explained the technical aspects of placing his cameras and sound equipment, the quicker they would lose interest and revert to chatting informally among themselves. Sure enough, after a tedious forty minutes of watching the crew exchange jargon and adjust yards of electronic cable, while Gordon droned explanations replete with technicalities, the sisters lost interest in the crew and their alien equipment. After offering the technicians cookies, tea and fresh-brewed coffee, the sisters temporarily abandoned their efforts to explain the events of the weekend and started a discussion of wedding arrangements, carrying on the sort of lively intimate conversation that couldn't be staged, even by the most talented reporter.

Sitting as unobtrusively as possible in a darkened corner of the room, Eve shot an inquiring glance at Gordon. He nodded, answering her unspoken question. She sat back and relaxed, knowing that the equipment was all fully operational and that Gordon was capturing the scene on tape.

In view of the fact that Patience would be marrying at Thanksgiving, the sisters had decided to decorate Eternity's famous wedding chapel with bronze and yellow chrysanthemums and branches of pine. "So that it will smell wonderful," June said, beaming. "It will feel as if we've captured the holiday spirit and brought it right to your wedding. Oh, Patty, this is such fun! Why didn't any of us do this before?"

"I can't think why none of us ever got married!" Violet exclaimed.

"In my case it's easy to explain," Constance said mildly. "It's because I was never asked by a man who seemed even half as interesting as my own company."

The sisters laughed. "There is that," June said. "The supply of entertaining men never seems to meet the demand." She seemed not at all cast down by this realization and quickly returned to the decorative arrangements for her sister's wedding. "Well, Patty, if the flowers for the chapel are going to be in fall colors, what color are you going to wear? You'd look lovely in a deep rose, but does that clash with yellow?" She smoothed her skirt as if she were mentally visualizing the wedding gown she would choose if she was the bride.

"I'm going to wear my beige suit," Patience said.

"Your beige suit?" Violet's mouth formed an astonished circle. "But you bought that last year!"

"That's irrelevant." Patience knotted her hands in her lap. "It's excellent quality and I've only worn it once."

June and Violet exchanged appalled glances. "Yes, you wore it to Judge Fritzheim's funeral!" June exclaimed. "Patty, you can't wear the same suit to your wedding that you last wore to a funeral!"

"Why not?" Patience's mouth thinned into a stubborn line. "What about that saying? You know, something old, something new, something borrowed, and so on?"

"But your wedding dress isn't supposed to be the something old!" Violet protested.

"I don't see why not. People wear antique gowns all the time, don't they? Heritage Gowns is one of the town's most successful stores."

"That's different." June's forehead wrinkled in distress. "Heavens, Patience, you run an antique store! You of all people ought to know the difference between last year's suit and an heirloom gown! It's as if you were comparing yesterday's empty soup can to a nineteenth-century jam jar!"

"If it makes you happier, I'll buy a new silk blouse," Patience said, sounding defensive. "I should be able to find one in a nice cream color, perhaps with a touch of lace at the throat."

"Last winter's beige wool suit and a new blouse. The perfect outfit," Violet muttered. "At least, it's perfect if you want to apply for a job as the town librarian."

Patience flushed. "Good heavens, Vi, I'll be seventy years old next birthday! What do you expect me to wear? White satin and a veil?"

"I expect you to wear something that suggests you're pleased to be getting married!" Violet retorted. "A velvet dress maybe. Something in burgundy would be subdued and yet...festive!"

June cheered up. "That's a lovely idea, Vi. Burgundy velvet would be charming. Or how about hunter green, like the pine branches? Dark green can be such a rich color—"

"I'm wearing my suit," Patience repeated doggedly. "Let's face it, I'm a piece of mutton, and it's no good pretending I'm a joint of tender lamb. Louis will have to take me as he finds me. Old and tough."

Constance, who'd been silent so far, spoke up at that. "Well, dear, it may be true that mutton can't pretend to be lamb, but who's to say you shouldn't put a frill on the roast even if it is mutton? Particularly since it seems to me that Louis Bertrand is definitely the sort of gentleman who enjoys frills." Her eyes twinkled. "On his ladies, that is, if not on his roasts."

"Then perhaps he should have asked Carlotta Ormsby or Dodie Gibson to marry him, instead of me!" Patience snapped. The coffee cup she was holding rattled as she returned it to the saucer. Her sisters stared in silent astonishment as she reached for an exquisite lace hanky tucked into her sleeve and pressed it to her nose. Tears welled up in her eyes.

June and Violet exchanged horrified glances. "Patience, dearest, we certainly didn't mean to upset you," June said.

"Of course your suit will be fine. Very...elegant. Louis will love it." Violet almost managed to sound sincere.

Patience wiped her eyes and gave her sister a wry smile. "Vi, you're a hopeless liar." She put the hanky away and squared her shoulders. "Heavens, I'm sorry to have been so grouchy."

Constance smiled. "My dear, you're not—"

"No, I was being ridiculous, and you're all quite right. Last year's suit is a dreadful excuse for a wedding dress, but it felt...safe. Familiar." She shrugged deprecatingly. "My goodness, it seems getting married at my age is just as nerve-racking as it would be if I were forty years younger!"

"I'm sure it's worse," Constance said, reaching over the arm of her chair and giving her sister's hand an affectionate squeeze. "You're old enough and wise enough to know what an important step you're taking. How intimidating that must be!"

"It *is* intimidating." Patience cleared her throat. "The truth is I feel all jittery inside. When Louis and I are together, everything seems wonderful. As soon as we're apart, I start wondering why on earth he wants to marry a cranky old spinster like me."

"You're not cranky," June protested. Her eyes twinkled. "At least, not most of the time."

"Besides, brides are supposed to feel nervous and on edge," Violet said with all the authority of a maiden lady who hadn't dated in at least a generation. She took her sister's coffee cup and carried it to the sideboard. "Never mind, Patty. If you want to wear your beige suit, you can." She smiled mischievously. "And I shall wear burgundy velvet. I've seen the perfect dress in Emma Webster's shop."

On this note, the conversation changed from what the sisters would wear for the ceremony to what would be served at the reception afterward. Complete harmony was soon reestablished as they ran through a list of favorite dishes and recipes, many of which they planned to cook themselves and freeze in advance of the wedding. After about twenty minutes, Eve realized that although nobody was taking notes or giving orders, the sisters had arrived at a clear understanding of what needed to be done for the reception, who was going to be responsible for what, and the precise role the catering service was going to play in the affair. Not bad for a quick lesson in how to establish positive family dynamics, she thought, smiling absently at Gordon.

"From my point of view, we have enough," Eve said to him. "Everything okay technically?"

"Perfect," he said, signaling to let the cameraman and the sound technician know they could stop recording. "Give us fifteen minutes to pack up the gear and we'll be out of here."

The sisters stopped in mid-discussion of whether to have ice cream for dessert, as well as wedding cake. "But what about the interview?" Patience asked. "When is that going to start?"

Eve smiled. "You already gave us a wonderful interview. I couldn't possibly have asked for anything better."

The sisters stared at her, torn between doubt and dismay. "But we were talking about such trivial things," June said. "Aren't we all going to sound silly when you broadcast that on television?"

"Not at all," Eve said. "You're going to sound like a group of people caught up in making wedding arrangements for a much-loved member of the family."

Constance looked perturbed. "I trust it won't end up boring your viewers. Not to mention embarrassing us."

"In the first place, none of you did or said anything to be embarrassed about," Eve said. "But apart from that, I've already promised you that this program isn't intended to humiliate anyone. Please trust me on that. My edit will be entirely tactful."

Patience was only half reassured. "But why did you need to film all that ridiculous gibble-gabble about what I'm going to wear?"

"It was anything but ridiculous," Eve said with complete sincerity. "If this program is going to be worth watching, I need to give our viewers some insight into the dynamics of modern marriage. I hope to show that decisions about relationships are never easy, at any stage of our lives. From a personal point of view, listening to your discussion this morning, I realized for the first time that bridal couples share a lot of the same anxieties and pleasures, regardless of their backgrounds or their personal situations. I'm sure viewers will be as fascinated as I was to realize that age doesn't necessarily take away all the tensions surrounding the arrangements for a wedding ceremony."

"But all that fuss over what an old woman is going to wear," Patience murmured. "By the time you become a senior citizen, you're supposed to have more important things to worry about other than clothes!"

"What could be more important than the dress you choose for your wedding day?" Eve leaned forward, smiling warmly. "Everyone already realizes that a young bride gives a lot of thought to the dress she wears. It'll be intriguing for our viewers to see that being mature doesn't necessarily make the decision any easier. In fact, you've whetted my appetite." She grinned. "No pressure of course, but I'm really looking forward to seeing what you eventually decide on."

"In my next life I'm going to be a man!" Patience exclaimed.

Eve laughed aloud. "Any special reason why?"

"A dozen at least, jealousy chief among them. Louis is just breezing through the arrangements for this wedding. He's already told me that whatever I decide will be fine. Fine, my foot! He's only being so darned accommodating so he can escape from all the difficult decisions!"

"At least he'll have to choose his own wedding outfit," Eve said.

"Hah, big deal! He'll wear a dark suit and one of his trademark vests with his grandfather's big gold watch tucked into the pocket. Then he'll put a dark red carnation in his buttonhole and everyone will say how distinguished he looks. Now tell me life is fair!"

"It isn't," Eve said, sharing a rueful laugh with the sisters. "I'd register an official protest with the authorities, but I don't quite know how to contact the appropriate party."

While she and Patience had been chatting, the technicians had carried most of the gear out to the van. Gordon came up to her as they stacked the final load. "We'd better hurry, Eve, if we're going to grab a sandwich before our next interview."

"Please do stay and eat with us," Constance offered. "I believe June has prepared a delicious chicken casserole, and there's plenty to share."

"It'll be ready in twenty minutes," June said.

Gordon spoke before Eve had a chance, giving the sisters one of his most charming smiles. "Thanks, you're very kind, all of you. I wish we could stay, but Eve and I really need to have a working lunch. We've lots of technical filming details to discuss, that sort of thing." He put his hand beneath Eve's elbow, drawing her to his side in an unmistakably possessive gesture. "Are you ready to leave, honey?"

Eve sighed, the harmony she'd felt earlier in the morning and her admiration of Gordon's professional skills dissipating in a flash. Five months ago, when Gordon decided he was in love with her, she'd made the mistake of not rejecting his advances flat-out. He was a nice guy, she respected him as a colleague, and at the time, she'd felt oppressed by the solitariness of her life. For the past few months she'd tried to work up a spark of enthusiasm for the idea of Gordon as a husband, and she'd dated him on those nights when the emptiness of her apartment seemed even worse than the alternative—sharing dinner with a kind, talented, good-looking man who bored her.

A month ago, Gordon had stopped suggesting that they marry "sometime" and proposed that they get married before Christmas. Confronted with an ultimatum and a deadline, Eve had panicked. She was thirty-two years old and she longed to have a child. Gordon would be a kind father and a faithful husband, so she wasn't entirely sure why she was hesitating. She'd promised him an answer by Thanksgiving.

Unable to beat herself into saying yes, she couldn't quite bring herself to deliver an unequivocal no. For the past several weeks, she'd berated herself for her being too much of a workaholic and too emotionally shallow to make a com-

mitment. Now she realized she'd been neither shallow nor
work obsessed. She'd simply been smart. Smart enough to
realize instinctively that marrying Gordon because her bio-
logical clock was ticking and she found him agreeable were
lousy reasons for getting married.

Gordon, however, wasn't willing to have his ultimatum
rejected, and so far nothing she'd said had convinced him
she wasn't a candidate for a second trip into the marital
combat zone. His refusal of Constance's invitation to lunch
and the possessive way he put his arm around her waist were
just two of the many ways he tried to assert a claim that
didn't really exist. Eve was annoyed, but in all honesty she
had to admit that her own past ambivalence justified some
of his behavior.

Not wanting to start a scene in front of the sisters, particularly since they were David's great-aunts and presumably
more than capable of reporting back to him, Eve made no
protest. She didn't want any garbled maiden-aunt version of
a fight with Gordon to reach David's ears. So she added her
warm thanks to Gordon's and followed him out to his car.
They were going to have a working lunch all right, she decided. She was going to lay it on the line for him: he needed
to keep his feelings out of the workplace and his hands off
her person, or it was going to become increasingly difficult
for them to work together.

The town had mostly emptied of its weekend contingent
of wedding guests, and they were able to find a quiet table
at the Bridge Street Café. Eve ordered a chicken-breast
sandwich, surprised to discover she was hungry again.
Gordon's possessive behavior was the sort of thing that
usually reduced her appetite to zero and drove her to crunch
an entire roll of antacids. Today she felt mildly irritated, but
that was all. Obviously murder and mayhem agreed with
her, she thought wryly. Or maybe she felt more in harmony
with herself because events over the weekend had forced her
to step back from the pressures of her career and get some

perspective on her life. Murder and mayhem did tend to shed a different light on personal problems.

Gordon added his order to hers, then leaned across the table, gazing deep into Eve's eyes. He was extremely good-looking, she thought abstractedly, with the sort of amiable expression and ready smile that went perfectly with his easygoing disposition. At moments like this, she wondered if she was crazy not to leap at the chance to marry him.

"You're mad at me, aren't you?" he asked, gaze tender.

"No, not mad. Irritated would be a better word."

"Why?" he said, looking crestfallen. "Eve, honey, how have I managed to upset you? Tell me, and I'll try to put things right."

"You refused Constance Powell's invitation to lunch without consulting me." She took a sip of ice tea. "I don't like it when you speak for me, particularly in a work situation. You shouldn't just assume my wishes are the same as yours. For all you know, there might be important background information that I need to get from the Powell sisters in an informal off-the-record setting. Like lunch."

He looked contrite. "You're right. I shouldn't have refused their invitation until I'd checked with you, but we work so well together I always feel we have a sort of telepathic communication where the program is concerned. I think of us as a team. A couple—"

"We're not a couple," she said flatly. "And professionally you're right, we're a great team, but the fact is, I'm the boss."

He stroked his thumb over her knuckles. "I know you are," he said, "and I have no problem with that because I respect your work enormously. I couldn't work for someone I didn't respect."

She sighed, ashamed of her crabbiness. "The feeling's mutual, Gordon. I was thinking only this morning how much I admire your work. I'm really looking forward to seeing the film you shot today at the Powells'. I think it's going to be spectacular.''

He flushed with pleasure. ''Thanks, Eve.'' He clasped her hands. ''Honey, I know in your heart of hearts you realize we're going to get married sooner or later, so why do you insist on putting off the inevitable?''

''Gordon, please—''

He hurried on, not letting her interrupt him. ''Why don't we get married right here in Eternity this month? I'd say this week, but I'd like us to be married in the chapel, a real old-fashioned wedding with all the trimmings.'' He smiled coaxingly. ''You know what the legend says—if we exchange vows in the chapel, we'll live happily ever after.''

''I think we'd need more than a legend to keep the two of us happily married.'' She removed her hands from Gordon's clasp, reaching automatically for her antacids. She already had the roll unwrapped before she realized what her fingers had done. She refolded the silver paper and dropped the roll back into her purse. Antacids, in the quantities she'd been eating them, couldn't possibly be good for her. And a dozen packs of double-strength pills wouldn't cure the problem of her relationship with Gordon. What that needed was a refreshing dose of honesty, something Eve had been remarkably reluctant to dispense.

She drew a shaky breath. There was something frightening about rejecting Gordon in the unequivocal terms that left no room for doubt. She procrastinated a little. ''Actually I think the legend about the Eternity chapel is more subtle than most people imagine. All it promises is that people who marry there will stay together for life.'' She flashed him a rueful smile. ''For the two of us, that would probably be a guarantee of eternal misery, rather than a promise of lifelong wedded bliss.''

He chuckled, not a whit put out. ''That's my Eve! Always a cynic. But you're such a cute cynic I still love you.''

She decided not to dispute his claim that she was *his* Eve or ask him how a cynic could be cute. "At least you don't seem to have any illusions about me," she said. "Tell me something, Gordon. Since you realize I'm nothing at all like you, why do you want to marry me? You're so good-natured yourself you deserve somebody equally as kind and easygoing. Why in the world do you want to spend your time with someone as scratchy and ambitious as me?"

He flushed and didn't answer for a moment. Then he looked up and gazed deep into her eyes again. "Because I'm in love with you, Eve." He cleared his throat, but his voice remained raspy with emotion. "Everything about you seems wonderful, even things like your ambition and your determination, which would be unattractive in other women."

There was a compliment buried in there somewhere, Eve thought wryly. Gordon, it seemed, was in love with her even though he didn't really like her. Whereas she liked him and found many things about his character admirable, but she was never going to fall in love with him. What's more, she'd done him a major disservice in not telling him in clear, unmistakable terms that marriage was out of the question. She pushed aside her glass and leaned forward.

"Gordon," she said gently, "I'm truly honored that a man as worthy as you has fallen in love with me, but I can't possibly marry you. Trust me, it wouldn't work, and we'd make each other bitterly unhappy."

"Why?" he demanded. "We like each other. We respect each other professionally. We have interests in common. We've talked about our beliefs and our family values, so I think we could raise a child together."

What he was saying made a lot of sense, Eve reflected, so why was she so sure a marriage between the two of them wouldn't work out? The answer came in a flash of unexpected insight. *Because my feelings for him are tepid.* She didn't desire Gordon sexually, and there was no real emotional connection between them. He left the deepest level of her heart untouched; in some fundamental way, they lacked the capacity for intimacy.

"Gordon, you're a very attractive man, but there's no...spark between us." She reached for his hand, feeling no more than a mild spurt of affection as his fingers interwove with hers. "You see? We don't connect," she said. "There's no passion, no fire between us."

His grip tightened. "You're just talking about sex," he said. "But sex isn't especially important to me because it doesn't have much to do with making a marriage work in the long-term. Sex fades all too fast, Eve. You, of all people, ought to realize that passion is nothing compared to good solid friendship."

"How do you mean? Why do I know that?"

He reddened. "Well, I was around when your marriage to David was breaking up. Remember, I'd just started at the station when things began to go wrong between the two of you. Everyone knew how in love you'd been, how attracted you were to each other, and look what happened to your marriage." He leaned across the table, tense with sincerity. "I'll say it again, Eve. Sex isn't everything. In fact, I'm convinced it isn't important in a marriage as long as the partners like each other a lot."

He was wrong, Eve thought with sudden overwhelming conviction. For her, at least, he was totally wrong. Sex might not be everything in a marriage, but without physical passion there was no glue to hold the relationship together, no gateway to lead into the unique world of marital intimacy. Marriage was made up of a thousand splintered moments that combined to create the magical whole. But surely some of the most important moments were spent together in bed when a man and a woman shut out the rest of the world and shared everything that they were—their hopes, their fears, their longings—in an outpouring of mutual desire and satisfaction.

She didn't quite know why she understood this so clearly today, when for months she hadn't been able to put her feelings into words. Perhaps, if she hadn't seen David again, she might have been able to convince herself that friendship was an okay basis for marriage. But after the incredible pleasure she and David had shared this past weekend, she knew better. Maybe she was oversexed. Maybe she had a skewed understanding of what marriage ought to mean. But the truth was she could never substitute a friendly union with Gordon for the passionate fire of her relationship with David. The end of her marriage might have been hell, but the beginning, God, the beginning! The first few months of her marriage to David was the standard against which she secretly judged what it meant to be truly happy.

The waitress arrived with their lunch before Eve had time to probe her feelings further. "Here're your sandwiches, folks. Sorry for the delay. Enjoy!"

"Thanks." For once, Gordon didn't manage to produce his usual cheerful smile. "What were you thinking, Eve?" he asked as soon as they were alone. "You looked a million miles away just now."

"Nowhere near as far as that," she said. "I was thinking that I've treated you badly."

"No, of course you haven't—"

"I've taken advantage of you," she said, admitting the truth to herself, as well as to him. She drew a deep breath. "Gordon, I wanted to fall in love with you because I was lonely, and I knew you'd be a great father for the baby I'm longing to have...."

He smiled in relief. "You see, we are in agreement!"

"No," she said. "Gordon, I wish I could marry you, but I can't, and I should have realized it a long time ago. You're a good friend, and maybe we'd even manage to stay friends after we got married if we worked really hard. But I'm greedy. I want more than friendship from my husband."

"What do you want that I can't give you?"

She smiled sadly. "I want the moon and the stars and all the planets, too. I want to fall madly, deliriously, insanely in love with my husband."

"But you could fall in love with me," he said plaintively. "Surely you could if you tried."

She realized then what it was she'd been trying to grasp a few seconds earlier. The truth that came to her was so simple and so shocking that she didn't know whether to laugh or to cry. "I can't fall in love with you because I'm in love with David," she said. "And I'm afraid I always will be."

Chapter Eleven

Having spent a productive day in Boston shopping for replacement diving gear, David wasted the entire drive back to Eternity trying to convince himself he was heart-whole and fancy-free. He was sure that what he felt for Eve was simply a nostalgic burst of sexual attraction for a beautiful woman. Despite the incredible hours of lovemaking they'd shared last night, his deeper feelings remained untouched.

He admired Eve's work, of course. How could he not when she was so talented? But that didn't mean he missed her insightful conversation or longed for her company or yearned for the soft warm sound of her laughter. No sirree. He was past the age of believing in romantic fantasy and understood the practical basis on which marriage needed to be built. He would never again fall into the trap of marrying a woman striving for professional success and especially not the same career-obsessed woman who'd already made his life a living hell.

He was smarter now than he'd been when he fell in love with Eve. He had his life planned out. Once he and Matt finished salvaging the *Free Enterprise,* he would buy a house in the suburbs, marry a sweet home-loving woman who had no professional ambitions and settle down to raise a family. It was a great plan. So why did it have him breaking out in a cold sweat?

He knew the answer to that when he arrived in Eternity and realized that, instead of driving straight home, he was roaming the streets, searching for the "Roving Report" van and hoping for a glimpse of his ex-wife. These were not precisely the actions of a man caught up in the throes of indifference, he reflected ruefully. Was he so damn frightened of his feelings that he couldn't risk being honest even with himself?

The truth was he was half-out of his mind with worry. He was scared that Eve wouldn't consider marrying him again, scared that she wouldn't be interested in a man who was no longer dedicated to the goal of climbing high and fast up the corporate career ladder, chewing up rivals and spitting them out with a triumphant gnash of his teeth. He had good reason to be scared, he decided. Eve was the one who'd demanded a divorce, and from her point of view, nothing in the past two years had changed for the better. Other than the fact that he managed to give her a great time in bed, why would she want to start their failed marriage again?

Besides, he decided gloomily, peering through the gathering darkness in search of the van, even their lovemaking might not seem special to Eve. She was so wonderfully responsive, so warm and generous in her sexuality that half the men in America could probably give her pleasure in bed.

He immediately felt murderous jealousy toward half the men in America. When he realized he was scowling ferociously at some innocent middle-aged male who happened to be standing at the traffic lights, he finally managed to laugh at himself.

I'm behaving like a lunatic, he thought. *Takeover of brain cells by testosterone. The ultimate and unmistakable sign of a man in love.*

He spotted the van at last, parked outside Marion Kent's jewelry store. Eve came out while he watched, smiling as she said goodbye to Marion and had a few words with one of the cameramen. His heart began to pound. Lord, she was beautiful!

He pulled to a halt behind the van, then stuck his head out the window. "Hi, Eve. Hi, Marion."

Eve barely nodded. Marion gave him a friendly smile. "Hi, David. Haven't seen you in a while."

"I've been busy. How are the babies?"

"They're gorgeous, of course, but quite a handful. I think Geoff is turning prematurely gray."

"And loving every minute of it, I'll bet." For once, David regretted that he hadn't paid more attention to his mother's gossip. He vaguely remembered hearing that Marion and her husband had split up, then spent a summer hovering right on the brink of divorce. He wished he knew Marion well enough to ask what had happened, how she and Geoff had reconciled and if they were truly as happy now as they appeared. Marion seemed to have found the perfect balance in her life. She was a devoted mother, but she still managed her store and found time to create custom jewelry designs in addition to caring for her twins. Maybe life did sometimes provide second chances, he thought, turning to look at Eve. God, he hoped so.

Eve finally finished going over the following day's assignment sheet with a good-looking man in his thirties whom David recognized instantly as a rival. He resisted the urge to bristle or strut. "Any need for a chauffeur?" he asked Eve, trying to sound like a normal person and not a man suffering from a terminal case of longing. "I'm available."

A faint flush crept into her cheeks. He didn't know if it was a good or bad sign that she appeared uncomfortable with him. "Thanks, but I have the rental car back at the chapel," she said, her voice sounding a little breathless.

"Leave it there. I can drive you to your first appointment tomorrow morning," David said.

"Okay. It's a deal." Eve climbed into the Jeep without quite meeting his eyes. David turned to wave to the people on the sidewalk and realized Marion was staring at the pair of them somewhat quizzically. He wondered if his state of adolescent longing was as visible as he suspected. Suddenly aware of the comic side of the situation, he gave Marion a huge grin. "'Bye, Marion. We have to get home," he said. "We need to feed our pregnant mother."

Marion looked surprised. "Oh, how...great. I didn't realize you were pregnant, Eve."

"I'm not," Eve said sharply. "David and I are divorced, remember?" She bit her lip, then smiled in silent apology. "I guess David's talking about our...about the cat." Her eyes suddenly twinkled. "Say, would you like a kitten when ours are born?"

"Heaven forbid! We've got enough babies!" Marion laughed and waved goodbye. David rolled up the window and sped toward the lighthouse.

"*Our* cat?" he queried. "*Our* kittens?"

Eve stared at the passing traffic. "A slip of the tongue. Cat is definitely all yours."

"I'm in a generous mood. I'm willing to share."

"Thanks, but my life-style doesn't lend itself to caring for pets. You were quite right to point that out when we were married."

"It's a relief to know I did something right. In retrospect, I can only remember all the occasions when I behaved like a total horse's ass."

"We both made mistakes." She looked away from him and spoke quickly, her voice excessively bright. "I had a good day, how about you? This is a nice town, full of nice people. I can understand why Pete Pieracini is so protective of his turf."

"I had a frustrating day, I guess. The face mask I want is out of stock in every dive shop in Boston, and the weather forecasters are predicting the imminent arrival of two major storms, which will screw up what's left of our diving schedule.''

"Oh, dear, that sounds bad," she said.

"Yeah. But it gets worse."

"How?"

"I can't stop thinking about you, Eve. You're there, dammit, wherever I go, whatever I do."

She became preoccupied with buttoning her jacket. "Having me on your mind is worse than the imminent arrival of two winter storms?"

He looked away when he made the admission. "Yes, it's worse, because I don't know what to do about it."

She didn't say anything. He parked the Jeep in front of the cottage and cut the engine. In the sudden quiet David heard the rustle of wind in the sage grass, the soft indrawn sigh of Eve's breath and the heavy pounding of his own heart. He wanted more than anything in the world to reach out and take her hand, but the gap between them seemed like the chasm between two skyscrapers. If he reached out and missed, the landing could be fatal.

"Eve, we need to talk," he said.

Her smile was strained. "A whole new concept in our relationship."

"We talked a lot this weekend," he reminded her. "It's been . . . good."

"We spent a lot of time in bed, too." She drew a quick, shallow breath. "It seems old habits are hard to break."

"What happened last night wasn't just about sex or hiding from our problems," he said.

"I know."

"Then what was it about, Eve?"

She'd twisted the button on her jacket so many times that it came off. She stared at it sightlessly for several seconds, then clenched her fingers around it and swung her head up, meeting David's eyes for the first time since she'd gotten into the Jeep. "I think it might have been about love," she said.

His hands shaking, David reached for her, closing the chasm and landing safely in Eve's arms. "Yeah," he said. "I kind of thought that myself."

THE PHONE RANG, rousing David from a blissful state of grogginess. He pushed Cat off his stomach—when the devil had he...she jumped up onto the bed?—and reached for the phone. "Hello."

"Mr. Powell? David? This is Marge Macdonald."

Caleb's landlady sounded distressed. He sat up, ignoring Eve's mumbles of protest. "Yes, Marge, what can I do for you?"

"I've been talking to Joyce," she said. "You know, you spoke to her, too. She told me you had a real nice talk."

"Sure," he said. "Caleb's sister. I hope she's okay."

"She's fair." Marge Macdonald fell silent for a moment. "For a while, I wasn't sure I should tell you this, but I thought about it some and I decided you need to know."

"We'd be grateful for any help you can give us."

"The other day you asked me if Caleb was worried about anything, and I said no, because I didn't want you to know—" Marge pulled herself up short and started again. "I told you Caleb had been involved with another woman," she said, the admission coming out fast and breathless. "He didn't want to be, kept telling me I was a good friend and he wanted to spend his life with me, but there was this other woman. He couldn't break free from her. It was like she had some magic hold on him, you know?"

"Yes, I can understand," David said, his grip tightening around the phone. "But you said Caleb never mentioned her name."

"That's right. Caleb never told me. Said it was better if I didn't know anything about her, that I didn't want to tangle with her. But when I was with his sister today, we started chatting. Nothing special, just remembering a picnic we went on this summer. Joyce told me how glad his family was that Caleb had found me. How he'd had this girlfriend a couple of years back that got her hooks into him and wouldn't let go. Joyce said this woman's name was Amy and she'd been a real piece of work. Caleb never had much sense about women, according to Joyce. First he got involved with his wife and her pills, and then this Amy. Like I told you, Caleb never breathed a word to me about no Amy, but Joyce knew the name real well."

Eve was now fully awake. She sat up, leaning close to him in an effort to hear the conversation. "Marge, I really appreciate your calling," David said. "Did Joyce happen to know Amy's last name or where she lives? And has she passed this information to the police?"

"She's gonna give 'em a call, although when I showed the detective Amy's name and the phone number written in the back of Caleb's notebook, he didn't seem to think it was important. I wasn't gonna say anything, then I got to thinking as how you both seemed to find that note about Amy real interesting and I remembered Eve said to call her if anything came up. I guess if he was involved with this Amy, you need to know, right?"

"We sure do." David tried again to get her focused. "We're glad you called, Marge, very glad. Especially if Caleb's sister was able to tell you where Amy lives or what her last name is."

"She doesn't know her address, but she knows her name. Joyce never met this Amy, mind, because Amy was married when she and Caleb started dating, so he didn't exactly introduce her around. Joyce says there was something real strange about their relationship right from the start. She says as how she seemed like a quiet, polite little thing on the surface, but she had Caleb so tied up in knots he didn't know which way to turn. If she'd asked for the Brooklyn Bridge, Joyce thinks Caleb would've tried to buy it for her."

"She must be some woman," David said. Hanging on to his patience, he asked for the third time. "And what was her last name?"

"Nichols," Marge said. "Her name was Amy Nichols."

Amy Nichols! The name exploded into David's consciousness, momentarily stunning him into silence. He paused so long that Marge spoke again. "Hello? David? You still there?"

"I'm still here," he said. "Marge, I think what you just told us might be very important."

"Is it going to help find out who murdered Caleb?"

"It might," David said grimly. "It very well might. Marge, I'll get back to you as soon as we know anything more. And thanks for the tip. Ask Joyce to think hard and see if she can come up with an address for Amy, will you? Some clue as to where we might find her."

Eve was already out of bed, picking up their clothes from the floor. She pulled on her sweater and tossed David his socks. "I heard what Marge said. She's found out Amy's last name. Nichols. Why are you looking as if you've been poleaxed?"

"Amy Nichols," he said. "That was the name of Ned's wife."

"Ned?" she repeated. Memories clicked into place. "Oh my God! Ned Nichols! Do you mean that Ned?"

"The very one. Good ol' Ned. The guy who robbed my clients of almost two million dollars, tried to shoot himself and then finally committed suicide in prison."

Eve stood, belt dangling from her fingers as she mentally connected the pieces. "We'd better not jump to conclusions here. It'd be an amazing coincidence if Caleb's girlfriend and Ned Nichols's wife turned out to be one and the same Amy."

"But it's certainly a compelling possibility, wouldn't you agree?"

"I sure would." Reluctantly she admitted, "Still, the world's full of amazing coincidences."

"And I guess it's not that unusual a name," David said.

"But it's not exactly John Smith or Mary Johnson, either."

David paced the bedroom, his mind buzzing on the brink of overload. "If Caleb was once head over heels in love with Amy and anxious to get her back, we have to accept that he knew she was here in town. And that she knew likewise. Which means little Amy Lewin has been lying through her teeth when she denies being acquainted with Caleb."

Eve nodded. "But that doesn't necessarily mean they were up to no good. In fact, lovers who split up usually prefer to avoid each other, and they often lie about their past."

"True. But we invited Amy and Matt to share a pizza with us last night just so you could check her out. Did you conclude she was lying? In your opinion, is she what she appears on the surface?"

"I don't know," Eve admitted. She shook her head in frustration. "I thought I'd be able to make a pretty firm judgment about her honesty once we spent some time together, but she was too... opaque. I've interviewed a lot of people since I started work at 'Roving Report,' but I can't remember ever encountering a woman who was harder to read. Even after last night, I have no *sense* of her. No idea whether or not she knew Caleb. No idea whether or not she feels anything for Matt."

"Nor me," David said. "But whatever she may or may not feel for him, I'm a hundred percent sure Matt's in love with her, and if Amy Lewin turns out to be Amy Nichols, ex-wife of Ned, ex-lover of Caleb, it's going to be traumatic for him."

"Really traumatic," Eve agreed. "We have to face the likelihood that if all these women are one and the same, then there's a good chance Amy developed her relationship with Matt strictly in order to set him up."

David couldn't see the exact shape of it, but he felt a cloud of dread form on his mental horizon. "Matt's already upset about what he considers Caleb's betrayal. He'll be devastated if it turns out Caleb and Amy were *both* using him."

Eve winced. She sat down in the armchair, and Cat immediately curled into her lap. "David, tell me exactly what you suspect Amy of doing."

"Too many things," he said. "I'm leaping to conclusions like an Olympic hurdler."

"Take me through your leaps one by one. I think I fell by the wayside right around the first jump."

David tried to order his chaotic thoughts. Strange how the simple fact of hearing Amy's last name could change his entire concept of what had been happening over the past few weeks. If Caleb and Amy were old acquaintances, if they'd been working together to rob the *Enterprise* of its treasure, so many puzzles became easier to explain.

"Let's go back to the beginning," he said. "To Amy Nichols and her husband, Ned."

"Is that the beginning?" Eve asked.

"I think so, from our point of view. I never met Ned's wife, but I have a clear impression of the sort of woman she was. She didn't testify at Ned's trial, but from some of the evidence he gave, it's obvious she had the guy twisted up in an emotional morass. He testified that he stole because Amy had an almost pathological need to spend money and that somehow she made him feel he was a failure as a man if he couldn't provide it."

"How did she spend the money?" Eve asked. "On possessions, or on high living?"

"Both, I guess. Jewels, cars, trips, you name it. Ned knew he had to provide her with a luxurious life-style or she'd leave him, and he was unable to bear that thought. In the end he understood what she'd done to him, how her manipulations had corrupted his judgment. He even understood that she didn't really love him, but he still couldn't break free."

"That's exactly the sort of thing Caleb's sister was complaining about to Marge, isn't it?" Eve said. "On the other hand, we've seen Amy and Matt together, and I didn't detect any sign that she was obsessed with money or riches, did you?"

David shrugged. "No, but that may not mean much. Ned wasn't a stupid man and neither was Caleb. Presumably Amy's techniques for exploiting her lovers are a bit more subtle than sitting down every night and demanding champagne and diamonds. On the other hand, I agree with you that it's hard to visualize the Amy Lewin we met last night as a scheming woman, involved in a nefarious plot to get the men in her life to shower her with riches. Her character seems so...bland."

"Bland isn't the right word," Eve said. "*Concealed* would be better. And she doesn't like you."

David was surprised. "How can you tell? I didn't feel any negative vibes."

"I noticed that she didn't want to shake your hand, and every time you came near, she moved back so that there was no chance of the two of you accidentally touching. The desire to avoid you was about the strongest sign of emotion she gave all night."

David thought about that for a moment. "If she's really Amy Nichols, she might well have reason to dislike me," he said. "After all, I'm the man who uncovered her husband's fraud. I was the star prosecution witness at his trial. Maybe she blames me for his suicide. And in a roundabout way she's right."

"Of course she isn't!" Eve protested. "Besides, she'd already divorced Ned months before he killed himself. She's in no position to claim emotional distress or blame you for anything."

David sat down on the edge of the bed. "When it comes to feelings, people aren't always logical or consistent," he said. "Amy could divorce Ned at the first sign of trouble and still be genuinely distraught over his death." He looked up and caught her gaze. "Consider the two of us," he said. "I hated you the night you asked me for a divorce. Hated you with a passion, because you wanted to end our marriage when I loved you so damn much."

"Oh, David!" She put Cat off her lap and came to kneel on the floor beside him. "I was hurting," she said, her expression dark with remembered anguish. "I just wanted the pain to stop. I didn't care how I did it or how much I wounded you in the process."

"I understand that now." He framed her face with his hands, aching with the intensity of his longing. "Marry me, Eve." The words came out of the most deeply buried layers of his subconscious, but as soon as they were spoken, he knew he meant them more than anything he'd ever expressed.

Her cheeks paled and her blue eyes clouded with panic. "I don't know," she said. "David, I'm not sure... Oh God, we made such a wretched mess of it last time!"

"Maybe we both learned something from picking up the pieces," he said. "I think I did."

"I'm not ready..."

"We can go slowly," he said. "Let's take it one step at a time. Do you love me?" He wondered what the hell he'd do if she said no.

Color flooded her cheeks, then retreated, leaving her paler than before. "I love you," she admitted. "Only you. Always." She gave a broken little laugh and dashed the back of her hand across her eyes. "I'm just not sure I can live with you, that's the problem."

He was so relieved that the love was still there for both of them that he wanted to grab her and dance a jig. With a great effort of will, he managed to do nothing more violent than press a quick hard kiss on her lips. He decided to back off for a while. He could live without her immediate promise to marry him. For a week or two. Maybe. But he was a determined man, and he knew there wasn't a chance in the world he was going to let her slip away from him a second time.

He smiled and hauled her up on the bed, holding her close. "I'm willing to settle for being your lover for now. But be warned, I plan to keep nagging until you agree to make an honest man out of me." He shot her a sideways glance. "Besides, Cat needs a respectable home to bring up her kittens."

She laughed, but he saw the strain behind her smile. He kissed her lightly on the nose. "Okay, now that we've got the important things taken care of, maybe we should get back to our discussion of Amy Nichols."

"All right." As he'd suspected, Eve grabbed eagerly for the change of subject. She began to tick off the points on her fingers. "Let's assume the Amy who was married to Ned Nichols is the same Amy we know here in Eternity. Amy Lewin Nichols persuades Ned to steal two million dollars for her spending pleasure. Then Ned gets arrested and she turns to Caleb Crewe for comfort." Eve stopped in midstride. "That poses a problem right away. Why would she turn to a man like Caleb?"

"Because she fell hopelessly in love?" David suggested.

Eve shook her head. "The woman you've described would never be motivated only by love."

"Then I can't begin to guess. Amy Lewin is good-looking. Very good-looking. If she craves money and high living, you'd think she'd go after some rich elderly executive willing to trade in wife number one for a younger, sexier model."

Eve thought for a moment. "The woman you've described wants power, along with her jewels and expensive vacations. With a man who's already rich Amy wouldn't be in control. She'd be the supplicant, always waiting for her husband to dish out rewards, always the subservient person in the relationship."

"You're suggesting that she needs to be in control of her lovers?" David said. "That persuading them to steal for her is part of her pleasure?"

"It's a possibility, don't you think? Maybe she gets her kicks from knowing that she's twisted an honest man until he's willing to do anything to keep her, even commit a crime. You told me once that Ned was an honest man who lost his moral bearings. From what you and Matt have said, I'm guessing that Caleb was an honest, decent sort of guy until he met Amy. Maybe that's the point. Maybe she's only interested in honest, decent guys."

David found the picture Eve was painting uncomfortable. "You're making her sound like a black widow spider crossed with Prince Machiavelli."

Eve grimaced. "I interviewed a woman exactly like that once. She'd set up a drug-dealing network that covered half the college campuses in New England. She had an IQ well above the genius level, and she could have had a glittering academic career. Instead, she got her kicks from running hard-and-fast on the wrong side of the law. She liked the challenge of outsmarting the rest of the world. She took on organized crime, the college authorities and the law-enforcement agencies, and for a few years she won. It could be that Amy has the same sort of twisted lust for power. An insatiable desire to corrupt."

David remembered Amy as he'd seen her the previous night, sitting placidly in the armchair, teasing them because Cat was a pregnant female and neither of them had realized it. He shook his head. "It's easy to agree with what you're saying until I actually visualize Amy Lewin. Then I think we're creating a monster out of a woman who's so ordinary we'd never notice her in the normal course of events."

"But she isn't so ordinary," Eve said. "She's stunningly good-looking, and yet she doesn't act like a beautiful woman. She doesn't seem to send out any sexual vibrations at all. Why not?"

"I can't begin to guess." David's voice was dry. "I guess you could say my sexual attention has been focused elsewhere these past couple of days."

Eve blushed, but looked rather pleased at the backhanded compliment.

"I guess the question now is what we do next," she said. "Do we talk to Detective Pieracini?" She shook her head. "No, bad idea. Lousy idea. Can you imagine his reaction if we walk in and suggest he should investigate Amy Lewin on the grounds that Caleb wrote the name Amy in his notebook and you once helped prosecute the husband of a woman called Amy Nichols?"

David flinched. Expressed in such bald terms, the theory they'd constructed looked little short of ridiculous. Were they making mountains out of very small molehills? He got to his feet and took a restless turn around the bedroom. "Pete'd be right to ignore us," he said. "Right now he's taking statements, waiting for lab reports, coordinating with the Boston police and dusting half the surfaces in Eternity for fingerprints. He's not going to drop all that because we believe—no, have a vague hunch—that Amy Lewin once had an affair with Caleb."

"How about if we told him we suspect Amy Lewin may have killed Caleb?" Eve said.

The rumble of Cat's purr echoed in the sudden quiet. "That would certainly raise the stakes," David said at last. "But knowing Pete, my guess is he'd tell us we were risking a suit for slander and carry on dusting for prints."

"She's the most logical suspect for putting rats in our beds and destroying your diving gear. We'd already decided that looked like a classic act of revenge, and Amy definitely dislikes you."

"She could have put those obscene pictures in the light-house, too," David said. "Remember how she was the one who sent us in there?"

"And when it looked as if we might leave without finding the photos, Amy was the one who pointed out the broken display case with the pictures inside."

"This is all speculation," David said. "Pete still isn't going to listen to us."

"Maybe we should talk to Matt." Eve got up from the bed and paced the room. "He must know more about Amy's background than we do. Besides, he needs to be told what we suspect."

"We can't approach Matt." David's friendship with Matt went back to college days, and he knew that his friend was a lot less self-confident than he appeared. Matt's mother was an alcoholic and he'd grown up emotionally abandoned by an ambitious, indifferent father and a step-mother who disliked children. Myriad unresolved hurts swirled beneath Matt's happy-go-lucky surface, and David dreaded having to approach his friend with the news that Amy might have deceived him. Matt was already depressed by the probability of Caleb's betrayal. He would be devastated to learn that the woman he loved had been conspiring with Caleb to steal treasure from the wreck of the *Free Enterprise*.

"Matt's head over heels in love for the first time in his life," he explained to Eve. "If it turns out we're wrong about Amy, he'd never forgive either of us for suspecting her. Talking too soon could literally destroy our friendship. And even if we're right, he sure as heck wouldn't cooperate with us to investigate Amy's background. We need solid proof she was conspiring with Caleb before we breathe a word of this to him."

Eve sighed. "You're right. Of course you are. But solid proof means we need something like documents, or incriminating photos...."

"Or even one of Pete Pieracini's much-loved finger-prints."

"But how are we going to get that sort of hard evidence?" Eve asked. "If the police with all their resources haven't found anything, we aren't likely to do any better."

"We might," David disagreed. "If we searched Caleb's apartment, we'd specifically look for links between him and Amy Lewin. The police aren't doing that. If they come across a snapshot of Amy and Caleb arm in arm on the deck of his boat, it won't mean a thing to them. They'll put it right back in the album."

"True." Eve gave a frustrated shrug. "But we aren't going to get the chance to search Caleb's apartment, so we're stymied. The police aren't looking for a link between Caleb and Amy, and they won't start looking for one until we've already established that the link exists. At which point they don't need to look. A classic case of the vicious circle."

David refused to surrender to her seeming logic. "We're both approaching this with too much negative personal baggage," he said. "We're not thinking straight. Eve, you're a talented investigative journalist. If you were working on an assignment for 'Roving Report,' you wouldn't give up this easily. Imagine you're in the midst of filming an important program and you want to get the inside scoop on Amy Lewin. How would you do it?"

Eve straightened, energized by the appeal to her professional expertise. "I have a research team of course, and in this sort of case the initial procedure would be routine. I'd have them run a credit check on both Amy Lewin and Amy Nichols—that's easy to do and can turn up information you wouldn't believe."

"A credit check isn't going to show that Amy Lewin was working with Caleb or that she invaded the cottage and planted dead rats in our beds, so what would you hope to turn up?"

"You'd be surprised at how often a credit check will give you evidence of what you're looking for, even if not in the way you expect. Aside from that, I guess I'd ask the team to look for proof that Amy Nichols and Amy Lewin are one and the same person. Even if they established that, it wouldn't prove Amy was involved in a conspiracy with Caleb Crewe—it wouldn't prove she was involved in anything—but it certainly ought to justify asking her some tough questions."

"We can't access bank records or driving-license bureaus," David muttered. Then he jumped up, ignoring the howl of protest as Cat tumbled to the floor. "That's it!" he said. "Her social security number! We can go after her employment records and show that Amy Nichols is registered under the same social security number as Amy Lewin. After that, it should be much easier to track her movements over the past couple of years and establish her connection to Caleb Crewe." He stopped in midstride. "Always assuming she didn't use fake ID."

"As far as we know, there's no reason for her to do that," Eve said. "After all, she and Caleb presumably planned to leave Eternity with the treasure long before anyone considered checking into her background. Or his."

"Great, then let's go." David marched to the bedroom door.

"Wait! Don't get too cheerful. I hate to rain on your parade, David, but did Amy have a job during the time she was married to Ned Nichols?"

"No, but that doesn't matter." David was seized by a surge of adrenaline so strong his hands were twitching. "I can call in a favor from my old boss, Cyrus Frank. He can give us Amy Nichols's social security number, providing he's willing to disclose it. That would provide us with at least half the information we need."

Eve looked puzzled. "Why would your former boss know Amy's social security number?"

David grinned, unable to avoid feeling a little smug. "As Ned's wife, she was part of the company health plan, and I know they kept track of plan members by means of social security numbers. That's the way most health plans work. Cyrus can access that number for me with a couple of phone calls to the personnel department. Always providing he's willing, of course."

"Then let's get started." Eve glanced at her watch. "It's almost nine o'clock. Do you know his home number?"

David took his Rolodex off the dresser. "I think I have it," he said, flipping through the cards. "Yep, here it is. Home and office." He dialed the number and gave Eve a thumbs-up when his old boss answered.

"Cy, this is David. David Powell. How are you doing?"

"All the better for hearing from you. I thought you were hunting pirate gold in the Caribbean."

"You're a few months out of date," David said. "This time I'm going after Confederate gold off the coast of Massachusetts."

Cyrus snorted. "Damn-fool waste of time. What provoked this call? Are you broke? If you want your old job back, you're hired."

David laughed. "Cy, I'm not broke, and I'm so out of touch with the market, your clients would sue you for incompetence if you let me loose on their portfolios."

"A couple of months and you'd be right back on track. You have a magic touch with investments, David. You're wasting your talents harpooning doubloons, or whatever the hell it is you do. You can produce more gold on the stock exchange than you'll ever find rotting on the ocean bottom."

"Gold doesn't rot, but thanks for the compliment, if that's what it was. I'll give your offer some thought."

"Do you mean that?"

"Yes, I mean it." He glanced at Eve. "I may be moving back to New York. But the real reason I called, Cy, was to ask a big favor."

"Ask away, but I'm a hard-nosed old bastard. If I want to refuse, I will, even though I like you."

"It's about Amy Nichols," David said. "Ned Nichols's ex-wife."

There was a momentary pause and when he spoke again, Cyrus Frank had sobered. "Yes," he said. "How can I help you? That was a bad business all-around."

"Call someone in personnel and ask them to look up Ned's file. I need to know his wife's social security number. They should be able to find it listed somewhere in Ned's application for medical insurance."

"Why do you want this information?" Cyrus asked, his tone suddenly all business.

"I recently met a woman I think may be Amy Nichols, but she's going under a different name," David said. "I'm trying to confirm her identity by comparing social security records."

"It's not illegal to use a different name, unless it's for the purpose of committing a crime."

"That's the problem. I think Amy may have killed someone."

"Killed someone! Who?"

"One of her lovers. Who may have been stealing on her behalf."

Cyrus didn't speak for a while. "Have you a shred of evidence for suspecting her of such a thing?" he demanded finally.

"Not evidence that would hold up in a court of law. That's precisely why I need her social security number. It's a long, involved story, Cyrus, but that number could be the crucial key."

There was a heavy silence. "I took you at your word the last time you asked for a favor," he said after a moment.

'And I wasn't disappointed. I guess I can trust you one more time."

David's grip around the phone relaxed fractionally. "Thanks, Cyrus. I appreciate your confidence. How long do you think it might be before you can get hold of Ned's records?"

"About a minute," Cyrus said. "I don't have to contact anyone to get Ned's personnel file—it's right here in my study. When we were making the legal preparations for his trial, I duplicated the disk containing his personnel records, so that I could work on his case at home. I can check for the information you want myself. Hold on."

Neither David nor Eve spoke as they waited for Cyrus to come back on the line. "I've accessed Ned's file," he said, returning to the phone. "We have two entries for Amy Nichols in connection with the company health plan. She was born on January 12, 1962, in Ithaca, New York. And her social security number is 555-36-4420."

David let out the breath he'd been holding. "Thank you, Cy. Thank you very much. I owe you one."

"Yes, you do. Think about that job offer I just made if you want to give me a worthwhile payback." Cyrus hung up without waiting for David's reply.

"That was terrific," Eve said. "You have all the makings of a decent research assistant." Her eyes gleamed with laughter. "Ask me nicely, honey, and I'll see if I can find you a place on my team." As soon as she'd spoken, she went bright red and turned away. David knew why. During their marriage, they'd both been so damn sensitive about their career successes that he would have reacted with icy withdrawal to Eve's teasing. What fools they'd both been, he thought ruefully.

He touched her arm. "Gosh," he said. "I'm really flattered. Between you and Cyrus, this seems to be my night for job offers."

She swung around, her face flooding with relief that he hadn't taken offense at her teasing. "You told Cyrus you might consider going back to your old job. Were you serious?"

"That depends," he said, holding her gaze. "If you and I get married again, I can't very well go off chasing treasure all over the world, can I? Especially if we have kids."

Eve shoved her hands into her pockets, looking worried. "But do you want to be a stockbroker?" she asked. "I thought you were tired of living in New York?"

"It wouldn't be my first choice," he said. "But I want to be your husband, and all the rest comes way down the list in terms of importance."

"Oh."

Eve fell silent. He wished she would run into his arms and reward his willingness to compromise with a promise to marry him. She didn't of course, but he supposed it was progress of a sort that she didn't protest yet again that marriage between the two of them was doomed to failure.

He took her hand. "It's getting late," he said, "and we've still only solved half the problem. We know Amy Nichols's social security number. Now we have to find out Amy Lewin's."

"Yes, you're right." As usual, she eagerly seized the change of subject. "How are your contacts at the *Courier*? You did so well with your old boss. Any chance you can bribe or flatter someone at the paper into accessing Amy's file?"

"No chance," he said. "Katharine Falconer runs a tight ship."

"Darn. Maybe I can get my research team on it tomorrow morning. They can sometimes work miracles."

"No need to wait." He grinned. "I'm just full of hot ideas tonight. Come on." He grabbed her hand and ran downstairs to his computer, switching it on and pulling up another chair for Eve as he waited for it to come on-line.

"With luck, I may be able to access the *Courier*'s records myself."

"How?" Eve asked. "David, it can take hours—days—to find the access codes you need to break into a company's files."

"You sound as if you speak from experience," he said, moving his mouse to access his address file. "Ah, here it is." He gave a grunt of satisfaction as the listing for the *Courier*'s research center appeared on screen. He activated his modem and dialed the number.

"What are you doing?" Eve asked.

"Last year, when Eternity celebrated the two-hundred-year anniversary of its incorporation, my great-aunts made a donation to the town and paid for all the back issues of the *Courier* to be scanned and made accessible to researchers by modem. It's a great system and a great resource for local history buffs, not to mention serious historians. When Matt and I were researching the fate of the *Free Enterprise,* we scanned the data base for references to the shipwreck and accessed the articles without ever leaving the cottage. It's a tremendous time-saver."

"It sounds like a wonderful gift your family made," she said. "You mentioned it before. But what has a research data base got to do with finding Amy Lewin's personnel records?"

"Nothing in the normal course of events. Except twice I misdialed the number to access the data base and found myself staring at the paper's personnel files."

"Good grief, surely you can't remember the number you misdialed!"

"Not precisely, but I remember it was the last digit I got wrong. My fingers slipped on the key and I think I hit a even instead of six."

The computer whirred and bleeped, then flashed a message onto the screen. REQUESTED NUMBER NOT AVAILABLE.

"Damn. I guessed wrong." David quickly keyed in another number. "Maybe I keyed one down instead of one up. Five, instead of six."

The computer bleeped again. REQUESTED NUMBER NOT AVAILABLE.

David scowled at the screen. "Dammit, I know I did this! I accessed the personnel files by mistake. What number did I dial?"

"The *Courier* could have changed the number," Eve suggested. "Maybe they found out that too many people were making the same mistake you did."

"Could be," David said. He glanced down at the computer keyboard and his gloom lifted. The pad of number keys at the right of his keyboard mimicked a touch-tone phone, with the six centered between a nine and a three. "That's what I did," he muttered. "My finger slipped down and I keyed in a three instead of the six."

He dialed the number, and after a few beeps and whirs, a heading appeared. COURIER PUBLISHING CORPORATION.

He and Eve exchanged delighted smiles. A list of menu choices appeared beneath the heading and he moved the mouse to PERSONNEL RECORDS.

The screen darkened, then lit up with a new message. ENTER APPROVED SECURITY ACCESS CODE.

"Good grief," David muttered. "This always looks a lot easier in the movies."

"Let me try," Eve said. "You'd be surprised how unimaginative people are at inventing passwords." She leaned across and tapped in a single word—Falconer. The screen flickered. The hard drive hummed and obligingly coughed up a new series of commands, including ENTER FILE NAME.

David gave a small whoop of triumph. "How the devil did you guess that Katharine Falconer uses her own name as an access code?" he asked.

"Because I've done this sort of thing before," Eve said wryly. "At least twenty percent of people use their names or birth dates as security passwords, even though all the manuals advise them not to."

David finished entering Amy's name. A new header appeared at center screen. RECORD OF EMPLOYMENT: AMY M. LEWIN. Beneath the heading were listed Amy's biographical data, tax and salary information, her three-month performance review and her application to enroll in the company health plan.

He scanned the information quickly. Amy M. Lewin was born in Ithaca, New York, in January 1962 and had been divorced since 1992. No record of her ex-husband's name. She was hired at an hourly wage of $8.50, which was raised to $9.00 after an "excellent" three-month review. Her social security number was listed as 555-36-4420.

He looked up at Eve. They smiled at each other in faintly punch-drunk approval.

"Bingo!" she exclaimed softly. "We've got her."

Chapter Twelve

Eve's euphoria faded when David began pacing the room, his expression forbidding. "What's the matter?" she asked. "For someone who's just completed a pretty nifty detective job, you don't look too pleased."

"Detection is fun when you're playing Clue," David said. "In real life, it hurts real people."

"You're worried about Matt," she said, understanding at once. "Because he's in love with Amy."

David nodded. "I have to talk to him," he said. "We've been friends for a long time, and before we take this any further, he deserves to know what we've discovered."

"Let me come with you," she said. "I know from experience that when people are confronted with news they don't like, they tend to blame the messenger. If I'm with you, he'll have two messengers to blame."

"So he can be furious with both of us, instead of just with me? Is that an improvement?" David asked. Nevertheless, he went off to call Matt looking slightly more cheerful. He came back to say that Matt had invited them to the motel.

"Let's go right now and get it over with," Eve said, not looking forward to the next couple of hours. This was the sort of situation that could very easily destroy a long-term friendship if it wasn't handled right.

"Maybe we'll get lucky," David said. "Maybe he'll be ble to convince us that Amy was never involved with Caleb Crewe, then we won't have to take any of this stuff to the olice."

"How could he convince us that Amy didn't know Caleb nd had nothing to do with his murder?" Eve asked.

David looked bleak. "I can't imagine," he said.

HE NEW LOCK on Matt's door at the motel gleamed silver a the fluorescent lights of the parking lot.

Eve found her steps slowing after they got out of the Jeep. he'd been relieved and excited when they discovered that Amy Lewin and Amy Nichols were the same person, but she vas beginning to realize that suspecting Amy of being se- retly involved with Caleb Crewe didn't solve all the mys- cries of the past few days.

She took David's arm, forcing him to match her pace. We need another couple of minutes before we march into Matt's room and start flinging around accusations," she aid. "So many things have happened over the past couple f days that I keep losing track of the details. But in retro- pect, thinking back to the night when Matt's room was andalized, don't you think it's odd that Caleb was dumb nough to invade Matt's room, trash the place so that it ooked like a robbery and then steal nothing but the harts?"

"You mean because stealing only the charts immediately ade Matt and me suspicious of him?" David asked.

"Yes. And if he was working in cahoots with Amy, why ould he need to *steal* the charts? We thought before there's good chance Amy has a key to Matt's rooms, and she must ave a pretty good idea of Matt's schedule. She could slip to his suite when she knows he's away, take the charts to e instant-copy shop and return the originals all in the space f an hour. Why have Caleb run the risk of breaking into a otel room when they could get all the information they needed without you or Matt having a clue that your security was even breached?"

"Good question," David said.

"I sure hope you have a good answer."

He looked down, gaze troubled. "Only that criminals often seem to do dumb things."

"Definitely not a good answer," she said. "The more I think about it, the more it seems that Caleb was flat-out stupid to steal *only* the charts. It was like pointing a finger of suspicion straight at himself."

"And Caleb wasn't stupid," David said. "Far from it." He spread his hands in a gesture of defeat. "Eve, none of this affects the fact that we need to talk with Matt. Let's get this session with him over before we play detective again. We need to tackle one problem at a time. Right now, our problem is warning Matt what we suspect about Amy."

"Okay." She hooked her arm through his as he rang the doorbell. Matt had obviously been waiting for them and answered the door within seconds, wearing his trademark black jeans and a baggy sweater. He leaned forward to kiss Eve's cheek, frosted beer can held out to the side. He gave an exaggerated sigh when he saw her arm linked with David's. "Eve, sweetie, how come you're still hanging around with this good-for-nothing guy? Haven't you noticed yet that I'm twice as handsome and twice as smart?"

"Mmm. And twice as conceited, too." She smiled to take the sting from her words, wishing they didn't have to destroy his good cheer by raising doubts about the woman he loved.

"So what's up, old buddy?" Matt punched David's arm in casual greeting, then invited them to take a seat with a wave of his beer can. He tore open a package of pretzels and set it in the center of the coffee table with a flourish. "Okay. Your gourmet refreshments are now served. Dig in. I can offer you beer, Coke or apple juice. Take your pick."

"Nothing, thanks." David jingled the change in his pockets. He looked as edgy as she felt, Eve decided.

"I'm fine, thanks," she said. "Nothing for me, either."

Matt slumped deeper into the chair, stretching out his long legs and propping his beer can on his flat stomach. He yawned. "What's up, guys? Much as I love your company, I've had a hell of a long day, so if you don't mind, let's cut to the chase."

Eve and David had spent the fifteen-minute drive to the motel planning exactly what to say and how best to alert Matt to the squalls looming ahead. It had seemed a lot easier in the car than it did in his sleepy, unsuspecting presence.

David shifted on the narrow sofa, almost visibly girding himself for battle. "Look, Matt, there's no way to ask this tactfully, so I guess I just have to go ahead and ask straight-out. It's about Caleb and Amy. Do you think there's any chance they could have known each other before we all arrived in Eternity?"

"Why the big buildup to such an innocuous question?" Matt asked, puzzled. "Anyway, you already know the answer. Amy never met Caleb. She'd never even heard his name until he was murdered. Good grief, you were with her when the news came in to the newspaper. You must *know* she'd never heard of him."

"Actually we wondered why she didn't recognize his name," David said. "It seemed strange that you'd never mentioned it to her. After all, we worked with him every day, and you see Amy every night. It's only natural to discuss the day's work."

"You know damn well that in our trade you learn to keep your mouth shut, even in bed," Matt said. His eyes gleamed teasingly. "Besides, we had better things to do than talk about Caleb."

"When you love someone it's hard not to discuss your daily activities," Eve ventured.

Matt didn't deny that he loved Amy. "We talked some," he said, beginning to sound exasperated by their persistence. "I tend to keep the various parts of my life separate. I didn't talk to David about Amy any more than I talked to her about Caleb."

It was certainly true that he hadn't discussed his new love with David, Eve reflected. When she and David had met Amy at the *Courier* offices, they hadn't even known for sure that she was Matt's girlfriend.

"Amy knew David and I were excavating a shipwreck," Matt continued. "But I never discussed the details of the operation with her, and so there was no reason for Caleb's name to come up in conversation. In fact, it's such an ingrained habit for me to be cautious, my subconscious probably screened his name out whenever I talked with Amy about my work." He took a swallow of beer and yawned again. "Dave, old buddy, I wish you guys would stop beating around the bush. What are you really trying to get at?"

"All right, I'll tell you why we came," David said, his voice flat. "Caleb's sister claims her brother had an unhappy love affair with a married woman called Amy Nichols and that the affair was ongoing."

Matt waited, not saying anything, and Eve realized he found the information so irrelevant that he didn't understand that David had finished his point and expected him to reply. For the first time since Amy Lewin's social security number had flashed up on the computer screen, she began to question Amy's involvement with Caleb Crewe. She didn't doubt that Amy Lewin had once been married to Ned Nichols or that Caleb Crewe had been in love with a woman called Amy Nichols. But she wondered if she and David were stretching that pair of facts into an enormous theoretical balloon that was all hot air and no substance. There were a dozen good reasons Amy Lewin might not want people to know she'd once been Mrs. Ned Nichols, none of them related to Caleb. The fact that Ned was a convicted embezzler who'd killed himself in prison, for a start. No wonder Matt was looking so blank, Eve thought.

"We believe that Caleb Crew might have been in love with Amy Lewin," she explained. "We think your Amy Lewin and Caleb's Amy Nichols might be the same woman."

Matt's blank expression was replaced by an astonished stare. "My Amy? Involved with Caleb?" His gaze flicked from David to Eve. He looked as if he wanted to laugh, but was too shocked. "Sweetie, what have you and David been smoking?"

His words were teasing, but underneath Eve could hear the throb of anger. This session was going much as she'd feared. Not surprisingly, Matt was hurt by the suggestion that a woman he loved and trusted might be two-timing him, and his anger was turning not toward Amy, but toward them.

She was glad when David cut into the mounting tension with an abrupt question. "Do you remember a colleague of mine called Ned Nichols?"

"Of course I do. He worked with you until he went nuts and started plundering the company profits. Sure, I remember your talking about him, although I never actually met him."

"His wife's name was Amy," David said. "Amy Nichols. And we've run checks on her social security number. It's the same as Amy Lewin's."

Matt didn't say anything, but his hand clenched tighter around his beer can and all trace of laughter drained from his expression. He stared at the television, his gaze suddenly as gray and blank as the screen. "Are you sure?" he asked at last.

"There's no doubt about it," Eve said gently. "The woman living here in Eternity and working at the *Courier* is the same woman who was once married to Ned Nichols. Amy Lewin and Amy Nichols are the same woman."

Matt's face had about as much expression as a diver pulled unconscious from the ocean. "That doesn't mean she was also involved with Caleb Crewe," he said.

"No," David agreed. "But since Caleb had an affair with a married woman called Amy Nichols and, according to his sister, was still involved with a woman in Eternity called Amy, it's pushing the long arm of coincidence rather far to believe that the Amy living here in Eternity is a different woman."

"Coincidences happen all the time," Matt said stiffly.

His eyes had turned dark with pain, and Eve knew he didn't really believe his own protests. She wished with all her heart that he could have found some other woman to fall in love with. She wished that his face wasn't so revealing. She could almost see the thoughts chasing through his head. Any minute now, he would realize that if Amy had lied about her past and about knowing Caleb Crewe, she had probably lied about a lot of other things, too. Including what happened the night Caleb Crewe was murdered.

With exaggerated care, Matt set his empty beer can next to the untouched package of pretzels. "What are you going to do about this?" he asked.

"We have to tell the police," David said. "Matt, I'm sorry, really sorry, but I guess you have to face the fact that Amy may know more than she's been telling about Caleb's murder."

"Why the hell is that?"

"Matt, if Amy knew Caleb, why did neither of them admit to knowing the other? Don't you think it's likely she was involved with him in some scheme to rob the *Enterprise* of its treasure? We need to point the police in her direction."

Matt turned away, refusing to meet David's eye. He said nothing.

"I know how devastated you must feel," Eve said.

"Do you? I doubt it."

"Matt, we'll both be thrilled if the police come back with the news that Amy had nothing to do with this," David said. "But we need some answers."

"Yeah, I guess you do." Matt sounded so weary, so depressed, that Eve wanted to take him in her arms to comfort him, but she was rebuffed by the emotional barricade he'd erected. At this point, she could tell that Matt didn't want comforting—at least not from her or David.

He got up and walked over to the bar, bending down to open the fridge. When he stood up and turned around, he was holding a gun.

Eve stared at him, horrified. "Matt, we don't need a gun, for heaven's sake."

He looked at her, eyes blank, voice cold. "You don't. I do. Unfortunately."

My God, he's going to commit suicide, Eve thought, her stomach plummeting with fear. She got up quickly. "Matt, don't! Amy's not worth it. Nobody's worth killing yourself—"

"Eve, stand still. Don't move!" David's words were harsh with the urgency of his command.

The jagged note of fear in his voice shocked her into obeying. She came to a halt about two feet away from Matt. A sick, incredulous understanding began to build deep inside her. *Matt,* she thought. *Oh my God, not Matt.*

Matt gave David a brief sad smile, but his grip on the gun had tightened, and he was pointing it straight at Eve. "This was never supposed to happen," he said. "That's why we tried so hard to keep you in the dark, so we'd never need to do this. But I can't let you go to the police, not for the next few days, anyway. Don't try to get the gun away from me, David, or I'll shoot Eve." He looked at her, mouth tightening in frustration. "Damn, I hate this! It's all Caleb's fault."

"Why is that?" David asked, sounding almost casual.

"He backed out of our deal at the last minute," Matt said. "The truth is he was jealous of me and Amy, of our wonderful relationship."

"I suppose he was still in love with her," David said.

"Everyone who knows Amy falls in love with her." Matt spoke with total conviction. "Caleb was crazy about her."

"She must be a very...special...woman," David said.

"She is." For a split second, Matt's smile was one of unalloyed happiness. "She makes a man feel strong and sure of himself."

Eve bit back the impulse to point out that inspiring her partners to commit terrible crimes was a rather strange way to make a man feel sure of himself. Not to mention the fact that her two previous lovers had both ended up dead. A high price to pay for self-confidence.

"What happened between you and Caleb?" David asked, taking a couple of steps toward Matt. "What went wrong the night he was killed?"

Matt might be mentally unbalanced by his obsession with Amy, but his reflexes were still in great shape. He saw David move toward him and reacted instantly. "Get back!" he ordered, his aim never wavering. "Don't try anything, Dave, or I swear I'll shoot Eve."

"That wouldn't be very smart," David said quietly. "People would hear the shot."

"Are you willing to gamble Eve's life on the chance that I won't shoot her?"

"No."

Matt gave another sad smile. "You're a good guy, David, but you'd go a lot further in life if you could only learn to lie a little."

"I didn't think lies were necessary among friends."

"That's where you need them the most," Matt said bitterly.

"When did we need to lie to each other?" David asked.

Only since Amy arrived on the scene, Eve thought.

Matt didn't answer the question. "You know what?" he said. "Caleb didn't like the idea of lying to you. We argued about that a lot. He said he didn't mind defrauding the government, or Lloyds of London, but you were a friend, and he wanted to cut you in on the deal."

"I'm flattered." David allowed only a hint of irony to color his voice. "I guess the gun you're waving at Eve means you don't share his high opinion of friendship and its obligations."

"You know I do," Matt said. "You're the best friend I ever had. But I'm a realist. If Caleb had known you for as long as I have, he'd have realized you're a damned straight-arrow kind of guy. You'd never agree to any sort of illegal deal."

"Why did you?" David asked.

"I need the money," Matt said. "Amy has very expensive tastes." He sounded almost proud, as if he was discussing an endearing character quirk, such as an insistence on baking her own bread or always wearing purple underwear.

Eve finally recovered her wits enough to speak. "Matt, you know you can't get away with this. What are you going to do if David and I both move at the same time? Mow us down in a hail of bullets? I don't believe you're capable of such a thing."

"Don't put your theory to the test," Matt said. "I love you, sweetie, but in comparison to Amy and twelve million dollars in gold sovereigns, you just don't stack up."

"But you don't have twelve million dollars," Eve said. "You and David haven't found the treasure yet. What's more, you need David's help if you're going to locate it before the winter storms put you out of business."

"He doesn't need me because he's found the treasure," David said. "That's what this is all about, isn't it, Matt?"

"Of course not—"

"Matt, there's no point in lying anymore. That was the reason for the mysterious failure of the pressure gage on my air tanks and the fishing net that kept us both tangled up outside the hull of the ship." David sounded impatient with his failure to have seen something so obvious. "I kept wondering how a saboteur could have controlled those incidents, even if he gained any benefit from them. But for you, the control was easy, because you were right down there with me. You faked your shortage of air. You deliberately tangled yourself in that fishing net. And in the process you kept me away from the place in the ship where you'd found the treasure."

"I didn't know your regulator was going to jam open," Matt objected. "It was a sheer fluke that it happened at the same time I got caught in the net."

"A damn convenient fluke," David said. "Where did you find the treasure? Somewhere close to where you laid that trap of fishing nets, right?"

Matt shrugged. "I lied to protect you, David, because you're my friend. But I guess it's too late for lies if you're determined to set the police on Amy's trail. So I'll admit you're right. Yes, I've found the treasure, and yes, it's hidden behind those fishing nets. Now all Amy and I have to do is bring the chests to the surface." He gave a grin that was a parody of his familiar, jaunty smile. "Then we're outta here, folks. Rio de Janeiro here we come!"

"When did you find the gold?" David asked. "How? Why didn't I know about it?"

"That's easy. Caleb took Amy and me out every weekend when you thought we were in Boston."

"Amy dives?" Eve asked.

"She's been certified since she was a teenager," Matt said. "We've been going down to the wreck every weekend working the aft section of the ship, and that's where we found it. Two huge trunks, filled right to the brim with gold sovereigns."

"Even working overtime, you couldn't be sure you and my would find the gold before I did," David said.

"Amy...we..." Matt drew a deep breath. "I had a contingency plan in case you found it first," he said crisply.

An accident on the ocean bottom? Eve thought, shivering. God knows, there would have been a dozen ingenious ways to arrange that, and no witnesses to contradict Matt's version of events.

David didn't waste time asking Matt to explain what he meant by a contingency plan. He'd obviously reached the same conclusion as Eve. "How did you plan to bring up the treasure?" he asked.

"We arranged with Caleb that we'd raise it this past Saturday night," Matt said. "He brought in the special gear, the pulleys and the buoys. He was supposed to rendezvous with us on the beach so that Amy and I could get ready for night dive. Then Caleb got cold feet. We knew he was getting ready to sell us out to you, David—that's why I faked the robbery of those charts. I had to find a way to point suspicion at him and away from me." His voice took on an apologetic tone. "He was so damned stubborn. Amy really had no choice but to kill him."

"It was Amy who fired the fatal shot?" David asked.

"She's a very decisive woman."

"Matt, listen to me," Eve pleaded. "If Amy shot Caleb and the gold is still on the bottom of the ocean, then you haven't committed any crime. For God's sake, take a hard look at yourself! See what this woman is doing to you and walk away from her before you get into even worse trouble."

"He can't do that." The door to the bathroom opened and Amy Lewin came out. Her chestnut hair was piled in a thick, lustrous knot on top of her head, and her stunning figure showed to maximum advantage in faded jeans and a jade green turtleneck. Like Matt, she was holding a gun—in her case, a .357 Magnum—and it looked almost obscenely large and heavy in her slender hands.

Amy walked up to Matt and stood close beside him. Eve had wondered why her personality always seemed so bland, and now she knew. Amy had been hiding behind a mask so thick that it had cut off all the natural human vibrations. Now that Amy had chosen to toss her mask aside, the impact of her presence was literally breathtaking. The blatant force of Amy's sexuality affected even David. Eve saw his eyes widen and color flare briefly in his cheeks before contempt replaced his reflexive masculine response to a truly beautiful female.

Matt's reaction was far stronger. He literally shuddered, his expression changing from melancholy to helpless longing. "What do you want us to do, darling?" he asked.

"This has gone on long enough," Amy said. "We don't owe them any explanations." She jerked her head toward the door. "You take her. I'll take him." She walked up to David and pointed the gun straight at his heart. "Listen up, big boy." Her voice was raw with hatred. "We're going to walk out of here arm in arm, and you're going to look like you're loving every minute. Same with Evie over there. She's going to lean up against Matt, real close, and look like she's having fun."

"And if we don't?" David asked. "What if we scream and yell? How do you expect to get away with murdering two people in a motel parking lot?"

Amy's smile was tinged with scorn. "It's nearly midnight on a Monday, and the good people of Eternity are all tucked in bed. I expect to get away with it long enough to bring up that treasure and hightail it to Brazil."

Eve didn't believe that Matt and Amy had a chance in a million of getting away with murder in the motel parking lot. The trouble was, though, her opinion didn't count. Matt and Amy were cockeyed enough to believe they could suc

ed, which meant they'd shoot first and worry about es-
pe afterward.

Eve realized that her mouth was dry with terror. She
dn't taken Matt's threats seriously, because she simply
dn't believed him capable of killing her. That had been a
d mistake. She and David should have jumped Matt when
e odds were two to one in their favor. Amy looked as if she
as more than capable of killing anyone who got in her way,
d Matt was besotted enough to go right along with her
structions.

"Where are you taking us?" she asked as Matt grabbed
er arm and pulled her toward the door.

"For a little boat ride," he said, shoving her through the
oor.

Behind her, she heard a scuffle. Matt spun around, drag-
ng her with him, holding her against him, arms pinned to
er side. Eve saw the flash of motion as David's elbow went
nashing into Amy's ribs. Amy doubled over, coughing, but
e managed to retain her hold on the gun and David side-
epped quickly as she swung her arm up, trying to aim. In
 move almost too quick for the eye to follow, he got be-
nd her and brought his arm around her throat, immobi-
zing her in a stranglehold. Amy clung desperately to the
n, but David was much the stronger of the two, and in a
w seconds, he'd forced her fingers open and taken pos-
ssion of the weapon.

Matt's voice was harsh with panic. "Let her go, or I'll
oot Eve!" To show he meant business, he braced his back
zainst the door, sliding the gun up Eve's neck until it was
essed against her temple.

"Seems we have a standoff," David said, panting. "You
oot Eve and I'll shoot Amy. Is that what you want, old
iddy?"

It was a good thing Matt was holding her so damned
ghtly, Eve thought. Otherwise her legs would have given
ay beneath her. In TV hostage dramas, crazed gunmen

held weapons to the heads of innocent victims all the time
The reality wasn't even remotely like that. It wasn't even like
interviewing the perp and the victim after the incident was
all over. She was so scared, she was afraid she would vomit
all over Matt's restraining arm, and each breath she drew
caused a painful cramping in her stomach. At the same time
she was aware of a distinct sense of unreality. This was Matt
Packard holding a gun to her head. The friend who'd shared
more happy evenings with her and David than she could
count.

"Matt, be reasonable," David said, his voice steady but
implacable.

"I am being reasonable," Matt said. "Amy and I are going to take care of you two guys, then we'll bring up the gold
and fly off to a new life in Brazil. Once we're there, it
doesn't matter what you tell the police."

"That's not going to happen," David said. "Amy doesn't
plan to leave Eve and me alive, and you know it."

"That's not true, is it, babe?" Matt sounded almost
pleading.

Amy didn't reply, and David tightened his grip around her
neck. "Face it, Matt, the only way you're going to get out
of this room is by killing Eve. And then I'll kill Amy, and
you, too. You know I'm faster with a gun than you are." He
spoke almost gently. "Give it up, Matt. It's all over. Don't
add Eve's murder to the list of sins on your conscience."

The gun trembled against Eve's temple. She closed her
eyes, praying that Matt's finger wouldn't slip on the trigger. Then she felt his body go limp and his arm fall from
around her throat. She had just enough presence of mind to
pull herself out of his arms and drop to the floor.

"No! No! Don't let her go!" She heard Amy's agonized
scream from far over her head. She rolled to the side,
hunching against the wall as Amy, demented with rage, tore
herself out of David's grip and launched herself straight at
Matt.

"Give me the gun," Amy yelled, almost incoherent with frustrated fury. "Give me the damn gun!"

Matt warded her off, his gestures limp and defeated. "It's all over," he said sluggishly. "Amy, it's too late. Face reality. We've lost."

"*This* is reality." Amy brought her hand down in a sharp chopping movement on Matt's wrist. He winced, but he managed to ward her off, still clinging to the gun.

Amy wasn't willing to give up, and she clawed at his face, literally berserk with rage as she tried to wrest the gun from his grasp.

"Amy, stop. Enough," David said. He stepped forward, intending to haul her away from Matt. Just as he moved, Eve heard the muffled explosion of Matt's gun and Amy fell forward, collapsing against Matt's chest.

"Oh my God!" Eve got to her feet, but David ran across the room and stepped in front of her.

"Amy?" Matt said, pushing her head back from his chest and staring into her eyes. "Amy! For God's sake, speak to me!"

Silence echoed off the walls.

Matt gave a howl of anguish that sounded more like an animal caught in a trap than a human being recognizing death. He swept Amy into his arms and carried her to the sofa. Still moaning, he put his fingers against her neck. Then he looked up, his eyes staring unseeingly toward David and Eve.

"She's dead," he said. "I killed her."

"It was an accident," David said. "Matt, it wasn't your fault."

Matt brushed his fingers over Amy's eyes, closing them. "I killed her," he repeated dazedly. "I killed her." He looked down at the gun he was still holding and turned it slowly toward his mouth.

"No, Matt, don't do it!" Through a haze of horror, Eve saw David hurl himself at his friend. David grabbed for the

gun. There was an explosion, a flash of blue flame. Matt
slumped against the back of the sofa and David fell across
his chest.

"Oh, dear heaven!" Eve rushed across the room, heart
pounding, stomach lurching with dread. *Please don't let
David be dead,* she prayed. Just as she reached his side,
David sat up, holding Matt's gun.

Eve knelt on the floor, reaching up to touch his face. "Are
you all right?" she asked urgently. "Dear God, David,
where did you get hit?"

"Nowhere," he said, standing up and pointing to a spot
high in the far wall where plaster was flaking around a bullet hole. "Only the wall got wounded."

"You saved Matt's life," she said. "He sure as hell didn't
deserve it."

David looked down at Matt, who was staring vacantly
into space, hands splayed at his sides. "I was paying back
old favors," he said, unloading the bullet clips from the
guns. "Let the legal system take care of him. Without his
help, I'd have been food for the Caribbean fishes on at least
two occasions."

"He was willing to cheat you and rob you."

David took her into his arms. "Yes, but in the end he
wasn't willing to kill me. Or you."

"He came too damn close for comfort." She choked on
a hastily swallowed sob. "I thought you were dead."

"I'm not that easy to get rid of." He kissed her softly on
the forehead. "I love you, Eve. Don't ever leave me,
please."

"I love you, too." She tightened her arms around him,
overwhelmed by the need to be close, to feel the strong
thump of his heart against her breasts. "Marry me, David," she said.

He cradled her head against his chest. "Sometimes," he
said, "you have the most wonderful ideas."

Epilogue

The marriage of Patience Powell and Louis Bertrand was undoubtedly one of the happiest occasions ever seen in the fraternity chapel. Accompanied by his son, Paul, the groom waited at the altar, looking tall, distinguished and appropriately nervous for an anxious soon-to-be ex-bachelor. Overcome by emotion, he pulled his dashing scarlet silk handkerchief from his breast pocket and dabbed at his eyes when the bride, preceded by her three sisters, entered the little chapel.

Patience had settled the problem of who should escort her down the aisle by deciding to walk triumphantly alone. Encouraged by her sisters, she had chosen a satin dress of burnished gold in a style that carried hints of the Edwardian era in its high, antique-lace collar and deep buttoned cuffs. With her snow-white hair swept on top of her head, she looked as elegant and beautiful as every bride is supposed to look. Even the technicians from "Roving Report," a crew not noted for their sentimentality, were seen exchanging sappy smiles when Bronwyn Powell declared the couple husband and wife.

The chapel had been jammed to capacity for the service, but the overflow crowd had now departed for the reception at the old family mansion, where the culinary talents of the

Powell sisters and the caterers would be jointly on display a
the overflowing buffet tables.

The "Roving Report" crew had packed up their gear
with Gordon declaring confidently that they had the per
fect finale for the upcoming program on winter brides. Th
bright lights necessary for taping had all been switched off
leaving the chapel bathed in soft shadows and its usual glov
of diffused lamplight.

The flowers and pine branches arranged so lovingly b
June and Violet Powell remained on the window ledges an
at the center of the simple stone altar, their scent lingerin
in the air and their rich colors radiant in the gleam of can
dles. Glancing around her, Eve thought there couldn't be
more serene and beautiful place to be married in the whol
world.

Bronwyn Powell had finally finished shaking hands wit
guests and posing for group photographs. She returned t
the chapel and stepped once again into the center of th
sanctuary. She smiled at the dozen or so guests still waitin
at the front of the chapel.

Opening her service book, she turned first to Eve, then t
her brother David. "Are you ready?" she asked them qui
etly, her gaze warm with approval.

David kissed his mother, then glanced to where Eve wa
sitting, across the aisle with her parents. "I'm ready," h
said.

Eve rose to her feet. Her mother smiled up at her, eye
misty. "Be happy, sweetheart."

Eve squeezed her mother's hand. "I will be. Thanks fo
coming, Mom." She bent down and kissed her father
"You, too, Dad."

Her father made the inarticulate harrumphing sound tha
meant he was deeply moved. She gave him another quic
hug, and then walked the two or three steps to David's side

"I thought you could never look more beautiful than you did on our first wedding day," he said, taking her hand. "I was wrong."

Her heart contracted with love. "Thank you," she said.

"We're going to make our marriage work this time," he promised her, his voice harsh with the force of his conviction.

"Yes," she said softly. "We are."

HARLEQUIN®

Weddings, Inc.

If you enjoyed visiting Eternity, Massachusetts, and meeting the people of Weddings, Inc., Harlequin would like to invite you to even more weddings! Just collect three (3) proofs-of-purchase from the backs of any of the Weddings, Inc. titles and Harlequin will send you a free short-story collection featuring weddings!

Just select the book you would like, fill in the order form and send it, along with three (3) proofs-of-purchase for each book ordered, plus $2.25 postage and handling, to: WEDDINGS, INC., P.O. Box 9071, Buffalo, NY 14269-9071 or P.O. Box 604, Fort Erie, Ontario L2A 5X3.

☐	#83228-6	WITH THIS RING	(1487)
☐	#83238-6	TO HAVE AND TO HOLD	(1488)
☐	#83258-3	JUST MARRIED	(1489)
☐	#83295-5	MARRIAGE BY DESIGN	(1490)

Name:_____

Address:_____

_____ City:_____

State/Prov.:_____ Zip/Postal Code: _____

(Please allow 4-6 weeks for delivery. Offer expires January 31, 1995.)

WED-POPR

ONE PROOF-OF-PURCHASE

097 KCC

Take 4 bestselling love stories FREE

Plus get a FREE surprise gift!

HARLEQUIN®

INTRIGUE®

Harlequin Intrigue
invites you to
celebrate

It's a year of celebration for Harlequin Intrigue, as we commemorate ten years of bringing you the best in romantic suspense. Stories in which you can expect the unexpected... Stories that walk the fine line between danger and desire...

And to help celebrate, you can RETURN TO THE SCENE OF THE CRIME with a limited hardcover collection of four of Harlequin Intrigue's most popular earlier titles, written by four of your favorite authors:

REBECCA YORK	Shattered Vows (43 Light Street novel)
M.J. RODGERS	For Love or Money
PATRICIA ROSEMOOR	Crimson Holiday
LAURA PENDER	Déjà Vu

This unique collection will not be available in retail stores and is only available through this exclusive offer.

Send your name, address, zip or postal code, along with six (6) original proof-of-purchase coupons from any Harlequin Intrigue novel published in September, October, November or December 1994, plus $1.75 postage and handling (check or money order—please do not send cash), payable to Harlequin Books, to:

In the U.S.	In Canada
A Decade of Danger and Desire	A Decade of Danger and Desire
Harlequin Books	Harlequin Books
P.O. Box 9071	P.O. Box 604
Buffalo, NY	Fort Erie, Ontario
14269-9071	L2A 5X3

(Please allow 4-6 weeks for delivery. Hurry! Quantities are limited. Offer expires January 31, 1995)

DDD-POP

 HARLEQUIN INTRIGUE
A DECADE OF DANGER AND DESIRE
ONE PROOF OF PURCHASE

092-KCG

"HOORAY FOR HOLLYWOOD" SWEEPSTAKES

HERE'S HOW THE SWEEPSTAKES WORKS

OFFICIAL RULES — NO PURCHASE NECESSARY

To enter, complete an Official Entry Form or hand print on a 3" x 5" card the words "HOORAY FOR HOLLYWOOD", your name and address and mail your entry in the pre-addressed envelope (if provided) or to: "Hooray for Hollywood" Sweepstakes, P.O. Box 9076, Buffalo, NY 14269-9076 or "Hooray for Hollywood" Sweepstakes, P.O. Box 637, Fort Erie, Ontario L2A 5X3. Entries must be sent via First Class Mail and be received no later than 12/31/94. No liability is assumed for lost, late or misdirected mail.

Winners will be selected in random drawings to be conducted no later than January 31, 1995 from all eligible entries received.

Grand Prize: A 7-day/6-night trip for 2 to Los Angeles, CA including round trip air transportation from commercial airport nearest winner's residence, accommodations at the Regent Beverly Wilshire Hotel, free rental car, and $1,000 spending money. (Approximate prize value which will vary dependent upon winner's residence: $5,400.00 U.S.); 500 Second Prizes: A pair of "Hollywood Star" sunglasses (prize value: $9.95 U.S. each). Winner selection is under the supervision of D.L. Blair, Inc., an independent judging organization, whose decisions are final. Grand Prize travelers must sign and return a release of liability prior to traveling. Trip must be taken by 2/1/96 and is subject to airline schedules and accommodations availability.

Sweepstakes offer is open to residents of the U.S. (except Puerto Rico) and Canada who are 18 years of age or older, except employees and immediate family members of Harlequin Enterprises, Ltd., its affiliates, subsidiaries, and all agencies, entities or persons connected with the use, marketing or conduct of this sweepstakes. All federal, state, provincial, municipal and local laws apply. Offer void wherever prohibited by law. Taxes and/or duties are the sole responsibility of the winners. Any litigation within the province of Quebec respecting the conduct and awarding of prizes may be submitted to the Regie des loteries et courses du Quebec. All prizes will be awarded; winners will be notified by mail. No substitution of prizes are permitted. Odds of winning are dependent upon the number of eligible entries received.

Potential grand prize winner must sign and return an Affidavit of Eligibility within 30 days of notification. In the event of non-compliance within this time period, prize may be awarded to an alternate winner. Prize notification returned as undeliverable may result in the awarding of prize to an alternate winner. By acceptance of their prize, winners consent to use of their names, photographs, or likenesses for purpose of advertising, trade and promotion on behalf of Harlequin Enterprises, Ltd., without further compensation unless prohibited by law. A Canadian winner must correctly answer an arithmetical skill-testing question in order to be awarded the prize.

For a list of winners (available after 2/28/95), send a separate stamped, self-addressed envelope to: Hooray for Hollywood Sweepstakes 3252 Winners, P.O. Box 4200, Blair, NE 68009.

CBSRLS

OFFICIAL ENTRY COUPON

"Hooray for Hollywood"
SWEEPSTAKES!

Yes, I'd love to win the Grand Prize — a vacation in Hollywood —
or one of 500 pairs of "sunglasses of the stars"! Please enter me
in the sweepstakes!

This entry must be received by December 31, 1994.
Winners will be notified by January 31, 1995.

Name _____

Address _____ Apt. _____

City _____

State/Prov. _____ Zip/Postal Code _____

Daytime phone number _____
(area code)

Mail all entries to: Hooray for Hollywood Sweepstakes,
P.O. Box 9076, Buffalo, NY 14269-9076.
In Canada, mail to: Hooray for Hollywood Sweepstakes,
P.O. Box 637, Fort Erie, ON L2A 5X3.

KCH